"This is why I didn't want a pretty bride," James muttered.

Ann's cheeks flushed crimson and she clenched her hands into fists. "You think an ugly girl will make you a better breakfast?"

"I need to eat, Ann. The animals need to eat. The crops need to be planted and harvested. And you can't even cook an egg."

"I'm sorry I'm a disappointment to you, Mr. McCann, but why are you berating me? If I'm another man's intended, you won't be bothered with me much longer."

James's cheeks burned. "I shouldn't have spoken to you that way. Forgive me."

He escaped out the back door before he could say something else he regretted. Despite the disastrous breakfast, in a single morning she'd impressed him with much more than her beauty. She'd risen early to clean the entire kitchen by dawn, made an attempt at breakfast and stood stoically through the dressing of a burn that would have likely made a grown man cry. None of that mattered. The agency intended her for another, and he had to keep reminding himself of that.

Forget for an instant and he risked falling in love.

Whitney Bailey is a city girl turned farm wife. She makes her home in the Midwest with her husband, four children and an assortment of sociable barn cats who meow at the window when she's trying to write. *A Mistaken Match* is her debut novel.

Books by Whitney Bailey

Love Inspired Historical

A Mistaken Match

WHITNEY BAILEY

A Mistaken Match

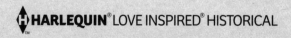

Recycling programs
for this product may
not exist in your area.

LOVE INSPIRED BOOKS

ISBN-13: 978-0-373-42545-7

A Mistaken Match

www.Harlequin.com

Printed in U.S.A.

Be careful for nothing; but in everything by prayer
and supplication with thanksgiving
let your requests be made known unto God.
—*Philippians* 4:6

For Patrick

Chapter One

June 1895
En route to New Haven, Ohio, on the Toledo and
Ohio Central Railway

The train's wheels clattered in perfect harmony with Ann Cromwell's racing heart. Each beat brought her closer to her new life, and her hands trembled as she thought of what awaited her at journey's end.

"Would you like an apple, miss?"

Ann had nearly forgotten she had a seatmate. She could pretend she hadn't heard her, but something told her this woman wouldn't give up easily. Her voice held the kind of friendliness that was the hallmark of a talkative traveler.

Ann waited a beat before blinking the sun from her eyes and turning from the window. Silver hair streaked the woman's temples and deep lines bordered her mouth. Slightly overweight, she carried it well on the tops of her cheeks and across her bosom. Once Ann faced her, the smile lines deepened.

"Would you like one? They're perfectly ripe."

Her outstretched hand held a large, red apple blushed with gold.

"No, thank you," Ann whispered, even as her stomach groaned.

"Are you sure? I have a whole bag."

Though the apple looked delicious, would it stay down? The queasiness in her stomach grew with each station stop. Ever since childhood, nerves always made her belly rebel. She'd last eaten yesterday from a food cart on the Pittsburgh station platform and only managed to force down a few bites before throwing the remainder of her ham sandwich in a rubbish bin.

"I'm quite sure." Ann kept her voice as soft as possible while still remaining audible.

The woman's eyes widened as she returned the apple to her bag. "My, what a sweet accent you have! Are you English?"

No one in New York had noticed Ann's accent. Only when the train boarded passengers in central Pennsylvania did her voice attract attention. Now in Ohio, it seemed impossible to keep from drawing notice—like a scullery maid embarrassingly visible in the parlor. She wasn't trying to be unfriendly, but conversation was the last thing she wanted.

The woman's eyebrows arched higher as she awaited Ann's response.

"Yes, ma'am. I'm from London."

"London? How exciting! What brings you to America?"

Before Ann could respond with her usual falsehood about visiting an aunt—the story she had crafted to help draw as little attention and interest from her fellow passengers as possible—something gave her pause. As she drew closer to her final destination, so grew the chance of someone catching this particular lie.

"If you don't mind, I think I've changed my mind about that apple."

The woman smiled broadly and fumbled with her bag to retrieve the fruit.

"Here, let me clean this up for you." She buffed the apple against the fabric of her skirt. Ann flashed a cursory smile of thanks and turned back toward the window. The apple lay heavy in her hand and her mouth watered at the heady scent of ripe fruit. Crisp and sweet, it tasted glorious after weeks of ship and train food. She savored each bite to prolong the silence. Each time Ann entered into a conversation, it led to questions she had no desire to answer.

All too soon only the apple's sticky core remained. She glanced about for a place to tuck the scrap.

"Let me take that from you."

The woman produced a small paper sack. Ann dropped in the core and wiped her tacky hands briskly against her skirt. Before she could turn away, the woman spoke again.

"I'm returning from a visit with my sister. She just had her tenth child." She paused, clearly waiting for a reaction, and Ann humored her by opening her eyes wide in a show of surprise. "Yes! Tenth! Her sixth girl. She needed help, of course, with some of her younger ones, and I was delighted to lend a hand."

The woman paused again. Her eyes softened, and she reached out and patted Ann's hand in a motherly way. "My children are all older now. My oldest daughter is near your age. I so enjoyed being near babies and young children again."

"How lovely for you."

The woman grinned. "My, your accent really is nice."

"Thank you." Ann had learned long ago how to mimic the melodic upper-class accent of her employers.

"Are you traveling on from Columbus?"

"Yes, to New Haven." Her own words sounded strange. She hadn't told anyone even a fraction of the truth in days.

The woman clapped her hands. "Isn't that wonderful! I'm from New Haven."

Ann felt a rush of thankfulness that she hadn't lied.

"Are you visiting someone?" the woman continued.

Ann shook her head. "No, not exactly. I'll be living there."

The woman waited a beat for Ann to continue. Ann smiled weakly.

"Who will you be living with, dear? I was born and raised in New Haven. I'm sure I must know them." The woman's voice grew softer than before, but no less friendly.

Ann cleared her throat. "James McCann."

The woman's brows knit together and she pursed her lips tight. Ann knew what her next question would be. She saved her the trouble of asking. "He's to be my husband."

Ann dreaded the interrogation sure to follow. But there were no questions—at least not right away. Instead, the woman's hand found Ann's again and she squeezed it tight.

"That is wonderful news. Really wonderful. James McCann is a fine young man. I wish you both much happiness."

Ann's heart jumped, and for a moment her walls dropped. She leaned forward. "You know him?"

"Yes, of course. Not terribly well, but everyone in town knows James."

"Is he a nice man?" Ann's voice cracked.

"Yes, he is." Her head cocked to the side. "But don't you know that, dear?"

"I've never met him." Ann's cheeks burned and she turned her head down, knowing full well the woman would soon guess the nature of their relationship. This reinforced why she'd avoided talking to anyone during her travels. She'd been assured that respectable women became mail-order brides all the time, but the idea still made her blush.

"Well, James McCann is a fine man. Any young woman would be blessed to have him."

Ann's gaze snapped back to the woman's face. No judgment or mocking that she could observe. Only a warm smile that creased her cheeks so deep her eyes almost disappeared.

"You said you didn't know him well," Ann murmured.

"He doesn't get to town much. His obligations on his farm keep him very busy. He's also quiet and keeps to himself mostly, but he's honest and decent. He's in church every Sunday, he comes from a fine family, and I know for a fact he pays his bill at the store in full each month." She wagged her finger to punctuate these last two points.

"And you say that any young woman would be blessed to marry him?" Ann tried to smother feelings of hope. Certainly this woman had no reason to lie? She'd imagined James McCann desired to send away to

England for a bride because he had few other choices. She certainly wouldn't be here if a pretty face and no references could get a servant girl more than a room in a brothel.

"Oh yes. He is—or rather was—a very eligible bachelor." She bobbed her head in emphasis, and the loose bun on top bounced along with her.

"Might you even say he is kind?" Her voice was plaintive, even to her own ears.

The woman pursed her lips and patted Ann's hand. "Very kind. Generous, too."

Ann exhaled at the news. The girls at the agency had guessed right. She'd made an ugly match in James McCann. Most of them had been matched with men living in western America, where she'd been told eligible brides were as rare as the gold the men sought. When she shared with them the news of her future home in Ohio, these girls had smirked knowingly. *He's either ugly or wicked*, they'd said. It relieved her to hear he was the former. She'd take an ugly, kind man over a cruel, handsome one any day. She hadn't entered into this endeavor with any romantic notions. She only desired someone who could provide for her. To expect more would be foolish.

"I never introduced myself. I'm Mrs. Margaret Ludlow. And your name, dear?"

This question could be her chance to make a new start with a new identity! But no. James McCann already knew her by her name of the past eight years. It would have to remain. "Ann. My name is Ann."

"Nice to meet you Ann—soon to be Ann McCann."

She'd never thought to test out her new name. The result sounded like a silly joke, and she mouthed it silently for the first time. It possessed a surprisingly pleasant cadence. She liked it, all things considered.

Before she could ask Mrs. Ludlow any more questions, the conductor entered the car and announced their impending stop in Columbus. Her stomach quivered and she immediately regretted eating the apple. Despite misgivings, Mrs. Turner at the agency had allowed Ann to make this journey alone. Moral support proved a powerful thing, and most girls were required to travel in pairs. Clients weren't happy when the brides they'd paid for got cold feet and failed to arrive. But Ann never intended to back out of the agreement. The orphanage had no more work for her, and her reputation as a servant for the upper class had been forever tarnished. Marrying James McCann was the best chance she had at a decent, stable future. Still, as the train edged closer to the station Ann wondered what would happen if she disembarked at the next station and disappeared into the crowd.

Mrs. Ludlow leaned over and pointed out the window. "We're almost to my stop."

"Your stop?" Ann's heart fluttered. She'd found some measure of comfort in thinking this woman would be with her until her journey's end.

"Didn't I say? I'm staying in Columbus with another sister for a few days. Don't worry. New Haven is only thirty more minutes."

Mrs. Ludlow moved with excited efficiency, smoothing out the wrinkles in her traveling dress and using her palms to beat away at the dust clinging to the hem. Her haphazard toilet made Ann conscious she'd been traveling all day without so much as a glance at her reflection. She fetched a pocket mirror from her bag and bobbled it on her knee as she repinned her hair at the nape and smoothed the locks around her temples.

Mrs. Ludlow glanced over as Ann tidied herself and nodded approvingly. Ann smiled inwardly under the woman's gaze. She'd been born into little, but God blessed her with beauty. She could only guess her looks had garnered a premium price as a prospective bride. No doubt the reason the agency accepted her application, despite their initial hesitation.

When the train finally ground to a stop, Mrs. Ludlow hoisted her carpetbag onto her lap. "There's my sister's husband," she said, pointing to a stout man grimacing at his pocket watch. "I'd wait with you until the train departs, but the poor man doesn't have an ounce of patience."

"Thank you, but I'll be fine. It was very nice meeting you."

Ann ached for her to stay.

"The pleasure was mine, dear. May I call on you sometime?"

The question jarred her. She would soon have a home—her own home—in which she could accept visitors.

"Certainly. Of course. I would like that very much." Ann stumbled over the words.

"I'll let you settle in before I do. Every married couple needs time to get to know each other."

Ann's stomach turned to ice at the reminder of her approaching wedding night. How much time did she need to get to know a stranger? "I look forward to your visit."

Mrs. Ludlow repeated her goodbyes several times and stopped at the door and waved before stepping from the train. Her brother-in-law hurried toward her and snatched the bag from her hands in chivalrous impatience.

Ann immediately missed Mrs. Ludlow. It had been weeks since she'd had a real conversation with anyone, and the woman's kindness had reopened a loneliness Ann had tried hard to deny. Soon new passengers boarded the car and Ann's heart dropped when the train lurched forward twenty minutes later, and she remained seated alone.

In that moment she would have welcomed even the most irritating of seatmates to distract her from thinking about what lay ahead. A new life in a new country. An intended husband whom she'd never met. After weeks of wondering and waiting, only a train stop stood between Ann and her future.

James McCann ran a calloused hand along the side of his wagon and grimaced. "I should have brought the buggy, Fred."

Frederick Renner ambled over, his portly frame casting a shadow over the wagon boards. James had wiped down the seats and swept out the wagon bed, but most of the boards were split at the ends and embedded with the grime of farm work. The entire contraption could have done with a fresh coat of paint.

"Doesn't look so bad to me," Frederick offered. "And haven't we already covered this? She's going to have luggage. Probably a trunk or two. They would never fit in the buggy."

"We could have left them with the stationmaster. I could have come back tomorrow with the wagon."

Frederick chortled. "Boy, are you in for trouble if you

think a woman would be content to be parted from all her worldly possessions for an entire day."

James sighed. His friend was right. The buggy was the more attractive vehicle, but the wagon was the practical choice. The only choice. He wanted everything to be perfect for his bride, but if the pain of losing Emily had taught him anything, it was practicality served one so much better in this world than beauty.

"Besides," Frederick continued, "if you're trying to impress her, I'm sure that suit will do the trick." He jabbed a chubby elbow into James's ribs.

James tugged at the dark suit jacket, the new fabric stiff and unforgiving. The collar seemed to grow tighter by the minute. He slipped a finger between his neck and the material. A sparse breeze raked over a trickle of sweat and teased him with coolness. If only the day hadn't turned stifling, maybe his heart wouldn't beat so quickly.

The puff and clatter of the approaching train rumbled softly in the distance. The small crowd on the station platform buzzed and pushed forward like a swarm of bees, and James moved to join them. Frederick tapped him on the shoulder and held up a large cardboard sign with *Ann Cromwell* neatly lettered in black paint. "Don't you need this?"

James waved him off. Like the unnecessary new suit and haircut, Frederick and his cousin Delia had insisted on the superfluous sign. "I'll know her when I see her."

"How exactly? You don't have a picture."

James exhaled. Frederick was a good friend, but he didn't understand why James sought a bride from outside New Haven. *He'd be flabbergasted if he knew how I expect to recognize her.* He pushed the sign back into Frederick's hands. "I just will."

The train entered the station and James's heart quickened. He clenched his fists at his sides, willing them to remain there instead of mussing his hair as he often did when he was nervous. In mere moments he would be face-to-face with his future wife, God willing. A young woman alighted from a third-class car and glanced back and forth across the platform.

It was her! Wasn't it? His legs carried him forward before he could hesitate. As he strode closer, her features and form grew clearer. Yes, it had to be her. Tall and broad shouldered with mouse-brown hair yanked back into a severe bun. He drew close enough to observe a constellation of pockmarks on her cheeks. Her small eyes darted about before landing briefly on James. He smiled. Her brows pulled into a crease and she glanced away.

His heart fell. *The sign!* Frederick had been right after all. He recognized his bride, but she clearly didn't realize he was her groom. His steps stuttered, but only for a moment. He couldn't very well leave her on the platform while he fetched it. He approached the woman and removed his hat.

"Excuse me, miss?" Did his voice always sound so hoarse?

The corners of her mouth turned down and her eyes narrowed in suspicion.

"Clara! Clara, dear, I'm so sorry!" A thin, middle-aged woman in a blue dress with similar mouse-brown hair and an equally painful-looking bun appeared at James's side and wrapped the young woman in a tight embrace. "We had the time wrong. I thought we were arriving early, and here you are, poor niece, left waiting all by your lonesome."

Warmth swept over James's cheeks as a vise of embarrassment replaced the drumbeat of nerves in his chest. The tall woman eyed him warily over her aunt's shoulder as he replaced his hat and backed slowly away. He drew a deep breath. Ann Cromwell stood somewhere at this station and he needed to compose himself so he could find her. The crowd quickly dispersed as trunks were carried to waiting wagons and reuniting families finished their embraces. He scanned the thinning platform until two figures caught his eye. Frederick, cardboard sign in hand, speaking with a woman dressed in a dark green traveling dress with her back to James. Frederick's eyes goggled.

James had no doubt the true Ann stood before his friend. Frederick's gaping surprise told him everything. He chastised himself for not being the first to greet her. Rivulets of sweat coursed down his back and his shirt clung to every inch of his torso as he rushed over to join them.

"There you are, James," Frederick said as James approached. "We've had a bit of confusion. Miss Cromwell saw the sign and thought I was you."

"I am so sorry to have kept you waiting, Miss Cromwell." Her diminutive size surprised him. The agency shared her height, but he never imagined she'd be so... petite. He stepped around the pair and at that same moment, she lifted her face to him in greeting.

"Oh my," he breathed. His heart stopped and his mouth went dry as a haystack. Golden blond hair framed a delicate face accented by high cheekbones. Her eyes, as blue as a robin's egg, blinked in the sun and her full, rosebud mouth turned up in a hesitant smile. "Are you the real James McCann?" Her voice held a teasing tone.

It took several beats for James to shake off the shock of finding a beauty instead of the plain, even homely woman he specifically requested. He removed his hat and held out his hand. She placed her impossibly small hand in his. "Yes, I am. Nice to meet you." *Oh no. There's been a mistake. A terrible mistake.*

"Do you have any trunks, Miss Cromwell?" Frederick asked.

"Please, call me Ann. And yes, I have one."

She handed him her claim ticket, and Frederick stepped away to wave down the nearest porter, leaving James to shift his weight awkwardly from one foot to the other. His heart raced, but no longer from anticipation. The cold flush of panicked sweat threatened to soak through his jacket.

The smile on Ann's perfectly pink lips slowly faded as the silence between them grew. He had to say something. Anything. "You're Ann Cromwell?"

Her brows knit. "I am."

"From the Transatlantic Agency?"

She laughed softly. A nervous laugh. "I gather my picture didn't arrive."

"It did…not." His mind fogged. His hat remained in his hands and he replaced it before the urge to muss his hair became too strong.

"I imagine the post can be rather slow from England to Ohio."

"Yes." Words failed him. He couldn't tear his eyes from her face. His mind skipped like a phonograph needle, playing the same thoughts over and over. *Some sort of mistake. An enormous mistake.* Thankfully Frederick returned and slapped him on the back. The jolt broke his trance.

"The trunk's being loaded. Are you two ready?"

James stared at his friend. "Ready for what?"

Frederick smirked. "Didn't you say you'd made reservations at Donahue's?"

"Yes, yes." He would follow his original plans for now. In a few hours he'd be at home and more than a few feet away from this woman and he could think clearly again. For now he struggled to keep his voice steady as Ann looked up at him through impossibly dark lashes. "I thought we could get some dinner in town before going back to my farm."

"That sounds lovely."

James offered her his arm, and Ann placed her hand on the sleeve of his jacket. He swore the heat radiated through two layers of material and scorched his skin.

Frederick cleared his throat. "It was very nice to meet you, Ann. *Very* nice. I'll see you tomorrow."

The brim of her hat obscured her face, but he could hear the smile in her voice. Ann's lilting accent sent a shiver through him. "A pleasure to make your acquaintance, as well, Mr. Renner."

"Frederick. Call me Frederick."

"A pleasure, Frederick."

Frederick winked at him and hurried away as fast as his short legs and ample frame would allow. He disappeared around a corner before James could think of a reason to convince his friend to stay.

Donahue's stood four blocks from the station, but the journey felt like miles. Ann asked polite questions about each building they passed, and James tried his best to keep his eyes directly forward as he answered. The smallest glance at her face disoriented him, and he couldn't help but notice how her beauty's effects extended to passersby. He caught smiles of admiration, eyes slit with jealousy and two men received pointed elbows from their female companions for the mistake of looking too long. Several men outside the tobacco shop sent streams of juice down their shirts in distraction. Every eye in New Haven seemed to be fixed on Ann, save for his. *Please, Lord*, he prayed during the brief moments of silence. *Grant me wisdom.*

James couldn't taste a bite of his two-dollar steak. He dutifully chewed the meat and swallowed, but his brain barely registered the meal. How many times had he walked past Donahue's Hotel and Fine Dining and wondered when he might have an occasion to eat there? Now inside, he couldn't be bothered to take in the grandeur of his surroundings or the extravagance of the meal. It all paled next to the beauty of the girl seated across from him.

Even as new rivers of perspiration trickled down his back and his hands trembled when he reached for the salt shaker, she showed no signs of being nervous. No one would guess she'd been traveling for days, let alone recently met the person she thought to be her future husband. Her cheeks were pink, her eyes were bright and her golden hair freshly styled. If only she knew what James had to say. His throat caught at the thought of telling her.

"I hope your steak is as delicious as mine," she murmured.

Her lilting voice brought his attention to the piece of steak on his fork. How long had he been holding it? James took a bite. It sat as coarse and flavorless as week-old mutton in his dry mouth. "Yes, delicious."

"Your friend Frederick seemed very nice."

"Yes, nice."

"Have you two been friends long?"

"Fairly long."

Ann pressed her pink lips together and took a long draft of water from her cut-crystal glass. He couldn't keep her at arm's length for the entirety of the meal without upsetting her, let alone for the weeks or even months it would take to sort all this out. Yet he knew he couldn't tell her in the middle of Donahue's. She was a foreigner in a new land and none of this was her fault. He must be tactful.

"Frederick and I have been friends since we were kids," he offered.

Her smile returned. "And he lives near you?"

"He lives here in town."

"Shall we be seeing him in town tomorrow, or is he visiting your home?"

"I'm sorry?"

She cocked her head to one side. "He said he would see us tomorrow."

Creamed spinach caught in his throat and his eyes watered. He took several gulps of water to keep from choking. "He did, didn't he?" he croaked.

How could he explain this one? He would have to tell her the truth. At least part of it. "The agency said some couples marry almost immediately," he blurted.

For the first time Ann's calm demeanor broke. Her cheeks flushed and her eyes widened. Her hand trembled as she reached for her water glass. "Yes, Mrs. Turner said some choose to marry rather quickly."

"So I'd made an appointment with Judge Vollrath at the courthouse for tomorrow. I'd planned for Frederick to meet us there and act as a witness."

Ann bobbled her water glass but righted it before any liquid spilled. "You did?"

"But I've decided to cancel," he added quickly. "It seems hasty." Why hadn't he started by saying that? Something about Ann Cromwell made it hard for him to put his thoughts in the proper order. He chastised himself as the red in her cheeks faded, returning them to their natural rosy hue.

"Mrs. Turner said many couples like to get to know one another before they marry. Assuming, of course, there is no—" she paused and her cheeks flushed again "—impropriety."

Something about her embarrassment made James's heart leap in his chest. It took everything he had not to reach across the table and take her hand in reassurance.

"I'm afraid I can't afford to put you up anywhere, but my Uncle Mac lives with me. Never leaves the house, in fact. Would you object to him serving as our chaperone?"

She shook her head. "That sounds quite acceptable. I don't imagine Mrs. Turner would object."

James speared an impossibly thin potato with his fork and pushed it around the gold-rimmed plate. His next questions required delicacy. He knew nothing of Mrs. Turner and the Transatlantic Agency outside a brief correspondence and their ad in the *New Haven Gazette*. Fine English Girls Seeking Home and Hearth in America.

"I completed a profile for Mrs. Turner. Did you do the same?" He tried to sound casual.

"We all did. She also conducted extensive interviews before she matched us."

James feigned immense interest in the pattern on his silverware. "So there were a lot of girls at the agency? And they all matched with someone?"

"Oh yes. Dozens of girls came in every week, and all very eager to live in America. Most were matched with men far west of here. The Great American Frontier, I believe?"

James chuckled. "If you believe the newspaper advertisements." So the agency teemed with potential brides, and he'd been matched with this one. She hadn't been sent due to a lack of other options.

Ann leaned forward and cocked her blond head. Her soft blue eyes gazed at him expectantly. "Is there anything else you'd like to know?"

Yes. Why on earth did the agency match me with you when I specifically requested a plain bride?

Chapter Two

Ann had hoped her meal with James McCann might break down this peculiar wall between them, but as he guided her to the wagon, she could almost palpate the barrier. She knew things would be awkward at first—the agency had prepared her for that—but she hadn't expected the bewildered greeting or the clear discomfort.

They were both nervous, she reminded herself. She simply hid her nerves better. If only he knew how her breath had caught in her throat when she first laid eyes on him. She'd been expecting an ugly man, not a handsome one who sent her pulse racing. Perhaps if he knew, he could make eye contact with her for more than mere seconds.

James released her hand the instant she alighted from the wagon, as if her touch burned him. She glanced back at her trunk for the first time. A beautiful quilt lay folded on top. A pattern of intertwining gold circles rested on a background of forest green and sky blue.

"What's this?" For a moment, she forgot the awkwardness between them and held up the quilt.

James glanced over as he juggled the reins. "It's a present from Frederick."

"A present for me?"

His cheeks flushed crimson. "For us. A sort of early wedding present."

"Who made it?" Ann unfolded the quilt to examine it further. Even from a distance she knew it had been made by an expert hand. Up close the stitching proved exquisite.

"Frederick's cousin is a seamstress's apprentice. She works over there." He pointed to a brick storefront with a bright blue awning squeezed between the tobacco shop and a mercantile.

"From this work she looks to be more than an apprentice." She made a quick count of the stitches. "Why, there look to be fourteen stitches per inch!"

"You know quilting?" He sounded surprised.

Ann smiled. "Yes, well, embroidery mostly. Though I love any kind of stitching. The more stitches in an inch, the more accomplished the quilter. This work is some of the finest I've ever seen."

"You didn't mention it in your letter."

There had been only two short letters exchanged between them before Ann had left. The expanse of the ocean made it difficult to have any kind of courtship. How very much like strangers they were.

"Your letter didn't say much either." Four paragraphs. He summed up his life in four short paragraphs.

They left the town behind, and James took off his hat and ran his hand through his thick sandy hair. The wind tousled it and gave him a decidedly boyish appearance. She studied his face. He possessed a straight, strong nose and finely lined lips. James McCann proved as handsome as they come.

"What do you want to know?" he asked.

Ann clapped her hands together. Finally! "How much time do we have?"

"The ride back to the farm is around forty-five minutes this time of year."

Her stomach dropped, but she tried not to show her disappointment. It had been years since she'd lived more than a few blocks from the nearest store. "Isn't that a rather long time?"

"Quite a short time. In the spring the skies open and this road turns to mud. That's why it's called Mud Pike. When the road turns soggy it takes two, maybe three times as long. On those days it's faster to walk."

The sticky heat of the summer evening clung to Ann's back. She tried to push the thought of walking to town as far away as spring felt.

"You're a farmer, aren't you?"

James nodded.

"Are you originally from New Haven?"

James only nodded again. Ann sighed. She needed a new line of questioning.

"How old are you?" She tried.

James turned to her. "Didn't the agency tell you all of this?"

"Yes, but I wanted to hear these things from you."

"I'm twenty-five. You're eighteen, right?"

"Nineteen in September."

Ann waited for him to ask her a question but he remained silent.

"Isn't there anything you wish to know about me?"

James took his eyes off the road and placed them

squarely on Ann. She shivered under his intense gaze. "The agency said you used to work as a maid."

"That's correct. I was eight years in service."

"You don't look like a maid." He sounded accusatory.

"May I ask what a maid is supposed to look like?"

His eyes narrowed. The effect made him look thoughtful rather than menacing. Ann sat up straighter and tried to look more confident than she felt. As his scrutiny continued, blood drummed in her ears and perspiration trickled down the back of her neck.

"I guess I never thought a maid would look like you," he answered finally.

"And you don't look like a farmer."

James eyes widened and his lips drew into a broad smile for the first time that day.

"Alright, then. What does a farmer look like?"

Ann narrowed her eyes in the same way James had, and tried to mimic the intense scrutiny he had applied to her. Her efforts had the opposite effect. His smile grew wider. And what a simply splendid smile. Straight teeth and full lips. The fading light darkened the green in his eyes, and fine lines crept out from the corners. He sat perfectly straight as he drove, and his work-broadened shoulders tapered into a lean waist. The fingers of the hand holding the reins were long and slender, but thickly calloused. He'd likely worked hard every day of his life.

"I've changed my mind. You do look like a farmer."

"You still don't look like a maid."

Ann sighed and crossed her arms. She wanted to get to know him better, but he didn't make it easy.

They continued the rest of the trip in silence and Ann tried to ignore the bumps in the road that bounced them closer and closer together on the wagon seat. She let out a breath when James announced, "There it is."

James's farm sat a quarter mile off the main road. A large whitewashed brick two-story with a gray slate roof and gracefully arched windows perched atop a small hill at the end of the drive. A deep porch sporting a sun-bleached porch swing ran along the front. The barn and other outbuildings shone bright with new red paint, and a neatly trimmed yard spread out in front of them. A well-tended garden filled with neat rows of green sat beside what appeared to be half a dozen fruit trees. Ann's heart leaped to find something else that day that exceeded her expectations.

James stopped the wagon in front of the porch steps and helped her down. As she stood waiting for him to return from the barn while he stabled the horse and put away the wagon, she admired the clumps of freshly planted white and yellow daffodils around the foundation. Had he asked a neighbor for some transplants for her benefit? James returned carrying her trunk and the quilt, and she tentatively held his elbow as they walked up the steps. His arm didn't stiffen this time.

An elegant panel of windows flanked either side of the front door, and it opened into a small but inviting entry. A long rag rug, shallow side table, oval framed mirror and a gilt framed photo of the very house they were standing in adorned the space. A graceful walnut railing curved along the staircase.

He set the trunk down at his feet and gestured to the left. "This is the parlor." A stiff horsehair sofa and chairs faced the fireplace. "And the dining room to our right." Six curved-back chairs surrounded a cherry dining table. A high cabinet with glass front doors held a small collection of matching china dishes encircled with blue flowers.

Ann smiled and nodded, hoping he could see how the house pleased her. Mrs. Turner had tried to prepare her for something small and sparse and her heart lifted in delight to see she couldn't have been more wrong.

"Where's the kitchen?"

"Through the door at the end of the hall. My father only put on a lean-to when he built the house."

Ann perked up at the mention of his father. "When will I get to meet him?"

"Who?"

"Your father, of course."

James set down the bags and rubbed his hands together. "I'm afraid you can't. He and Mother died some years ago."

"I'm sorry," she said, and meant it. "When will I meet your brothers and sisters?"

"No brothers or sisters. It's just me and Uncle Mac."

"I thought all farmers had many children."

James laughed. "Where did you get an idea like that?"

"In England, farmers always have scads of children."

"Did you grow up on a farm?"

Her thoughts turned to the orphanage and the Atherton house. The simplest answer felt the easiest. "No."

"Mother and Father wanted more but the Lord only blessed them with me. A farm is hard work with only one son to help. I pray God chooses to bless me with many children."

Ann's hands grew slick with sweat and her stomach lurched like a newborn foal finding its legs. He wanted children? Had her one request been overlooked? Ignored? Certainly her face reflected the nausea that lurched within. James tilted his head in scrutiny, and she drew in a deep breath to stifle the sickening dread that threatened to overtake her.

"Are you alright?"

What could she possibly say? Two dollars in coins jangled in her pocket book. It was all the money she had in the world.

"I must have eaten something that didn't agree with me."

He picked up her trunk and pointed toward the stairs. "I'm sure you're worn out after all your travels. Let me show you to your room."

Upstairs were three closed doors. James stopped at the first on the right and opened it. Inside a small side table and dresser sat below a plainly framed mirror. A single bed hugged the wall next to the window. He marched in and set her trunk down in the middle of the faded green rag rug and draped the quilt across the top.

"Uncle Mac has the room next to this one, but he's in bed already. You'll meet him tomorrow. My room's across the hall, but I'll be sleeping on the back porch."

"Is that really necessary? I'd feel horrid if you weren't able to get a proper rest."

"Don't feel bad on my account. I sleep out there most summer nights anyway."

"Oh."

"Can I get you anything?"

Her head and neck ached and the fatigue of travel and stress enveloped her like a heavy blanket. She could only think of the inviting-looking bed. Ann shook her head.

"Well then, good night, Ann. I'll see you in the morning." And with that, he left the room and closed the door behind him.

Ann sank onto the bed. A dull ache throbbed across her temples, and she closed her eyes and tried to sort out the day's events. The more she reviewed the day, the more peculiar it all felt. James had been nervous when they met, but something more hid behind his green eyes. It wasn't only surprise. Was it confusion? Disappointment? He'd had plans to marry her the very next day—plans he'd quickly changed. Though she was relieved—surely they could get to know one another a little while before they were betrothed—she couldn't help but wonder why the sudden change of heart? And what of that comment about wanting lots of children? Surely Mrs. Turner hadn't made a mistake?

She closed her eyes and replayed her exchange with Mrs. Turner in the cramped and stuffy offices of the Transatlantic Agency. Mrs. Turner had announced with resolution, "I believe you and Mr. James McCann will be as perfect a match as any." Ann took deep, measured breaths and tried to slow her racing heart. Mrs. Turner wouldn't make a mistake of this magnitude. Her business depended on it.

Ann rose and stared into the mirror above the dresser, hoping to find some clue to James's dismayed reaction at their meeting. The hint of a shadow traced under her eyes, and two stray hairpins poked their heads out like nosy children. She appeared as she expected after so many days on the train. She removed her brown felt hat and ran a hand over her forehead. The pain in her temples spread over her creased brow. Ann plucked out her hairpins and untwisted her coiffure. Her hair fell down past her shoulders and she groaned as the ache in her head eased.

She opened her trunk and retrieved the few things she needed for her toilet. The pitcher proved empty, and James hadn't shown her the privy. Did all men forget women had need of such basic necessities? The reality of sharing a home and life with another would drive anyone to distraction. Maybe that was all that was wrong between them—awkwardness and nerves.

That thought cheered Ann, and she convinced herself of it on the short walk downstairs with the pitcher. If houses in America were like those in England, the well pump would be directly outside the kitchen door. James had also failed to supply her with a lantern or candles. Thankfully, the summer sun had not yet set, and soft fingers of orange sunset lit her way.

She opened the kitchen door and found the room bathed in dusky light. James sat at a worn wooden table with his back to her. The floor creaked as she entered and he jumped from his seat, sending papers scattering to the floor. They both stooped to retrieve them and his fingers grazed hers. He snatched his hands back and ran them from the crown of his hair to the nape of his neck.

"I'm sorry I startled you. I came to fetch some water."

James's gaze fixed on the papers in her right hand. She passed them to him, but not before she saw the salutation.

"Why are you writing to Mrs. Turner?"

James colored and opened his mouth to speak but clamped it shut. He pulled out a chair and directed Ann to sit down.

"I'm sorry, Ann. I should have said something sooner. But when you got off the train, you caught me by surprise and I didn't know what to do."

"You're sorry? What has happened?"

James locked his eyes with hers. "There's no use beating around the bush. I never expected a woman like you." He raked a hand through his hair.

"The agency sent you to me by mistake."

Chapter Three

The room spun. Her hands tingled strangely and the pitcher fell from her fingers. James lurched forward and rescued the pitcher within an inch of its smashing into the floor.

"By mistake? That isn't possible," Ann protested. "Mrs. Turner gave me your name and you had mine. We exchanged letters. How could there be any confusion?"

James set the pitcher on the table and stared at it rather than at Ann. Had she done something wrong in the previous few hours? She mentally picked through the events of the evening, but couldn't uncover any clues.

"I think the agency made a mistake when they matched us. I had one request and you don't fulfill it."

Ann sank into the nearest chair. How could this be? Ann had suspected a mistake minutes earlier but brushed the thought away from her mind like a bothersome fly. Mrs. Turner didn't make mistakes, did she? "We've only just met. We barely know one another. How could you already be so sure?"

James met her eyes before dropping his gaze to the worn wooden floorboards. "I knew in an instant. From the moment I saw you."

"I don't understand." Mrs. Turner had prepared the girls for all sorts of excuses if their matches had a change of heart. They didn't work hard enough. They cooked terribly. Her mind raced through several reasons why a man might object to marrying her, but none could be ascertained with a glance. *He would have to know my heart.* She shuddered at the thought.

James met her eyes again. "At the train station today. You could see my surprise at the sight of you."

"You were nervous. To be honest, so was I."

James sucked in a lungful of air and pushed his words out in one long breath. "It was more than that. I was surprised because I expected a plain girl. An ugly girl, even."

Ann rubbed her aching temples. What on earth was he talking about? She'd also expected an ugly match, and had been pleasantly surprised. If only every girl at the agency, and every lonely bachelor in America could be so fortunate. "Forgive me, but I'm afraid I don't see the trouble."

James ran both hands through his hair until it stood up in tufts. "I requested the agency send me someone as plain as they come. That was my one and only request."

Ann shook her head. She knew James McCann might have many valid reasons for rejecting her as a wife, and she had steeled herself for all of them. But she'd never expected him to outright lie. She squeezed her hands together to keep them from trembling. "No man would ask for such a thing."

James sighed. "I did. Farm life can be hard. I knew a pretty girl would expect more than I could give her. I don't need that kind of nonsense."

Ann's cheeks grew hot. Her heart thudded so loud she feared he could hear it. "Why go through an agency at all? I'm sure America has as many ugly girls as England." She winced at the harshness of her own voice. She'd never been good at keeping her temper. Ann bit her lip.

James brow creased. "I thought someone who needed to find a husband through an agency would have no other alternatives."

A shiver coursed through her. James McCann had described her situation perfectly. Still, she bristled with irritation on behalf of all the other girls at the agency. "You thought all mail-order brides were desperate."

"No, no." He waved his hands as if to bat the words out of the air. "I meant no disrespect."

She sat up straighter. "What *did* you mean?"

"I thought a mail-order bride would be more content with this life."

"This life?"

"I've been working on this farm by myself far too long. Uncle Mac needs tending to. I need a helpmate."

"And why have you already deemed me unsuitable?"

James dipped his head and smiled sheepishly. "A woman like you couldn't know what hard work really is."

The hairs on the back of her neck stood up. "A woman like me? I'll have you know I've worked harder than most men all my life."

James chuckled and coughed to disguise it. "I know you worked as a maid, and I'm sure that is hard work, but it's not the same as farm life."

"You have no idea," she replied between clenched teeth. The labor of farm life seemed a sweet reprieve in comparison to her former occupation. Her neck burned with heat and she clenched her hands until the nails cut into her palms as she fought to control her wretched temper.

He dropped his gaze and turned away. "You don't understand. Regardless, you're to be someone else's bride. It's my fault. If I hadn't been so surprised by your beauty, I would have put you right back on that train the instant I laid eyes on you."

"Back on the train to where?"

"I know some other girl is supposed to be here instead of you, and you're supposed to be married to some rich banker in California. Or an oil baron in Texas. I'll send a telegram in the morning, so they know of the mistake, and a letter going into more detail. When we hear back from the agency, we'll make the proper arrangements."

How could she fight this? James believed the agency sent her by mistake. In her heart, for her own reasons, she agreed. She took a deep breath and straightened in her chair. "It could be weeks before we hear from the agency. What shall we do until then?"

"Only a few people knew you were coming, but I suppose there's no way to hide your presence now. We'll tell everyone the truth. We're getting to know one another. When you leave they'll assume you didn't like me."

Ann laughed bitterly. James didn't join her. "You aren't serious?" she asked.

"Those who know I chose an agency to find a bride already think I'm peculiar. It won't seem odd to them that you decided not to marry me. And with Uncle Mac here, there's no reason for anyone to think the arrangement improper."

"And what if you change your mind about me in the meantime?" Her stomach plummeted and her cheeks burned. Why had she asked that? He must think her positively desperate.

James's feet stopped tapping and his eyes locked with hers. "You aren't supposed to be here, Ann. We must right this mistake."

The resolve in his voice broke something inside her. Her body ached with exhaustion. She'd come so very far, only to be turned away. Soon she'd be completely alone in this world. Ann had been so afraid of rejection, but never in her wildest dreams had she believed it would be because of this. She blinked hard, but it didn't squelch the tears. They spilled over her lashes and spattered the tabletop.

James reached for her hand and squeezed it tight. She allowed him to hold it, though she desired to wrench it away. "Ann, you're a fine girl. Any man would be proud to have you as his wife. But I'm also certain if you're here, some heartbroken fool has been sent the homeliest girl in all of England." She forced a laugh, and he gripped her hand tighter. She wanted to squeeze his hand back until he yelped in pain. "Don't you see? We must make this right."

She nodded, but the desire to pinch his fingers between her own remained. Ann dried her tears with a handkerchief from her pocket, and James excused himself to fill her pitcher. The moment the door closed behind him she snatched the papers from the table and turned them over.

Dear Mrs. Turner,

It is with regret I must write to you so soon. Your
agency assured me you would deal with any issues
should they arise, and I have an urgent and pressing concern. As you must recall, my only request
for a match was the girl be plain. The match you
have sent to me, Miss Ann Cromwell, is the most
beautiful girl I have ever—

The letter ended there and she flipped the pages back
over a second before James returned. He handed her
the pitcher.

"I should have voiced my concern the moment we
met. Please forgive me."

Ann forced a weak smile. "It was an overwhelming
moment for us both."

His shoulders slackened and he let out a long breath.
"I appreciate your understanding."

Back in her bedroom, Ann splashed her face with
cold water and tried to absorb what had happened. Mrs.
Turner's voice echoed in her head, as clear as in her office. *This is your match, Ann. You must try to make it
work.* No dejected and miserable banker had greeted
his plain bride today, with only his immense wealth to
ease his disappointment. No lonely oil baron. If James
didn't want her, no one did. The agency intended her
to be here or nowhere.

As she readied for bed, Ann sorted through her hope-
lessly tangled thoughts. There had to be something she
could do. She'd been faced with a seemingly insur-
mountable hardship before. She would simply have to
work out her next course of action. She stretched out
on the bed and stared at a crack in the ceiling. She had

to think! She couldn't return to London. Even if she could somehow pay for the passage, it pained her to even contemplate the life waiting for her there. No, she could not go back.

She had only one choice. Stay in America. Hadn't she heard someone on the steamship call it "the land of opportunity"? But could a young girl really support herself here, with no family and no references?

Ann couldn't cook, of that she was certain, but her years of experience as a maid had to be an asset. She hadn't noticed many fine houses in New Haven, but there must be wealthy people nearby, and the wealthy were always in need of domestic help. She only had to seek them out and offer her services. She'd never imagined working as a scullery maid again, but without references, she would have to start again at the bottom. The wages were sure to be poor, and the tasks backbreaking, but they were backbreaking in England, too, and she'd survived them before. She was still young, strong. At least she would have food in her belly and a roof over her head.

Sleep didn't come easy that night. The house remained quiet but Ann's thoughts did not. Each time her eyes closed, she saw herself on the streets. Sometimes in England. Other times, America. No matter the location, the image sent her pulse racing.

When sleep finally overcame her, fear haunted her dreams. Night fell and a destitute Ann lived in a filthy alley overrun by rats. She found a quiet corner and curled into a ball in a desperate attempt at sleep. As she closed her eyes in exhaustion, a ghastly howl pierced the quiet of the night. A moment before she'd been alone. Now a screaming baby in a bundle of rags wailed into

Ann's chest. Its face reddened with each cry, and from its open cave of a mouth spilled forth the most horrible sound she'd ever heard.

Ann awoke with a start and shuddered. The room remained dark and she threw back the sheets now soaked with sweat. It had been over two years since she'd heard that cry. Two years of trying to forget. Now it echoed in her ears as if she'd last heard it yesterday. Ann hugged her knees to her chest and rocked back and forth.

Please, Lord, she prayed. *May I never have that horrid dream again.*

James couldn't get comfortable. He'd slept on the back porch countless nights before, but tonight the hammock sagged more than usual, his pillow lumped beneath his head and the still air drew every mosquito within a mile to his breath. He stretched a tattered quilt over his face but only succeeded in trapping several whining insects beneath it.

Why did she have to be beautiful? Certainly plain girls were everywhere, if the population of New Haven was any indication. Did the British consider Ann homely? James chuckled at the ridiculous thought. An island nation populated entirely by women as exquisitely attractive as Ann Cromwell would be a sight to see.

Hours passed and sleep never came. Soon it would be light and the chance for rest would be gone. A mournful moo echoed through the barn beside him. James flipped from the hammock onto his feet and stretched his arms until they touched the bead board of the porch ceiling. No sense waiting another hour to milk the cow.

It might help keep his mind occupied on anything other than the woman asleep upstairs.

When dawn peeked her head over the horizon, James had completed all of his prebreakfast chores, mucked out the horse stall and reorganized his hand tools. He would have repainted the whole house if it meant avoiding Ann for a few more minutes. His stomach grumbled loudly and he sighed in defeat. He would have to go inside eventually.

Lord, please let her hair be up, he prayed as he entered. James didn't think he could stand the temptation of seeing her blond hair cascading over her shoulders again as it had the night before. When she'd entered the kitchen, it had taken everything he had not to tear up the letter to Mrs. Turner right then and there. But that wouldn't have been fair to any of them. This wasn't where she belonged.

Something felt different when he entered the house. The soles of his boots left gray ghosts of dust on the floor as he walked. Odd. They'd never done that before.

Ann stood at the stove. He was thankful to note that her hair was pinned up. He grunted a hello, poured a cup of coffee and sat down.

"Would you like some breakfast?" she asked.

He nodded into his cup.

"Will your uncle be joining us?"

"Uncle Mac takes most meals in his room. If he doesn't come down shortly, you can take some up to him."

Ann cracked two eggs into the skillet from the basketful he'd collected early that morning and left in the kitchen long before Ann awoke. They sent up a sizzle and added a homey scent to the new and pleasant odor in the room. When had he smelled it before? Something was definitely different. The white of the baseboards gleamed whiter. The red-checked curtain over the window hung crisp and vibrant. And the floor had been scrubbed! He realized that his boots always left prints, only now he could see them as they contrasted against the gleaming wood.

She set breakfast before him. Two eggs and a thick slice of leftover bread she must have found in the pantry. His stomach rumbled and he shoveled in several bites. Raw egg white mingled with burned yolk. A large shard of eggshell crunched between his teeth. James stifled a gag and sipped his coffee. Coffee grounds mixed with the mess of egg in his mouth and he swallowed hard. His stomach churned. *Thank You, Lord.* He needed a reminder of why he'd requested a plain bride.

"You said you used to be a maid?"

"That's right."

"You've never been a cook."

"No, the house always had its own cook. I worked only as a maid."

James sighed. "Come here."

She stepped closer.

"Did you use lard?" She shook her head no. "Had you ever cracked an egg before?" Her cheeks colored and she shook her blond head again. "Why did you scramble them?"

"The yolks broke."

He sighed again and pushed away from the table. Ann stood stock-still until he grasped her by the elbow, and guided her to the stove. James retrieved an egg from the basket on the sideboard and cradled it in his palm.

"Think of this egg as money. If you hadn't gone and ruined those—" he cocked his head toward the table "—I could have sold them for almost two cents apiece. You wouldn't throw two cents out into the field would you?"

As the words came out, he was vaguely aware he was speaking to her as though she were a child. She cocked a brow and crossed her arms. "No, I would not throw two cents out into the field," she replied coolly.

"What you do is this. Make sure the skillet is nice and hot and drop in some lard. Roll it around until it sizzles. If it smokes, move it off the fire." He could make eggs in his sleep. Once the lard had melted into a shimmering puddle, he deftly cracked the egg with one hand. It hit the pan with a hiss and bubbled along its edges.

"I don't like my eggs scrambled. I like them over easy. It takes some practice and a soft touch." He took her hand and placed it on the handle of the spatula and covered her hand with his own. Together they turned over the egg. It sizzled again.

"The yolk didn't break," she half whispered.

James chuckled. "Not if you do it right. Fetch that plate," he directed.

She retrieved his dish from the table and scraped the offending eggs into the slop bucket. He took the plate and held it near the skillet.

"Can you do this yourself? You still need to be gentle."

"I think so." She slid the spatula under the egg and James held his breath as it crossed the short distance from skillet to plate. They smiled at each other as it came to rest.

"Perfect," he breathed. James raised the plate to his nose and inhaled. "Now, do the next one by yourself."

Ann yelped and jumped back from the stove. She'd grasped the blisteringly hot handle of the cast-iron skillet.

James's heart jumped to this throat and he snatched up her hand. The flesh on her thumb and first three fingers pulsed red and angry. Several white blisters appeared before his eyes. He plunged her hand into a pitcher of water on the kitchen table. "You must always cover the handle of the skillet with a towel," he gently scolded. He withdrew her hand and blew a cool stream of air on it. "Does it still hurt?" he murmured between breaths.

She bit her lip. "Yes," she gasped.

Without a word he slipped an arm around her waist and led her out the back door. The water pump stood a few yards away. He pumped the handle with one hand and plunged her fingers beneath the icy stream that bubbled forth with the other. Every few moments he removed her hand from the water, examined it and blew a new stream of air across the wet skin to ease the pain.

Each time he drew a breath he also took in the scent of her. Lavender soap and rose petals. *Focus!* He had to focus on her hand. If he broke the blisters, she risked infection. A curl of her golden hair escaped its pins and brushed his cheek. She turned her face to him and smiled weakly. He shivered.

The shudder of movement cleared his head. He'd let her entrance him again. "We need to get some salve on this," he said gruffly.

"Do you have butter?"

"Butter's no good. I have something better." He grasped her uninjured hand and drew her back into the house. He left her in the kitchen and returned with a tiny silver tin and strips of clean cloth. She wrinkled her nose as he slathered the foul-smelling paste on the burn, but he smiled at the sulfuric, acrid scent. It always reminded him of Mother.

"This smells awful." She drew up her mouth and pinched her nose.

He mimicked her grimace and laughed.

"What's so funny?" She tried to jerk her injured hand away but he held on tighter.

"Just trust old Doctor McCann." He slowly wound the strips of cloth around her slim fingers as he scrutinized the calluses dotting her palm. He still couldn't imagine a beauty like her assigned to more than the lightest of household tasks. Maybe she was simply thin-skinned?

She picked up the tin of salve with her free hand and eyed the contents. "What's in this?" she asked warily.

"Beeswax, honey and a few local herbs, among other things."

"What kind of herbs?"

"Guess."

Before he could stop her, she placed the tin under her nose and took a deep breath. Her eyes watered and her rosy cheeks turned beet red. She coughed daintily into the sleeve of her free arm but the cough turned into a choke. Soon tears streamed down her cheeks as she barked in ladylike fits. James laughed.

"*What* is so funny?" she demanded as she wiped at her streaming cheeks.

"I'm sorry, Ann. I didn't mean to laugh. You just looked so adorable."

His stomach turned to ice and his heart raced. He dropped her hand.

"I looked so what?" Her deep blue eyes narrowed.

Had she really not heard? "I have a lot of work to do outside," he mumbled. He had to get away from her. "I'll take my breakfast with me."

James snatched up his plate and stepped onto the back porch. The cool morning air washed over him like a sobering bucket of cold water.

The emotional ups and downs that came just from being around Ann were making him dizzy—and angry. He'd had such a simple plan: marry for practicality to a plain, decent woman who'd never leave him so twisted up inside. And then Ann walked into his life and ruined everything, from his peace of mind to his sleep to his breakfast. He stomped back into the kitchen.

"This." He pointed to the slop bucket with the ruined eggs. "This is why I didn't want a pretty bride."

Ann's cheeks flushed crimson and she clenched her hands into fists. "You think an ugly girl will make you a better breakfast?"

"I need to eat, Ann. Uncle Mac needs to eat. The animals need to eat. The crops need to be planted and harvested. And you can't even cook an egg."

"I'm sorry I'm a disappointment to you, Mr. Mc-Cann, but why are you berating me? If I'm another man's intended, you won't be bothered with me much longer."

James's cheeks burned. "I shouldn't have spoken to you that way. Forgive me."

He escaped out the back door before he could say something else he regretted. Ann was right. It didn't matter that, despite the disastrous breakfast, in a single morning she'd impressed him with much more than her beauty. She'd risen early to clean the entire kitchen by dawn, made an attempt at breakfast and stood stoically through the dressing of a burn that would likely make a grown man cry. None of that mattered. The agency intended her for another, and he had to keep reminding himself of that. Forget for an instant and he risked falling in love.

Chapter Four

James had been gone half an hour, and Uncle Mac still hadn't appeared. Did James still expect her to bring the older man his breakfast? She fried a second batch of eggs that, despite James's lesson, looked only slightly better than her first. She fished out a large piece of egg-shell with the tines of a fork and broke both yolks in the transfer to the plate. Ann exhaled loudly as the yellow liquid ran over the burned edges of white.

She scrounged a dented metal tray from the pantry, and arranged the tray with the plate of eggs, the coffee-pot and a cup and saucer. After surveying the meager meal, she added the last of the bread heel she'd found under an oilcloth. On impulse, Ann poured a cup of cof-fee for herself and sipped. *Wretched!* She spit the bitter mess back into the cup and replaced the coffee with a mug of milk. Her ill-suited suitor was right. She was hopeless in the kitchen.

Upstairs, she hesitated at the bedroom door next to hers. Ann had years of experience serving, but her em-ployers expected her to remain unseen. She cleaned rooms after the family vacated them, and if called to a room where her employers were present, she entered and exited as quickly as her legs and duties allowed. But that kind of detachment wouldn't do here.

"Mr. McCann? This is Ann Cromwell. I have your breakfast." Her knuckles softly rapped the paneled door. Was he even a McCann? Oh dear, she may have offended the man. Feet shuffled on the other side, but they didn't move toward the door. Had his nephew even shared with him news of Ann's arrival?

"Mr... Sir? Your nephew sent for me through the Transatlantic Agency. I'm to...to stay with both of you for a time." How had the burden of explanation fallen on her shoulders?

Ann waited several long minutes, knocking louder and louder at regular intervals, but still no one approached the door. The sounds from the other side assured her Uncle Mac remained both alive and mobile. She set the tray on the floor.

"I've left you a tray of breakfast, sir. I hope you enjoy it." *Unlikely.*

Back in the kitchen, she cleaned up the few dishes from breakfast and surveyed the room. It had been dusk when they arrived the night before, and the house had appeared neat and well-ordered. In the morning light she'd discovered the truth. Everything had been tidied recently, but by someone who knew every trick of creating the illusion of clean. Tabletops were spotless, but the spaces beneath were a tangle of cobwebs. Windows had been washed but their sills were trimmed with dust. Had James even noticed how she'd scrubbed the floors, wiped down the baseboards and chased spiders from every corner? And all before she'd prepared breakfast. *Ruined breakfast*, she chided herself.

She never expected to become a proficient cook overnight, but her first attempts in the kitchen were sobering. To earn her keep here, and cook for herself when she left, she'd need to learn. Perhaps James would give her a few more lessons.

Ann tried to shake the thought from her head, but it wouldn't budge. The whole thing had been a dreadful mess, and yet the memory stirred her heart. The thought of James standing beside her, his strong hand gently guiding her through each step of frying an egg sent goose bumps down her arms. When she'd carelessly burned her fingers, those same strong hands turned impossibly gentle as he tended her wounds. For a brief moment she'd forgotten she wasn't meant for James and had thanked God for her good fortune at being matched with someone so unlike the man who'd caused her so much pain in the past.

Just as quickly the memory soured. She didn't blame James for his outburst. He knew as well as she did they weren't meant for one another. It did neither of them any good to pretend. But did he have to remind her of her shortcomings? She knew them as well as anyone.

Ann's stomach knotted as it so often did when she grew nervous or upset. She chided herself. James McCann occupied far too many of her thoughts already, despite being no more than a begrudging temporary landlord and she his unwelcome houseguest. She needed a distraction. Polishing and scrubbing were good for that, but she'd already depleted the meager supply of soap and polish she'd found in the cabinet. Her needle lace had always been a comfort to her, so she fetched some from her room and set to work.

The simple piece—a square of linen on which she built up needle-lace scallops and flower petals one stitch at a time—didn't require enough attention to prevent her mind from drifting back to her situation. Despite James's beliefs, she knew no one waited for her. She would soon be alone in a strange country. Basic necessities to buy. Room and board to pay. The very thought of each expense made Ann's stomach go cold.

Embroidery proved a very poor distraction. Her hands trembled over the stitching as she contemplated her future, and after she ruined the third petal with her carelessness, she tucked the lace away in her apron pocket.

The creak of floorboards snapped her attention to the back porch. The wooden screen door swung open and James entered in his stocking feet. He'd walked through the kitchen with his dusty shoes on this morning. Did this mean he'd taken note of the markedly cleaner floor?

"Is lunch ready?"

Ann's throat constricted. A glance at the clock proved the day approached noon. "I'm sorry. I didn't know you wanted me to prepare something."

"That's alright. I don't think I could stomach another meal like breakfast."

Heat rose up the back of Ann's neck, and her fingers itched to snatch a plate from the table and launch it at his head. James smiled and teasingly winked. The angry heat receded a little.

"I've cooked my own meals for years. I think I can manage a little longer in exchange for a house this clean," he added.

He had noticed!

Before she could respond, James stepped abruptly

from the kitchen into the hall. His footsteps moved from the dining room to the parlor. He returned, his lips pulled down into a frown. "The other rooms haven't been cleaned. What have you been doing all this time?"

His accusation warmed her blood again. She rose from her chair and drew a deep breath to calm her temper. "I am not lazy, James McCann."

He gestured about the room. "No lunch and a dirty house. What do you call that in England?"

"I'll have you know it would have been my pleasure to clean your filthy house. You would have walked in the door and lost your senses at the great beauty of clean floors and windows not covered in grime. But you're out of supplies." Ann bit her lip to keep from saying more, though she feared the damage was done.

James's eyes widened and the taut muscles of his jaw relaxed. His voice grew soft. "I'm out of supplies?"

Ann stood up straight and clasped her hands submissively behind her back out of habit. She'd assumed this same stance whenever her employers addressed her while in service. She realized this immediately and let her hands fall to her sides.

"I used all of what you had cleaning the kitchen. I should have told you earlier." *If you hadn't stomped out of the house before I could.*

James dipped his sandy head and his cheeks colored. "Figures. I paid a woman from town to clean the house but she obviously cheated me. House is still dirty and she took the extra soap and polish with her."

He ran a hand through his hair and glanced at Ann. He looked…sheepish? Like a schoolboy caught with candy in his desk. "I'm sorry I accused you of being lazy. What have you been doing this morning?"

"I made Uncle Mac breakfast, though he didn't come to the door when I knocked. I left the food on the landing."

"It's my fault for not making proper introductions. We'll right that this afternoon. What else did you do?"

Her heart raced as she dipped her hand into her apron pocket. James would likely think her time better spent staring at the wall than working on needle lace. She withdrew the piece from her pocket. "I worked on this." She held out the handkerchief and cringed when he took it from her with dirty fingers.

She gestured to the cloth. "I'm sure you think such work is worthless, but I had nothing else to fill the time. I would have cleaned had I found more supplies," she repeated.

James examined the handkerchief as she spoke. Over and over, he turned it in his calloused hands. The more he studied it, the lighter his touch became, as if he handled a fragile porcelain cup. "You did all of this? The lace?"

She nodded.

His eyebrows raised and Ann saw a flicker of what appeared to be admiration. "No one helped you?"

Ann laughed at the absurd question. "Do you see anyone else here?"

James chuckled softly. "I meant—did someone help you with this before you arrived in America?"

"No. I began the work a week ago."

"After lunch we'll go into town for cleaning supplies. You'll take this." He gently folded the handkerchief into quarters and set it in her hand. His fingertips brushed her palm. The touch sent a warmth through her hand. She set her jaw and shook off the feeling.

James cobbled together a stew for lunch. "For Uncle Mac," he explained as he ladled the first steaming bowlful. He paired the stew with a mug of milk and they took the meal upstairs together. They hadn't even reached the top step before Ann spotted the breakfast tray. The spotless plate and empty mug suggested at least someone had enjoyed his meal that morning.

James rapped on the door. "Uncle Mac? Lunch is ready." Bedsprings creaked, but still the door didn't open.

"Best leave these here. There'll be plenty of time for introductions when we get back from town."

After lunch James retreated upstairs and returned wearing a clean shirt. His freshly scrubbed cheeks shone pink and water droplets clung to his tousled hair. Ann made a mental note to refill the pitcher in his room.

While James hitched the wagon, Ann stood outside and took in the expanse of land. Row after row of young green plants stretched in all directions. A small grove of oaks and maples, no more than five or six acres, anchored the east end of the field.

"May I ask what you did outside this morning?" Ann asked James as he helped her onto the wagon seat.

"Hoed the fields."

The field nearest Ann seemed enormous as she imagined someone clearing the weeds row by row. "When will you be done?"

James laughed drily. "A job like that is never done. Not until the corn grows tall enough to shade out the weeds. I'll be out here every morning until then."

"And when might that be?"

"Well…" James paused and rubbed his chin. "We have a saying. 'Knee-high by the Fourth of July.' When the stalks are that tall, we should only have a week or two more of weeding."

Weeks and weeks of hoeing this sweeping vista of green. Ann made a note to help him beginning tomorrow.

"What crops are you growing?"

James's eyebrows rose and his shoulders drew back. "Corn in the big south field and some wheat in the north field. Most everyone around here grows either corn or wheat as their main crop." He pointed to the next farm. "Hal Schneider has corn, too."

The meandering rows of corn on Ann's right weren't planted with nearly the precision of James's fields, and weeds were in abundance. In a few spots she couldn't tell the crop from the intruders.

"It looks like Hal Schneider needs to weed," she observed.

James glanced at the field. "Hal has a lot more than weeding to do."

"What do you mean?"

James's brow knotted and his mouth became a hard line. "The man has two young children and a house falling down around them. His wife died last year, and he didn't take it very well. He needs to tend to his children and himself as well as those fields." His voice held an edge of concern.

Ann strained to see the Schneider house, expecting to find children playing in the yard. It stood quiet and empty. She turned to James to ask him another question about his neighbor, but the top of an envelope jutting from his pocket caught her eye. So that was why he'd been so quick to suggest the trip to town. He needed to telegraph the agency and mail the letter to Mrs. Turner. Another reminder of her unknown future.

"Do you have much business in New Haven?" Ann tried not to sound too curious.

"A bit."

She waited for him to continue. He didn't.

"Am I to accompany you on your errands?"

He shook his head. "Nope."

It was like their trip from town to the farm all over again. Why must he swing betwixt friendly and withdrawn? Ann smiled through clenched teeth. "And what am I to do?"

"First you'll buy the supplies you need to clean. And then—" he turned to look Ann straight in the eye "—you're going to make yourself a new friend."

"What kind of friend?"

His eyebrows arched. "You'll see."

James sighed inwardly. He abhorred being so short with Ann, but what else could he do? Every time he let down his guard with her, his head spun. It was a familiar feeling. He'd felt it every time he'd been in Emily's presence. When she'd wanted something, he'd fallen over himself to do exactly as she'd asked, like a dutiful dog who only sees the good in its master. The need to please her had remained even as both his heart and God told him she was not the girl for him. At least now he knew how easily he lost his senses around a pretty girl. Better to focus on getting Ann to her intended husband and bringing his plain bride to the home where she belonged.

They drew into town and James turned onto the square and hitched the wagon in front of the first building. *Davis Mercantile* was neatly lettered in red and gold on the window.

"You can buy supplies in Davis's. Charge them to my account," he said as he helped her down.

"You aren't coming with me?"

"I have a few things to take care of first. Mr. Davis can help you find what you need."

James set off across the street. The post office sat on the other side of the square. Inside he handed the envelope to the clerk and asked him to calculate postage to England. He then spent ten minutes wording his telegram to the agency. Since he paid by the letter he had to get his point across as succinctly as possible. Afterward, he stepped into the library to fetch a book for Uncle Mac. Then he turned in the direction of the mill. He itched to confide in someone, and Frederick was his closest friend.

He stopped short on the wooden sidewalk a block away from the mill and chided himself. Ann had been in this town less than a day, and he'd left her unaccompanied. His weakness shouldn't mean she had to suffer through new experiences in a strange country alone.

He continued to the mill, but only stayed long enough to write a note to Frederick informing him he was no longer needed at the courthouse that afternoon. He gave the note to the foreman, who assured James he would deliver it to his friend.

He returned to the square and walked straight to the mercantile. The dark interior of the store was a sudden change from the sun-drenched sidewalk, and for a moment James couldn't see. He heard Ann's lilting voice well before he saw her.

"And you're sure this soap does a proper job?"

"Absolutely, miss. We don't carry Sunlight, but Fels-Naptha won't disappoint."

The store came into focus, along with Mr. Davis behind the counter. His dark mustache rose at the corners as he smiled in greeting. "I'll be with you in a moment, Mr. McCann," Mr. Davis called.

Ann stood at the counter and turned her golden head to face him. She smiled softly, and her shoulders dropped a hair, as if in relief.

"How will you be paying, miss?"

James strode to Ann's side. "Put everything on my account, Mr. Davis." He could hear the tremor of nerves in his voice. Why was he so nervous? He'd done business with William Davis for years.

Mr. Davis cocked a brow, but reached for the ledger book and entered the total without question.

Ann looked up at James, her blue eyes telling him something. Introductions! Apparently, he forgot even the most basic of social graces while in her presence.

"Mr. Davis, this is Miss Ann Cromwell. She'll be staying with me and Uncle Mac for a little while," he announced with far too much force.

"Delighted to meet you, miss," the shopkeeper replied. "It's always nice to have new people come to New Haven."

James silently thanked the man for not asking any questions. William Davis didn't get to be New Haven's most successful businessman by being nosy.

"Will there be anything else, Mr. McCann?"

"Did those new hand tools come in yet?"

Mr. Davis gestured to the farthest corner of the store. "Leroy just finished stocking them. Take a look. I think you'll find the new auger design superior to the old one."

James made his way to the back of the store while Mr. Davis wrapped Ann's selections and tied the bundle with string. He tried to concentrate on a shiny awl in front of him, but Ann's voice carried to him from the counter.

"This is a lovely town. On the drive in, I admired the many fine homes along the boulevard."

Mr. Davis chuckled. "I don't think any street here is fancy enough to be called a boulevard, but we do have some beautiful residences."

"In London, large homes employ several full-time servants."

"I imagine they would."

"Is that the case here in New Haven, as well?"

"Oh yes, miss. Half a dozen families here have servants."

"They do?"

Was James mistaken, or did her measured tone change? She sounded…anxious? Eager?

"Doc Henderson is the only one with live-in help. He has a cook and maid. Heard he's looking for a new one, though."

"A new cook or a new maid?" she asked.

He'd heard right the first time. Her melodic voice held a frantic edge.

"He employs one girl to do both."

"A maid of all work."

"If that's what you call it."

James stole a glance at the counter. Ann's lips were pursed and her large eyes cast down.

"In England, a servant who both cooks and cleans is called a maid of all work," she replied.

Mr. Davis's eyebrows arched. "Is that so?"

Was Ann looking for work? But why? They would be hearing from Mrs. Turner within a few weeks, and after that she'd be off to her true intended. Was living with him so miserable she'd rather work for someone than live with him? Heat flamed his cheeks. He had to treat her more as a guest, and pray it didn't lead him down a path to his own destruction.

Ann hoisted the packages off the counter but James arrived at her side in seconds and eased them out of her arms. "You shouldn't have to carry such a heavy bundle," he explained. Ann bit her bottom lip and murmured her thanks. Was she trying to stifle a laugh? He didn't doubt it. Everything Ann Cromwell did or said took him by surprise.

Chapter Five

Ann waited on the sidewalk while James placed her purchases in the wagon. She'd almost burst out laughing when he suggested the parcels were too heavy for her to carry. She was used to carrying basket upon basket of firewood up three flights of stairs for most of the year. The package of soap, polish and scrub brushes weighed nothing in comparison.

"Where to now?" she asked when he rejoined her on the sidewalk.

"Remember that friend I promised you? She should be in there." James pointed to the blue awning directly next to Mr. Davis's store. New Haven Dressmakers.

The shop appeared empty, but a bell clanging above the door brought a young woman bustling in from the back. Dark abundant hair piled high atop her head added even greater height to her tall and slender frame.

"Good afternoon, Delia. I wanted you to meet Ann Cromwell."

The woman's eyes widened and a broad grin broke across her face. In an instant she had Ann clasped in a hug. Ann stiffened and managed a feeble squeeze in return.

"So you're Ann! But didn't you mean to say Ann McCann?" The girl winked at James. Flames licked Ann's cheeks and she turned to find James's face suffused with pink. He took a half step back and bumped into a dress form, which teetered precariously before he righted it. James ran a hand through his thick hair and Ann's stomach tumbled. Did all men look so handsome when they were embarrassed?

She must change the subject, for both their sakes. "Were you the one who made that beautiful quilt?" she guessed. She recalled James saying this shop employed its maker.

The woman beamed. "Did you really think it beautiful? Frederick saw me working on it weeks ago and asked to buy it."

"And you are Frederick's cousin?"

The young woman placed a palm to her forehead. "Where are my manners, Mrs. McCann? I haven't introduced myself. I'm Ardelia. Ardelia Ludlow."

Ann shook her hand, and knew they couldn't let this woman's assumptions go uncorrected any longer. "It's still Miss Cromwell." She glanced again at James. His face flushed scarlet.

"Forgive my mistake." Her smile didn't dim and she laughed. "I'd say I'm still Miss Ludlow, but no one calls me that. My friends call me Delia, and you should, too."

Ann felt a twinge of the familiar and fumbled back to the jumble of memories from the day before. "I met a woman from New Haven on the train yesterday. She told me she had a daughter near my age. You both have the same last name."

Delia clapped her hands together and brought them under her chin. "You met Mother? What a coincidence!"

"This woman said she'd been visiting her sister."

Delia nodded her head vigorously. "That was her, alright. She visited my aunt in Pataskala. Just had her tenth child—can you believe it?"

"Your mother was so kind to help her."

Delia pointed to a cluster of chairs in the corner and a love seat. "Please, let's all of us sit and have a chat."

James rocked back and forth on his heels. The color in his cheeks diffused.

"Maybe I should leave you two alone," he offered.

"Nonsense!" Delia exclaimed. "Miss Cromwell, implore him to stay."

Ann bit her cheeks to keep from smirking. As if she could convince James to do anything.

"If I'm to call you Delia, you must call me Ann."

It didn't seem possible, but Delia's smile grew broader.

"Ahem." James cleared his throat. "Ann, did you bring that…uh…thing I asked you to?"

Ann bit back another smirk. So like a man to refer to a lady's handkerchief as a "thing." "Yes, I did," she replied, and fished the piece from her pocket. "It isn't quite finished."

No sooner had the lace left the folds of Ann's skirt than Delia snatched it from her hand.

"This needle lace is exquisite! Did you make this yourself?"

Ann nodded. Pride stirred in her middle.

"Handmade lace and embroidery are rare skills around here."

"It isn't as difficult as it appears. I am far more impressed with your quilt work."

Delia's dismissed Ann's compliment with a wave of her hand. "Everyone quilts. My baby sister is already better than me. But lace like this!" She chewed her lower lip. "I wish I could buy this piece for the shop today."

"Buy it?" Ann's voice rose half an octave. She paused and continued in a more ladylike tone. "You believe you could sell my lace?"

"Certainly. But I'm only an apprentice. Mrs. Williams, the shop owner, would have to make the decision to sell your work here. She'll be back tomorrow. Can I keep this and show it to her?"

James stepped forward. "Is it really all that special? That kind of lace, I mean?"

"Absolutely!" Delia stood and held the handkerchief a few inches from his nose. She traced a slim finger along one of the scallops. "See this pattern? It was made by embroidering scores of stitches, one on top of the other, to build up the design. There's no backing to guide it, like bobbin lace, just a needle and thread. Lace like this requires true talent."

Ann's mind raced with figures. It would cost one or two dollars a week for a boardinghouse. Twenty-five dollars to repay James for her steerage ticket, followed by the agency fee—the price of which she couldn't even guess. Still, she'd brought with her several dozen handkerchiefs. If they fetched half a dollar each, she might have some hope of supporting herself.

"Do you have any idea how a handkerchief like this might be priced?" Ann could barely contain the tremor of excitement in her voice.

Delia walked to the window and held the handkerchief in front of the glass. Sunlight streamed through the embroidery and painted a patterned shadow on the floor. "It's hard to say. We won't have many buyers in New Haven for something so fine, but we are getting more customers from Columbus. And it's English-made, which is very popular."

Ann laughed. In England her work was maid-made.

Delia looked up when she laughed and smiled back. "Five dollars."

It was good Ann remained seated. Otherwise she might have fainted. Had she heard right?

James coughed and backed into another dress form. "Did you say five dollars?" he croaked.

"Like I said, I'll have to check with Mrs. Williams, but I think that's how she'd price it."

Ann's head was spinning. "When will you know?" she breathed.

"You'll be at church this Sunday?"

Ann looked to James. He nodded.

"Wonderful. I can tell you then if Mrs. Williams is interested. If she is, I'm sure she'll wish to meet with you."

Ann moved through the pleasantries as if in a trance. It was only when James lightly touched her elbow that she realized they were leaving. She returned Delia's hug goodbye, and allowed James to guide her to the door. Once on the sidewalk outside, with the shop door safely shut behind them, James let out a long, low whistle. His green eyes met hers and he squeezed her elbow. "Five dollars!" he said, as if it were a fantastic secret between them.

His excitement added to her own. She drew a deep breath to retain her decorum. "Mrs. Williams might not think it's worth so much."

James laughed. "Even a few dollars is a lot of money for some old handkerchief."

Ann stiffened at the comment. "Needle lace takes years to learn and countless hours to create a few inches."

"I believe you. It's like nothing I've ever seen."

James's loose hair flopped over his right eye and he hadn't yet raked it back into place. The sight positively unnerved her. It was hard to concentrate as he gazed at her through the sand-colored strands. Why hadn't he swept it back?

A realization flickered. "You intended for me to meet Delia, didn't you? She was the new friend you mentioned?"

"Delia or Mrs. Williams. I thought you'd find something in common with them and could make a friend during your short time here."

"And you like it? The needle lace, I mean?"

He raked the hair from his forehead and met her gaze straight on. "Beautiful but impractical."

A shiver coursed through Ann's shoulders. He wasn't just talking about the handkerchief.

James extended his arm toward the wagon, and helped her alight onto the seat. "Where'd you learn it?"

"Hmm?" His strong hands had touched her lightly as he held her palm and arm, but the phantom sensation of his touch remained. Her other hand throbbed lightly from its burn, only serving as further reminder of the last time they touched.

"The lace. Who taught you how to make it?" James hauled himself onto the wagon seat and flicked the reins.

"We were instructed in basic embroidery at the orphanage. When I entered service, I took handkerchiefs out of my mistress's dresser and studied the needlework. Later, I would copy it."

"Why were you in an orphanage?"

James didn't know he'd asked Ann two questions. She'd lived in an orphanage twice in her life, but for very different reasons each time. Explaining the reason for her first stay was easy. Even thinking of telling him about the second made her stomach hurt. "Why are American children sent to orphanages?"

James squinted at Ann through dark lashes and nodded slowly. "Of course. I apologize for the callous question. You lost your parents. I'm sorry."

His voice grew soft as he apologized. She resisted the urge to reach out and touch his hand. To let him know she appreciated his words. The hand closest to her rested palm up on his knee, the reins slack upon his fingers.

He caught Ann staring at them and gripped the reins.

Ann averted her eyes. "Delia seems like a nice girl." She'd seemed like more than a nice girl. A few minutes with her and Ann felt she'd found someone she could confide in.

"All of the Ludlows—and the Renners, for that matter—are good people. You'll get to meet many of them at church."

"You aren't going to make me stay home? Hide me away until you hear from Mrs. Turner?" she teased.

James blushed. "I told you we'd tell everyone the truth. Or at least most of it. We met through an agency and you're staying with me and Uncle Mac to see if we suit. There's really no other way to explain why you're living in my house. Besides, half the people in town seem to know already."

He was right. Mr. Davis hadn't so much as blinked when James directed him to charge her purchases to his account. She now saw how ridiculous her inquiries regarding positions of service in New Haven had been. To all of New Haven, she would always be the intended Mrs. James McCann. It would be too awkward for any of them to hire her on. If she wanted a new position, she'd have to leave. Not only would she be starting yet another new life, but it must be far away from here.

Ann played with the hem of her sleeve and her breath caught in her throat. She must handle this next topic delicately. "We haven't yet discussed the terms of my staying with you."

He shot her a quizzical look. "What do you mean?"

Ann swallowed hard. "I—I don't have much money at the moment, to pay for room and board. However, if my handkerchiefs fetch as dear a price as Delia believes, I can repay you for everything. My passage. The agency's fee."

James waved a dismissive hand. "Don't you worry about board. If you clean the rest of the house as well as the kitchen and keep it that way, I'll consider it payment enough. The kitchen hasn't looked like that since Mother died."

"Oh." Had she detected a compliment? What a pleasant surprise.

"Of course, I'd hoped you'd cook as well as my mother, but I guess that was too much to wish for."

Ann bristled. She bit her tongue to keep her retort at bay. This man was never going to relinquish his prejudice against her.

"As for your passage and the agency," he continued, "I wouldn't worry yourself too much about that."

Ann cocked her head and puzzled over his comment. "Why not?" she asked finally.

"I'm confident the agency will refund their fee. They'd have to after the kind of mistake they made. And once you're properly matched with your intended, he can repay me for your ticket." He laughed. "I'm sure he'll be scandalized to discover I could only afford steerage. Maybe we'll tell him I sprang for a second-class ticket? Get a few more dollars out of him?"

He turned to Ann and his smile dropped. "I'm only joking, of course. I'd never be dishonest."

Ann barely managed a weak smile in return. If only he knew the cost of repayment rested squarely on her shoulders. Even if she procured money, she'd first have to think of supporting herself. "But you'll be alright until then?" she asked hopefully.

James cleared his throat and gave a nervous chuckle. "Yes, though the sooner we hear from Mrs. Turner and get you sent off, the better. Fact is, I used most of last year's profits to pay the agency fee and your passage. Until this year's crops are in, I'm stretched a little thin. I counted on a lot more help around the house and the farm this summer and fall. It'll cost to hire a hand during harvest."

Her insides clenched. If only a wealthy suitor really *did* await her, checkbook in hand.

"Did you post the letter to Mrs. Turner?" she asked, sure that he had.

James chewed his lip. "I did."

So it was done. The countdown had begun.

Back at the farm, James let Ann off by the door before pulling the wagon into the barn and tending to the horse. He took the few minutes of solitude to mentally review their trip to town. When he'd invited Ann to stay with him, he never imagined he could be so weak. He'd prayed over and over that morning for strength to focus on the task at hand. Such a simple task. Patiently await the arrival of his intended bride—a helpmate for the farm and the future mother of his children—all while sharing a home with the most breathtaking beauty New Haven had ever seen.

He stifled a chortle. Simple? This was the hardest task of his life. Every time he turned around, a compliment escaped his lips. Why did he keep doing that? The only antidote he could think of was to follow his praise with criticism. To remind himself he couldn't be caught up in the deceit of beauty again. Yet each time he criticized her, Ann's doe eyes reflected the wound. Then his chest would tighten to see he'd caused her pain, and he'd be caught up in her gaze all over again.

No, he couldn't do this to himself! His time with Emily would be for nothing if he repeated the same mistakes. From the moment they met, he'd been utterly blind to Emily's flaws. He'd ignored every warning God gave him and plunged ahead, hoping she'd grow a heart for farm life and family devotion.

The summer sun still hung high in the sky when he left the barn. His cheeks burned and his mouth felt dry as dust. He headed to the well pump for a drink of water and found Ann already there. She let the tin cup hanging by a chain drop with a clatter and wiped her mouth with the back of her hand.

"My, it's a mite warmer here than I expected," she called to James.

"Too warm for you, I'd imagine."

Ann's smile fell. "I said it felt warmer. I didn't say

I was swooning," she huffed. Her rosy cheeks flushed pinker.

I've done it wrong again! He couldn't teeter-totter between admiration and admonishment. There had to be something in the middle. He'd been praying for strength since she arrived. He now saw he needed something more. *Lord, I need strength, but please also grant me the gift of hospitality.*

Ann plucked a plain handkerchief from the pocket of her dress and soaked it under the icy water. She drew the cloth across the back of her creamy neck and sighed. His heart stirred. He prayed harder.

"I need to inspect your burn." The last thing he needed was to be in close contact with her again, but the task was unavoidable.

Ann held out her hand for inspection, and he unwound the bandages and turned her hand over in his. The scent of lavender tickled his nose and he held his breath. Her hand looked like any other hand. Only smaller and more delicate, and attached to a slim arm that led to an arching graceful neck...

Stop it!

The salve had done its job and the burns were healing nicely. "I'll give you the salve to reapply," he gruffed before pushing past her and drawing in a grateful breath of non-lavender-scented air.

Ann followed closely behind as he entered the kitchen. There he found Uncle Mac sitting quietly at the table. His hands were folded in front of him. His thick, gray hair parted severely to one side. His collared shirt was neatly tucked into his trousers but he'd missed the top button. When he saw James, the older man's eyes narrowed ever so slightly.

"I'm sorry you two didn't get to meet earlier," he began, addressing his uncle. "Miss Ann Cromwell, this is Uncle Mac. Uncle Mac, this is Miss Cromwell."

Ann stepped from behind James and the effect was immediate. Uncle Mac's gray eyes grew wide and his lips spread into a grin. He winked at James.

Ann clasped her hands in front of her and addressed Uncle Mac in a slow, melodic cadence. "It's lovely to meet you, sir. Thank you for allowing me to stay in your fine home." James was struck by the thought that she'd speak to Queen Victoria with the same respect if she were granted an audience.

"You may call me Ann," she continued. "And what shall I call you?"

"You can call him Uncle Mac. Everyone does," James answered.

"And what is Mac short for?" She continued to address the older man.

"It's short for McCann. His first name is Angus, but not even his family called him that. Isn't that right, Uncle Mac?" James strode forward and clapped a hand on the man's shoulder. Uncle Mac smiled again and nodded.

"I apologize for the eggs this morning." She spoke a little louder this time, but no less respectfully. "I hope they weren't too horrid."

Uncle Mac unfolded his hands and waved one as if to dismiss her comment.

"Was the stew more to your liking?"

Uncle Mac shrugged. "I—I can-can't talk," he replied.

Ann cocked an eyebrow in James's direction.

"Ann, will you join me on the porch a moment? I need to show you where I keep the milk pail," James said.

Once outside, James pulled both the screen door and outer door shut behind them. "I don't like to speak about Uncle Mac in front of him, as if he can't understand what we're saying."

"So he *can* understand me?"

"It's my fault for not explaining things sooner. I wasn't expecting him to be in the kitchen when we got home."

That was only half the truth. Emily had grown exasperated with Uncle Mac's speech the first time she met him. It was also the first time his heart began to cool toward her. Their introduction had hit a crescendo when she'd thrown up her hands and stomped out of the room. At the time, Uncle Mac had only a stutter. James had learned so much about Emily that day. Perhaps he'd held information back now for similar reasons—to test Ann for her genuine reaction.

"So he can hear us? He can understand us?"

"Every word. He has his own thoughts, but his brain won't let him express them. He wants to speak, but for some reason he can't. At least, that's how Doc Henderson explained it."

Ann placed a hand on her throat. "How terrible for him."

"Don't pity him. He would hate that most of all."

"What do I do?"

"Speak to him as you would to anyone else. He has ways to communicate, even if he can't speak."

"But he spoke just now. He said he couldn't talk."

"Through much practice, he's been able to hold on to a few phrases. A few words. But as time goes on, he loses more and more of them. When he first stopped speaking, he could still write out his thoughts, but not anymore."

"The poor dear." The smooth expanse of Ann's forehead creased in concern. "You said you were surprised to find him in the kitchen."

"Yes. He rarely leaves his room for more than a visit to the privy." James smiled. "If I had to guess, I'd say he came down so he could meet you. It's times like these I miss speaking with him most. If only I could ask him what he thought when he first saw you. I'd told him a plain girl was coming. Practically promised she could cook meals fit for a king."

His heart fell the instant he'd said the words. He'd aimed for teasing and had instead insulted her again! James grasped for Ann's fingers and gave them a squeeze. "He probably thought he'd stumbled into the wrong house when he saw the cleanliness of the kitchen. He's used to how I keep everything decorated with a nice layer of filth and cobwebs."

Ann bit her lower lip, but it didn't disguise the smile playing about her mouth. She squeezed his fingers in return.

Had he saved the moment? "I think he'll really enjoy having you stay with us," he added.

She released her lower lip and let the smile light her face. "Is there anything else I can do for him?"

James suppressed a sigh of relief. "Take him his meals and leave him be. He spends his days in his room reading. It's all he ever wants to do. He's terrified of the day his mind will rob him of that ability, too. That was one of my errands in town. Getting him books from the library."

He turned to reenter the house. Ann placed a hand on his arm to stop him. "How long has he been like this?"

"Longer than many of us realized. He hid it well for so long. Five years? Six?"

"You've been caring for him all this time?"

James nodded. "I farm and I cook and I take care of the house. Uncle Mac doesn't need much, but he can't lend a hand anymore. He helped with the animals and did all the cooking until a year ago. One day he milked the cow six times, poor girl." He chuckled softly, even as his eyes watered at the memory. He looked down to hide the tears and kicked at the whitewashed porch floor. "It was the day I realized I couldn't do it by myself anymore."

He broke his gaze with the floor to check Ann's reaction. Her perfect face contorted with concern.

"Is that when you first wrote the agency?" she asked.

"I waited a few months, hoping things would get better."

James ached to tell her more. How he'd spent every Sunday church service scouring the congregation for a suitable bride and always coming up short. The dull pain of envy that pulled at his chest every time he saw a young family strolling through town. He'd never wanted to send away for a bride, but the life he wanted was slipping through his fingers.

Ann's clear blue eyes were wide. Her hand remained on his arm and her slim fingers applied a firm pressure. "You needed help on your farm. With your uncle. There's nothing wrong with that. Everyone has their own reasons for using the agency."

Could she read his thoughts? James stared into her eyes. He'd thought they were simple pools of robin's-egg blue. He now saw the pupils were rimmed with a spectacular dark violet.

"I know my cooking is atrocious, but cleaning your home will never fill my day. Will you allow me to assist in meal preparations while I'm here? I promise my sandwiches are edible."

James smiled. "That would be nice, thank you."

"You shouldn't starve in the interval, provided the next girl is ugly enough for you," she added. "Though I hope she never knows about your specific conditions. Such a thing would destroy her."

His shoulders tensed. "I would never tell her. She would never know."

Ann tipped her head toward him. "Are you certain she wouldn't discover it?"

Heat rose in his cheeks. "Not even Frederick knew of my request. Only Uncle Mac, and he couldn't tell someone if he tried. And I never asked for an ugly girl. Simply a plain one." He imagined as he grew to know his match, she'd become beautiful in his eyes.

Ann shrugged. A blond curl slipped from its pin and fell against her neck. "I see how much help you need. If a plain girl is the most capable, I hope you find her. But perhaps—" Ann paused and pursed her lips "—perhaps a pretty girl could make you a good wife."

Something in his heart softened at her words and heat spread over his cheeks. He longed to grasp her wayward curl and twist it between his fingers. Instead he placed a hand over hers. As his sun-darkened fingers came to rest upon her pale ivory hand, the memory of Emily's alabaster skin flashed before him. This was why he couldn't trust himself with a pretty girl. They drove him to distraction. He could hardly form a rational thought.

James wrenched free from her light grasp. "I'm certain a pretty girl—a girl as beautiful as you—would leave the moment she laid eyes on this farm."

He stomped back into the house to get away from her, but not before a thought buzzed in his ear like an annoying fly.

But Ann didn't leave when she saw the farm. Ann stayed.

Chapter Six

After meeting Uncle Mac, Ann's heart ached for James. The burden of running the farm and caring for the old man must be enormous. She'd offered to assist with meals on impulse but soon realized how the act could assist them both. Her conversation with the shopkeeper had yielded one helpful bit of information. Maids in America were expected to both cook and clean. She could approach each meal as an opportunity to improve her cooking, and thus her chances at future employment.

She would purchase a cookbook the next time she was in town, though she wasn't sure how much good it would do. She'd perused one at the store and been utterly stymied by the directions.

Days passed and her optimism flagged. Each morning James rose early to tend to the animals and weed his fields, and she disappointed him a few hours later with burned eggs, or raw eggs, and coffee that was entirely too strong…not to mention rather chewy.

One evening she tried to recreate James's simple stew and instead served a burned and oversalted gruel. By the end of the week she'd burned more than half the eggs she cooked, and her first loaf of bread was so heavy James teasingly suggested they use it as a doorstop.

Before each meal she placed a tray of the same food outside Uncle Mac's door. And after each meal she retrieved a spotless tray. When Ann retrieved his dishes after serving the stew, Uncle Mac abruptly flung open his bedroom door and rewarded her with a broad grin. "Good," he mouthed, pointing to the empty stew bowl.

Ann surmised the old man's sense of taste had declined with his ability to speak.

Between meals she cleaned. Oh, did she clean! At the Atherton home and the orphanage, the scrubbing and dusting and polishing were done on a weekly or even daily basis. This home had gone ages without proper cleaning, and it proved filthier than she'd first realized. Years of dirt and grime filled every crease and crevice, and the cleaning left her no time to assist James in the fields as she'd planned.

Sunday morning she leaped from her bed, flung open the window casings and sent up a silent prayer of thanks. Her heart fluttered at the thought of seeing Delia, her one friend, and learning what Mrs. Williams thought of her lace. Good news could mean money in her pocket, the opportunity to repay James and the hope of supporting herself in America.

She raced to beat James to the kitchen, but he'd arrived first as always. He pulled a skillet from the oven as she entered.

"You didn't have to make breakfast," she said, relieved he had.

Her voice startled him. He bobbled the skillet before setting it atop the stove with a clatter.

"This isn't breakfast. It's johnnycake. We have a meal after church every week in the summer. Everyone brings a dish to share."

Ann stepped forward to find a deep golden cake. Steam wafted over the surface and carried a softly sweet scent.

"I could have made something," she offered, half-heartedly.

"You certainly could have. How about toast? Or sandwiches? Or toast?"

As always, James's eyes widened in surprise after he teased her, as if he didn't know from where the words had come. She found it oddly endearing. Ann poked an elbow into James's ribs, and he grasped it and gave it a squeeze in return. Her face warmed.

"I'll make something for next time," she assured him. She would be a better cook by next week. It wasn't possible to be worse.

"And I'll make another johnnycake just in case." James winked and Ann moved to elbow him again. He dodged her attempt but bumped into the counter and sent the open canister of flour off the edge. James caught it upright in his arms before it hit the floor. The jolt sent a billowing cloud of white flour erupting out of the canister and into James's face and hair.

Ann didn't breathe. Neither of them moved. James's eyes remained closed, and the wash of white gave him the appearance of a classic Greek statue. A Michelangelo in coveralls. The curve of his mouth turned slowly up at the corners. His lips parted.

"A little help?"

Ann drew forward and took the canister from his hands. His eyes remained closed.

"What can I do?" She couldn't hide the amusement in her voice. He chuckled. The shudder of movement sent a cloud off his shoulders.

"I'm afraid to open my eyes."

Flour coated his long lashes and dusted his lids. Reaching out to touch his face, flour sifted to the floor beneath her fingertips. As she worked, his warm breath caressed her skin. She resisted the urge to brush the flour from his lips.

Focus on the task at hand.

"Try opening your eyes now."

His lids rose slowly. Ann had thought his eyes were green. Up close they were clearly hazel with flecks of gold.

Ann's heart galloped. His face was so close. An unmistakable gentleness rimmed his eyes. She didn't see him move, but she sensed his strong body drawing closer.

Her heart strained. She couldn't do this. It would only bring both of them heartache.

"I'll fetch you some water," Ann mumbled as she turned away.

Was that a sigh behind her? She didn't let herself look.

"There's no time for that. I'll clean up under the water pump."

After rinsing off outside, James tromped upstairs with wet hair to change. When he returned he wore the same suit from the day they met. He'd looked so handsome that day. James was taller and trimmer than most men, and the tailored clothing accentuated his frame in ways his work clothes could not. His thick hair lay neatly parted, but when he caught her staring he reached up and mussed it back into boyish waves.

Outside, James hitched the buggy, rather than the buckboard. It only seated two. "Does Uncle Mac always stay home from church?"

"He prefers to stay home and read his Bible."

The trip to church was even longer than the one into town. A few miles into the drive they turned west, and soon the sights were strictly farmland with the occasional farmhouse dotting the landscape. As they approached each home, James recited their family name, followed by some odd bit of trivia. The Cooks' orchard produced the best apples for cider. The Zwebels had two of the fastest horses in the county. The Fladts ran an inn, but their own fifteen children took up most of the rooms. Ann watched as men readied their wagons and buggies, while their wives herded children and balanced covered dishes in each hand. Without exception, everyone waved their arms with abandon or called out a warm hello.

The wagon crested a hill and revealed a steeple in the distance. They rounded a corner and the entirety of the church came into view. The white steeple topped a brick building adorned with arched Gothic windows and ornate stained glass scenes. "My father donated the largest trees in our woods for the church's frame," James said.

Before the horses had even come to a stop in front of the hitching post, Ann scanned the crowd for Delia. She glanced toward the church entrance as a dark head disappeared through the doors.

"I see Delia!"

James looked up but she was already out of sight. Ann scrambled from the buggy and bounced on her heels as she waited for James to join her. Each passing stranger smiled in greeting and kept on staring. By the time James reached her side, Ann was ready to climb back into the buggy.

"No one here will bite," he said as he offered his arm.

She forced a laugh. "Of course not. They'll only nibble."

James laughed, but she only gripped his arm tighter.

From the outside, the church appeared remarkably similar to the one Ann attended back in England, but on the inside it couldn't have been more different. Quiet but lively conversations echoed against the stained glass. Where were the hushed tones? The uncomfortable reverence?

"Where are we to sit?" Ann asked, puzzled. She was accustomed to servants sitting in the back with several empty pew rows in the middle to separate them from their employers. Here, everyone appeared to be intermingled with no regard to wealth or class.

James pointed to an empty pew on the left, close to the back. "I like to sit here. Keeps me from blocking too many people's views."

Not only were the seating arrangements far different from what she was accustomed to, so was the sermon. In the Church of England, servants' obedience to their masters was always a popular topic, followed by servants being cheerful in their work. Ann had heard these sermons so often she imagined she could recite them from memory.

The pastor preached on loving thy neighbor as thyself. He asked the parishioners to treat each other as equals, and in the same way they wished to be treated. Ann tried to imagine the same message being preached back in England, to a congregation clearly divided by class.

At the end of the service everyone moved into a large tented area outside. Under the tent sat a long row of tables, and soon these tables filled with a bounty of food. Platters of sliced ham and chicken legs were followed by crocks of beans and potatoes. A mismatch of earthenware and porcelain bowls swam with tomato salad, string beans and scalloped onions. As each new dish was placed, Ann's stomach groaned a little louder.

James retrieved the johnnycake from the buggy and nestled it on the last table between a lattice-top blueberry pie and a crumble-topped cherry cobbler. It looked plain and homely next to its decorated neighbors. Discouragement pressed on her as Ann pondered how many weeks of practice it would take for her to learn to duplicate the simple johnnycake, let alone the gems surrounding it.

They'd no sooner entered the line for food before the first of many ladies approached with a shy smile and inquisitive eyes.

"Ann Cromwell."

"London, England."

"We're still getting to know one another. We don't know when the wedding will be."

She repeated the same answers to the same questions over and over. If few knew of her arrival before, everyone in the county knew now. Older ladies clasped her hands between theirs. Younger ladies eyed her up and down and squeezed her so tightly she almost couldn't breathe.

Had she detected a hint of malice in their greetings? After the sixth or seventh girl the revelation hit her straight on. The smirking smiles and too-tight embraces were the results of jealousy. Mrs. Ludlow had been right. James was a very eligible bachelor. If only these girls knew they had no reason to be jealous of her, and that he would be sending her away the first chance he got.

Ann forgot everyone's names as soon as she heard them. Friendly smiles and envious eyes blurred all the women together. It was no matter. Soon she would be leaving New Haven and would never see any of these women again.

By the time they'd reached the end of the line, Ann's plate overflowed and she'd grown eager for a few moments of quiet. As if reading her mind, James guided her to a table farthest from the crowd. She'd taken her first cautious bite of something foreign but delicious when a hand gripped her shoulder. Startled, she pulled away to find Frederick Renner.

"Enjoying the fine weather?" he asked, but didn't wait for an answer. Instead, he moved around to the other side of the table and thumped James between the shoulder blades before dropping his considerable weight onto the bench beside him.

James gave Frederick a playful shove and continued eating. Ann forced a smile and wondered if Frederick already knew about James's plan to send her away.

"So, Ann, I heard you've met my cousin Delia."

"Yes, I did. Do you know where she is?"

Frederick pointed, and Ann glanced behind her. Delia stood by the food tables and waved her long arms over her head when she noticed Ann looking her way. Her tall form moved swiftly toward them and Ann leaped to her feet to meet her. Delia greeted her with a ferocious hug. Tears welled up in Ann's eyes, and after

Delia broke the embrace Ann kept her back turned to James and Frederick so she could whisk the wetness away unnoticed. It had been too long since she'd had a friend.

"I have wonderful news for you, Ann."

"You spoke with Mrs. Williams?"

"She adored your handkerchief. Said she hadn't seen anything like it outside Columbus, and even there she wasn't sure they had anything so fine. She'd like to sell them and can give you sixty percent of the sale."

Ann never had a head for figures, but before she could even think James had done the math. "She'll get three dollars for each?" he asked.

Delia's brown eyes twinkled. "No…she'll get six! I thought each handkerchief would bring five dollars, but Mrs. Williams thinks she can sell them for ten!"

James choked on a bite of beans. His face turned red and he sputtered out a cacophony of hoarse coughs. Soon half a dozen men were on their feet and thumping his back. Finally, he drew a ragged breath and held up his arms in surrender. Still, a few of the more enthusiastic heroes had to be grasped by the wrists to stop the onslaught of thumps and whacks.

After a few raspy breaths, James snatched up his napkin and drew it over his face. He removed it to reveal an incredulous expression. "You mean to tell me people are willing to pay ten dollars for a single handkerchief?"

Delia grinned from her position beside Ann, where she'd seated herself during James's coughing fit. "Maybe more. Mrs. Williams set the price based on what she'd seen in Columbus. But as I said, she's seen nothing quite so beautiful."

Ann's stomach fluttered. She'd been as surprised as James at the news, but fought to retain her decorum. She took a large bite of berry pie and savored it until the butterflies settled enough for her to speak.

"That is wonderful news," she whispered. This was an immense understatement. Ann's very life depended upon her ability to find a livelihood and succeed at it.

Delia laughed and draped an arm around Ann's shoulders. "Can you bring more to the shop this week?"

"Yes. I have several finished."

"Mrs. Williams said she'd love to see them."

After Ann finished her plate, Delia insisted on making additional introductions, and led her about the picnic grounds. Next she guided Ann to a small field next to the church where a group of children played. A man crouched in the middle of a particularly boisterous fray. Children of all ages and sizes tackled him from every angle. Well-muscled arms reached out from the center of the pile and plucked boys and girls off his back. When he stood and shook off the last of them, the thick shock of sandy hair was unmistakable. It was James!

His face was the picture of mirth as children tugged on his arms and legs. His strong hands pushed them gently to the side until he was approached by a tiny girl with dark hair. He bent down and swung the child onto his shoulders. Ann's chest twinged.

"James adores children," Delia stated matter-of-factly.

The twinge repeated, only this time it migrated to her middle.

"And children obviously love James," she murmured.

"Sadie Schneider looks particularly charmed by him," Delia observed.

"Is she the one on James's shoulders?" Ann studied the child. Her dark brows and eyes gave her a naturally serious appearance, but her entire face lit up in delight as James galloped the two of them about. She had great fistfuls of his hair in her hands and used them to guide him like reins on a pony. Only the state of Sadie herself detracted from the happy picture. Her Sunday dress appeared crumpled and stained, and her shiny raven hair had not been brushed for some time.

"Yes. And that's her brother, George," said Delia. Sadie's sibling was unmistakable. He had the same dark hair and delicate features as his sister, along with the same serious expression. The older child appeared to have brushed his own hair, but his clothes were in need of a good scrubbing. He looked to be about seven and attempted to trip James as he ran. "Those are two of your neighbors."

Now Ann knew why the name Schneider sounded familiar. She looked around, expecting an impending introduction. "Where is Mr. Schneider?"

"Over there." Delia pointed to a man sitting slouched in the shade of a tree, far removed from both the children and the other picnickers. Despite the revelry around him, his head remained down turned and his hat was pulled so low only his chin was visible. A casual passerby might assume he was merely snoozing after the large meal. The dark brown hip flask jutting from his jacket pocket suggested otherwise.

"James said his wife died."

"At the end of last summer. He took it very hard."

"Is he drunk?"

"Either that or sleeping off his drinking from last night."

The incongruity of the scene unnerved Ann. A drunkard who brought his children to church but couldn't be bothered to leave the bottle at home. "Does he come for the food?"

Delia shrugged. "For the past year, I've never even seen him eat."

"Why come at all then?"

She sighed. "My mother visited Mrs. Schneider many times during her illness. She said toward the end, Mrs. Schneider made her husband promise he would bring the children to church every Sunday. If not for that promise, and my mother's bearing witness to it, I'm sure he wouldn't be here."

Mr. Schneider pulled the flask from his jacket and took a discreet swig. Ann turned away.

The crowd around them thinned.

"It looks like most people are leaving," Delia remarked. "I need to catch up with my family." She hugged Ann goodbye and joined a cluster of tall, dark-haired children who could only be her siblings.

James sidled up to Ann. "Ready to go?"

She nodded. It wasn't entirely true. The stream of introductions had wearied her, but the friendly faces had warmed her heart.

James headed toward the food table, and Ann followed. The few remaining dishes had been scraped clean. "All of the food today was delicious," she remarked.

"Almost all of it." He passed the dish of johnnycake to her. Only a tiny sliver had been removed.

"Someone enjoyed it."

He shook his head and laughed. "Every week someone takes a piece to be polite."

Ann had filled her plate until it nearly overflowed, but it hadn't occurred to her to try James's dish.

They walked side by side to the buggy, and Ann breathed a sigh of relief to see they were one of the last to leave. No more questions from strangers, at least not today.

"This was a beautiful day," he said, as the buggy drew away from the church. "I hope you enjoyed yourself." A contented smile played on his lips.

"Everyone was very friendly."

"I'm sure they were all dying to meet the girl who came all the way from England to marry me."

"I thought you said no one knew you'd sent for a bride."

"They didn't, but it's impossible to keep a secret in New Haven. Everyone talks to everyone, and nothing this gossipworthy has happened in months. If you think everyone's excitable now, I can't imagine what people will be saying after you leave. Too bad you'll miss it."

Ann studied his face. "Doesn't it bother you? To have everyone talking about you?" She couldn't imagine James was the type who liked being the center of attention.

Not like William. Ann scolded herself the moment the thought came into her head. She'd promised herself not to think of him.

James shrugged. "I expected as much when I contacted the agency. After all, you're the first mail-order bride any of them have ever met. But maybe that will work in my favor. After you leave, I'll tell everyone you were sent to me on a trial basis."

"What a horrid thing to tell them!"

James stared at her for a beat before bursting into laughter.

"Oh." Her face grow hot. "You were teasing...weren't you?"

"Yes, I was joking. But does it matter? Whatever I tell them, you'll be long gone by then. I doubt you'll even think back on your time in New Haven. Not with all those new jewels to distract you."

Ann's middle tightened. She doubted she could ever forget James or her stay in New Haven. She was also certain he wouldn't be making jokes if he knew what really waited for her, penniless and alone in a foreign country.

"Those children you were playing with? The Schneiders? They certainly like you."

James's face broke into a boyish grin. "George and Sadie. I wish I could visit them at home, but Hal Schneider won't answer the door. It's a wonder he brings them to church every Sunday."

"He made a promise to his wife."

James's head snapped toward her. "How on earth would you know that?"

"Delia told me. Her mother witnessed the oath."

James pursed his lips and nodded. "Margaret Ludlow's holding him to his word? Well, that explains quite a bit."

"I only spoke with her for a short while on the train, but I imagine she can be very persuasive."

James chuckled. "I can't disagree. That woman can persuade almost anyone of anything. She could probably sell one your lacy things for twenty dollars if she put her mind to it."

"Do you really see visitors from Columbus in New Haven?" She feared Delia's optimism over her hand-

kerchiefs selling to wealthy tourists might be well intended but misplaced.

"Sure. Frederick's family owns a furniture store next
to their mill. People travel here from bigger cities to
order beds and tables and the like."

"They would travel all the way here for something
they can purchase at home?" she marveled. Her mistress in the Atherton house traveled once a year to Paris
to procure clothes and furnishings, but Ann couldn't
imagine New Haven as the cultural epicenter of handkerchiefs and fine furniture.

"People think the craftsmanship is better, I suppose."

"Is it?"

He shrugged. "Does it matter? They're convinced
of it. If Frederick slapped his family's name on a pile
of kindling and called it a desk, someone would pay
top dollar."

Ann roiled at the irony. People flocked to New Haven
to buy quality furniture when they could likely find
items just as good to purchase at home. New Haven
positively teemed with eligible young ladies, but James
had dismissed courting any of them in favor of sending away for a girl he'd never met. Who or what had
convinced him a girl from England would make a better bride?

Chapter Seven

On Thursday morning, James came in from his chores to find Ann plating a breakfast tray for Uncle Mac. Two eggs waited for him on the table. He sat down and took a cautious bite.

"These eggs are perfect," he marveled.

She set a cup of coffee beside him. "Thank you."

"How many did you make before you got these two?"

Her pink cheeks darkened and she lifted her delicate chin in annoyance. "If you must know—three."

James chuckled. "Where are they now?"

"In my stomach." She rubbed her middle. "Oof. I'm not particularly fond of eggs anymore."

He suppressed the urge to laugh again. "I'd imagine."

Ann left with Uncle Mac's tray and returned wearing her hat and gloves.

"Will you be changing before we leave for town?" she asked.

He took another bite of eggs and shook his head. "I'm sorry. I know I told you last night we could go to town today. But a cow's about to calf and it looks like a hard one for her. I can't leave."

"Oh." Her disappointment was obvious. "Tomorrow, then?"

James shrugged. "I don't know. I left the farm two afternoons last week and now I'm behind. I know those lacy things are important to you, but I can't risk my crop on the chance some woman from Columbus will pay ten dollars for the privilege of dabbing her nose with one."

He still couldn't understand why she cared so much about this business deal with Mrs. Williams. She might as well hold on to the fancy handkerchiefs and pass them out to the new high-society friends she was sure to make once she met her intended match.

Ann crinkled her nose and tossed a dish towel at his head. He caught it and used it to wipe the corners of his mouth. Her full lips pressed together in amusement.

"May I go by myself?"

"Never thought of that. I expect you can. I'll hitch the wagon for you." He pushed back his chair and moved to stand.

Ann gestured for him to remain seated. "I don't want to take the wagon."

"Alright. You can take the buggy."

Her cheeks colored. "I've never driven a wagon before. Or a buggy. I've never even ridden a horse."

"Never? How is that possible?"

She threw up her hands. "Orphans weren't taught to ride, and then I entered service. A maid would never have access to her employer's horse or buggy."

"How do you propose you'll get to town?"

"I'll walk."

"It's five miles—one way!"

"I'd best be going then, shan't I?"

James stared. This fragile-looking girl was full of surprises. He hadn't even had a chance to answer before she strode past him and out the front door. James scrambled to his feet.

"Wait," he called from the doorway. "You know the way, don't you?"

Ann stopped at the bottom of the porch steps and cocked her blond head. "I believe I'll take a right at the end of the drive and follow this road straight into the center of town."

James laughed at the absurdity of his own question. "What I meant was…" He struggled for some reason to detain her and came up empty. "Have a safe journey."

"Is there anything I can retrieve for you in town?"

He plowed both hands through his hair. "No, I think we're… I'm fine."

"I'll see you later this afternoon?"

"If gypsies don't accost you along the way."

Ann's eyes widened in alarm.

"I'm only teasing," he added quickly.

Her eyes narrowed. "I knew that. I'll be back to prepare dinner."

James returned to his morning chores but couldn't shake his uneasiness at the thought of Ann walking alone. New Haven wasn't dangerous, but she was unfamiliar with the town. He hurried through the remainder of his work and avoided looking at the weeds in the nearest field. By the time he'd changed his shirt, checked on Uncle Mac and hitched the buggy, more than half an hour had gone by.

He expected to catch up with her quickly, but three miles passed with no sight of her form in the distance. James flicked the reins and Old Harriet labored from a trot to a canter. He was a quarter of a mile from the welcome-to-New-Haven sign before he caught a glimpse of Ann's light blue dress and straw hat.

James called out once he deemed Ann close enough to hear him.

"In need of a ride, miss?"

Ann's head spun around, a crease of worry on her forehead. The crease dissolved and a smile lit her face when she saw it was him.

"I see you changed your mind."

James slowed the buggy and she swung herself onto the seat before he could get down to help. He marveled at how her appearance remained unchanged in the last hour. The healthy glow in her cheeks was the only hint she'd walked nearly five miles at a lightning pace. She didn't even sound out of breath.

"I decided I had some business in town, after all. Frederick's been pestering me to take on some extra work at the mill later this summer. Figured I'd talk to him about it."

Her eyebrows rose in suspicion, but she didn't question him. Instead, she chewed her lip and played with the cuff of her sleeve.

"Would you consider accompanying me when I meet with Mrs. Williams?"

His heart skipped a beat.

"You'd like me to be there?"

"The truth is I'm terribly nervous. It might settle my nerves if I don't meet with her alone. There's always a chance Delia won't be there."

"Oh. Yes, of course I'll join you." What did she have to be nervous about? More important, why did he feel disappointed by her reason for wanting him near?

"Will you have time to meet with Frederick after?"

"Who?" He hadn't considered meeting with Frederick until the moment Ann boarded the buggy. Until then his only thoughts were of finding her. "Oh, Frederick! I can see him anytime."

"Splendid!" Her shoulders relaxed and she folded her hands on her lap. "I could use a friendly face."

She considered him a friendly face. James's chest warmed at the thought. He could certainly be friends with Ann, couldn't he? Just friends.

When they entered New Haven Dressmakers together, Delia grasped Ann's hand in a businesslike handshake and winked at both of them.

"Mrs. Williams?" Delia called out to the figure behind the small counter. James knew the older woman had been watching them from the moment they entered, but now she feigned interest in a ledger book. Not until Ann took a few steps forward did she look up and let her reading glasses hang from a slim gold chain around her neck.

"You must be Miss Cromwell." Mrs. Williams squeezed her large frame out from behind the counter. "I've been so looking forward to meeting you. Ardelia here showed me a piece of your work last week. It's breathtaking. I'm so glad you're interested in selling your work in my shop."

"It's lovely to meet you. Do you know my friend, James McCann?"

Mrs. Williams glanced at him. "Of course I know James. Everyone knows James."

She turned her attention back to Ann. Mrs. Williams appeared no more immune to Ann's magnetic beauty than anyone else.

"Do you mind if he joins us for our talk?" Ann asked.

Mrs. Williams's head drew back, as if startled by the question, but she nodded in the affirmative.

"I'll look after the shop," Delia announced before taking a seat behind the counter.

The older woman directed them to a semicircle of cream tufted chairs at the back of the shop. James cringed at the thought of sitting on the flawless fabric. He'd changed his shirt but not his pants after mucking out the barn. It might be best to stand. He crossed his arms and tried not to back into yet another dress form.

Ann floated onto her chair as if it were the most natural thing in the world. She'd confessed her nerves to him, but they weren't showing. Her every movement was graceful and poised, and her accent had taken on a new cadence the moment they arrived. The effect on the older woman was obvious. She gravitated to Ann like a fly to honey.

Ann produced a plump package from her bag and set it on the low table before them. One by one, she slipped each handkerchief from its tissue cocoon, and Mrs. Williams stated its price as assuredly as someone might state its color.

"Leaves and roses. Ten and a half dollars. Fans and scallops. Ten dollars."

Ann's calm demeanor remained constant throughout the meeting, but James sensed her excitement. She sat as straight as an arrow with her delicate hands folded in her lap, yet each time Mrs. Williams looked down at a handkerchief, Ann discreetly caught his eye. The first time James winked at her, and her cheeks turned crimson. The next time she looked at him, he simply smiled and nodded.

After the appraisals had been made, Mrs. Williams sat back in her chair and crossed her arms over her ample belly.

"Now, Miss Cromwell. I have one more opportunity for you. It may be weeks before we sell one of these exquisite pieces—"

"Did you say weeks?" Ann interrupted.

"One never can tell with these sorts of specialty items. But I have work you can start today, and I can promise payment in full when it's complete."

For the first time, Ann's mask of confidence showed a crack. She leaned forward and her eyes widened.

"I'll do any work you have."

She must be bored out of her mind to take on all this work. He felt foolish for having imagined she enjoyed being his houseguest. Her eagerness to occupy her time with anything but housework was sobering.

"I have a customer—" Mrs. Williams scooted forward on her chair "—who is to be married in a few short months. She came in last week for a fitting and I showed her your lace. She thought it was beautiful and has requested some for her wedding gown."

James didn't have to guess who she was talking about.

"You want her to make lace for Priscilla Vollrath," he stated.

Mrs. Williams paused and craned her neck back at James. "That's right."

"Who's Priscilla Vollrath?"

"The only daughter of our dear and honorable Judge Vollrath," Mrs. Williams explained. "She is used to fine things and has exquisite taste."

She was also one of the most vain and insufferable women James had the misfortune of knowing. There couldn't be a more difficult task in all the world than pleasing Priscilla. He stifled a laugh at the thought of Ann looking for a pleasant diversion by taking on this assignment.

"How much does she need?" Ann asked.

"Two yards. We'll attach it to the dress when you complete it, but it must all be done eight weeks from today. Is there any way you can produce it in time?"

Ann had to know she'd be long gone from New Haven by then. She must have pondered the same thing, because she chewed her lower lip while Mrs. Williams leaned farther and farther forward.

"The pay would be considerable," Mrs. Williams added.

Ann's head snapped up. "I'll have it completed in four weeks."

Mrs. Williams gasped. "There's no need to rush, dear."

"I'm afraid—" Ann caught James's eye "—my stay in New Haven should be over by summer's end."

"Ah, well then." Mrs. Williams fumbled for words. "I was under the impression your stay was indefinite."

The room grew suddenly hot. James raked his hands through his hair and shifted his weight.

"James and his Uncle Mac are my kind hosts. I would not be able to experience the beauty of rural Ohio without their hospitality."

She hadn't lied, but she had avoided all of Mrs. Williams's unspoken questions.

At that moment Delia appeared from the front of shop.

"Mrs. Williams? Miss Vollrath is crossing the street."

"Thank you, Delia." She turned to Ann. "Her timing couldn't be more perfect. You can meet your customer in a moment." Mrs. Williams hurried to the front of the shop just as the bell over the door jangled, signaling Priscilla's arrival.

Ann rose from her chair. Did his eyes deceive him, or did her legs quake for an instant? He pushed down the urge to wrap his arms around her in reassurance. Instead, he placed a light hand on her shoulder.

"I'll be praying for you," he whispered in her ear, steeling himself against the lavender scent washing over him. "Because you're going to need divine intervention to work for Priscilla."

Ann's heart galloped in her chest at the words of warning. James crossed his arms over his broad chest and gazed down at her. For a moment she longed for him to open up those arms and pull her into a reassuring embrace. But that wasn't going to happen. So she'd just have to be strong for herself—as she always was. Lifting her chin, she forced confidence into her voice as she said, "I believe I'm up for the challenge."

"Can you really make the lace that fast?" he asked.

"I'm certain of it."

As a maid she'd produced far more lace in far less time. Mrs. Atherton never gave thought to Ann's other duties when demanding a new piece. Even if she had to go without sleep for days, Ann knew she could finish this project with time to spare.

"Priscilla Vollrath can be quite a handful."

Ann sensed he was trying to scare her. If only he knew what really frightened her. It was not her new customer or the tight deadline. No, what she feared most was the letter from Mrs. Turner. If it arrived before she finished the lace, she could be leaving New Haven without a penny to her name. She had no hope that James was correct in his prediction of a rich man awaiting her. Mrs. Turner could not have been more explicit as to the terms of her match with James. If she could not make it work, she should consider herself on her own in this new country. No more matches. Until she'd arrived, Ann's pride never allowed her to imagine James would be anything less than thrilled to meet her.

The front of the shop could not be seen from their vantage point. Ann reared back her shoulders and rounded the corner. Mrs. Williams was in the middle of apologizing profusely to a small, slender girl in an elaborately feathered hat. The girl ignored the seamstress and glanced about the room, her face slack with boredom.

"...and if I'd known you'd wanted it in pink, I assure you I would have ordered it," Mrs. Williams continued.

"I shouldn't have to say it." The girl sniffed. "I told you once I like pink roses."

"Yes, er, I'm sure you did."

When the girl turned her back, Mrs. Williams rolled her eyes heavenward and threw up her hands in exasperation.

The seamstress turned in Ann's direction and a broad smile spread over her face. "I have wonderful news," Mrs. Williams said to Miss Vollrath's turned back. "Miss Cromwell believes she can produce the lace in time and to your specifications."

No specifications had been discussed, but before Ann could wonder what she meant, the girl looked over at her and shot her a broad and toothy smile that was anything but genuine.

"Miss Cromwell, how lovely to meet you." The girl

let a thimble she'd been fingering drop onto the nearest
table. It hit the wood with a clatter and bounced onto
the floor. She ignored it as she moved to sit in a nearby
upholstered chair.

"Lovely to meet you, as well, Miss Vollrath."

Ann offered the briefest of curtsies, and the girl's
eyes brightened, clearly impressed by Ann's accent and
deference.

"You may call me Priscilla," she said, as if bestow-
ing Ann with a great honor.

James stepped forward to Ann's side.

"Nice to see you again, Priscilla."

His warm baritone took an edge off Ann's nerves.
Please stay.

Priscilla sniffed. Ann recognized it at once as Priscilla Vollrath's version of hello, reserved for those she
felt beneath her. She'd had the same greeting directed
toward her more times than she could count.

"Well, I'd best go see Frederick. You ladies have a
nice day. Ann, I'll be back to fetch you in a few hours,
if that's alright."

Ann only nodded. She knew it was too much to ask
him to stand in the corner of the shop all afternoon as
moral support.

Priscilla tapped her fingers on the arm of her chair
and exhaled.

"Please sit down, Miss Cromwell. We have much
to talk about."

The discussion that followed reminded Ann more of
her life in England than anything else she'd encountered
since arriving in America. She was in service again,
with Priscilla as her mistress. The needle lace Ann
had already produced appeared adequate, Priscilla ad-

mitted, but not fit for her wedding dress. Sketch pads were requested and produced. Soon they were covered by Ann's hand in swirls and loops of charcoal representing lace.

According to Priscilla, Ann's designs were both too heavy and too light. Too intricate and at the same time too sparse. They examined Ann's handkerchiefs for inspiration, and Priscilla commenced pointing out the shortcomings of each. Cups of tea were poured, sipped and disparaged. After an hour of criticizing, Priscilla stood and announced a begrudging satisfaction with Ann's new designs.

"I never thought this wedding would be so much work." She pouted.

Ann followed her to the door. "It sounds like everything will turn out quite lovely."

"The finest wedding in three counties," Priscilla corrected. "That's what Father promised."

"And it will be," Mrs. Williams and Delia replied in unison, and with far too much enthusiasm.

"Yes, it will be," Ann agreed.

Priscilla nodded and thrust her nose into the air before exiting the shop.

As soon as she disappeared out of sight, Mrs. Williams and Delia dropped themselves into the nearest chairs. "This wedding cannot come too soon," Mrs. Williams announced as she fanned herself with one hand.

"I don't know how you held your composure, Ann," Delia said. "And to think—you'll be dealing with that girl every week!"

During their meeting, Priscilla expressed doubt Ann would remember all of her instructions. She had insisted on a review of her work, to be held in the shop once a week on an ever-changing day of Priscilla's choosing.

"I think she'll be pleased with the end result," Ann said.

"I hope so, dear, but her instructions were so vague and contradictory. How will you know what to do?" Mrs. Williams asked.

Ann lifted two handkerchiefs Priscilla had referred to—and criticized—repeatedly. "She wants the pattern from this one but edged with the border from this one."

Delia leaned forward and squinted at the lace, then back at the dozen sketches laid out on the table. "You're right! But how on earth could you tell? All I could hear were her complaints."

Complaints were Ann's specialty. Her former mistress, Mrs. Atherton, could turn a phrase in such a way that even a compliment came out as a criticism. How odd to find Ann's years of service had granted her the very skills necessary for dealing with customers like Priscilla Vollrath. "You have to know what to listen for," Ann answered.

Mrs. Williams hoisted herself from her chair and staggered toward the counter in mock weariness. "Why don't you take your lunch now, Delia? I'll mind the shop."

Delia glided to the back and reemerged with a small woven basket. "Would you like to join me? I take my lunch on the other side of the courthouse. Egg salad. I don't have much but we could share."

"I'm not hungry, but I would love to sit with you." Not hungry was an understatement. Ann wondered if she'd ever eat another egg again.

They crossed the dusty street and walked down the block to benches shaded by the impressive stone courthouse. Several others were enjoying picnic lunches and waved. Delia unwrapped the wax paper from her sandwich and again offered Ann a bite before eating.

"Did you really tell Mrs. Williams you could produce the lace in four weeks?"

Ann nodded.

"But why? Priscilla's wedding isn't until September."

Ann drew in a deep breath. Should she tell her? She'd hope to leave town with her pride intact. But it would be such a comfort to confide in a friend.

"I very much doubt I'll still be in New Haven by September."

Delia's warm brown eyes widened.

"You already plan to leave? But you barely know one another!"

"James asked for an ugly wife," Ann blurted.

"What?" Delia let out a nervous laugh.

"When James wrote to the agency he asked for a plain wife. An ugly wife. But they matched me with him instead. He's only allowing me to stay until the agency sorts out the mistake."

"Why would James ask for a plain wife?"

Ann sighed. "It doesn't matter. He's as ill-suited a match for me as I am for him."

Delia wrapped a long arm around her shoulders. "There must be something to be done. If there's been a mistake and James will be matched with someone else—surely there's another suitor for you, as well?"

"No, there isn't. Mrs. Turner—she's the woman at the agency—she told me James was the only suitable match for me that she had."

Delia pulled back and looked Ann straight in the eye,

her forehead creased in confusion. "That doesn't seem possible. A beauty like you?"

Ann's cheeks warmed under the scrutiny. "It's true. Dozens of other girls passed through the agency before I matched with James."

"Hmm." Delia pursed her lips. "And if this doesn't work out, you'll have to return to England?"

Ann's stomach dropped to her knees. "N-no," she stammered, an icy cold spreading across her belly at the very thought of returning. "England is the one place in the world I will never again call home."

Chapter Eight

Delia clucked her tongue. "You can't return to England? What do you mean?"

Ann rubbed her forehead. "It's a long story."

"I have all the time in the world."

But did Ann have the strength to share the memories that weighed on her so heavily? Just thinking of what she was about to say brought tears to her eyes. She'd pushed the memories down deep for so long, she'd come to believe they might be gone forever. Now she felt ready to reveal them and discovered they had always been under the surface. Each moment from her past surged forward with a bright clarity that brought an ache to her chest.

"I entered service at the age of ten. Mother and Father had died of fever, and with no relatives to take us in, my siblings and I were sent to an orphanage. After many months scrubbing floors for my keep, they noticed my hard work and arranged a position in a nice house for me.

"I was the Athertons' scullery maid. Each morning I rose at five and started the kitchen fire. During the day

I toiled in the basement, almost never seeing the sun. I rarely crawled into bed before twelve, and for the first six months I cried myself to sleep."

Delia's forehead knotted in pity and Ann waved it away.

"It wasn't really so horrible. I had a roof over my head, regular meals and a few coins in my pocket. But I missed my brothers and sisters dreadfully. My entire body ached with loneliness. I was in service seven months before I met a single member of the family I served."

"Who hired you?" Delia interrupted.

"The housekeeper."

"And you never met any of them for seven months. Not one?" Delia sounded incredulous.

Ann chuckled. It must sound absurd to anyone outside that life. "Servants strive to be invisible. My work rarely called me out of the kitchen, but when it did, I scurried away at the first hint of an approaching family member. We attended church with them, but walked a distance behind on the way, and servants sat in the rear of the sanctuary. I first met Mr. and Mrs. Atherton at Christmastime when they called me into the drawing room and presented me with a bolt of cloth with which to make myself a new uniform. I'd been in their service eleven months by then."

Delia raised a brow. "I thought you said it was seven months."

"I said it was seven months before I met a member of the family—their son William. I had been tasked with fetching something from an upstairs closet and ran headlong into William Atherton in my haste. I was only eleven. William was fifteen. For me, it was heart-wrenching love at first sight.

"For the next several years, I looked forward to even the slightest glimpse of him. When I was promoted to chambermaid, my new duties put me in the Athertons' living areas. The other maids claimed they rarely saw him, but I would encounter him on the servant stairs or rummaging through the kitchen pantry as often as twice a week. Once, I found him outside my quarters in the attic. He claimed to be lost. I walked in the park one day on my afternoon off, and we passed on a bridge. We only nodded to one another—anything more would have been wholly inappropriate—but the moment thrilled me. For days I could barely concentrate on my work."

Ann licked her lips and sent up a silent prayer for courage. She never thought she'd share this story with anyone, but now she'd begun and wasn't sure she could stop.

"I told myself our meeting in the park was coincidence, but the next week I passed him on the same bridge at the same time. That's when I knew he'd come there to see me. The week after, he pressed a slip of paper into my hand as we passed. On it he professed his love."

The familiar ache of embarrassment and regret turned in her stomach. Delia reached out and placed a cool hand on Ann's arm but didn't interrupt.

"I should never have believed what he'd written. We'd barely spoken to one another. But I had longed after him for nearly five years. It never occurred to me that my naive infatuation was nothing like his desire for me."

Ann drew another deep breath. A tear slipped down her cheek and she brushed it away.

"First we met in corridors, far from prying eyes. He brought me little presents and pledged his undying devotion. My love for him was deep and aching, and when he spoke, I could only believe his feelings were as sincere as mine. If I'd let one kernel of doubt into my heart, I might have avoided everything. Instead, it took just one promise of marriage. One promise to give up his inheritance and family and run away with me. That one promise led me to stumble down a path from which I could never return."

A pain in Ann's arm stopped her breath. Delia's grip had tightened to the point where the skin had colored white around Delia's fingertips. She released her grasp and murmured, "Sorry," before taking up the same vise-like hold on Ann's hand.

"A month later he was gone. Back to university. I didn't suspect anything was wrong until my breakfast left me every morning. A few more weeks passed and I knew with certainty that I was with child. I wrote to him straight away and told him everything, but months went by with no reply. He was never going to help me. That's when I foolishly thought I could help myself."

Delia's grip tightened. The discomfort was nothing compared to the pain gripping Ann's heart.

"If I live a hundred years, I'll never be more ashamed of anything than I am of the various things I did next. Hot baths, jumping off park benches and drinking castor oil and pennyroyal tea. Everything I'd ever heard of for girls in my condition, I tried. Yet my attempts failed.

"I knew if the Athertons found out, I would be cast into the street. I never stopped writing to William, but I never received a response. I had no choice but to conceal my condition, and it was startlingly easy. Our uniforms were full at the waist, and the other maids with whom I shared a room always dressed and undressed in the dark to save lamplight. I concealed it so well, I nearly forgot about it myself. Until the night of the dinner party.

"That night the spasms in my belly grew strong and frequent. I set the table for the Athertons and their guests, and excused myself to my room. I hoped I only needed to rest before dinner service. By the time I reached the attic, the pain grew so severe I could hardly stand. Within the hour I gave birth to a baby boy. He had a head of dark hair and the most darling little nose.

"When I didn't appear at dinner, Mrs. Atherton sent another maid, Jane, to look for me. I owe my life, and the life of the baby, to Jane's indiscretion. Instead of divulging my condition to the Athertons in private, she marched into the dining room and announced she'd found a baby in my room. The family doctor was a dinner guest that night, and when he heard the news, he came to my room straight away. I believe God placed Dr. Shields there. Without him as witness, Mrs. Atherton would have tossed both the infant and me out of her house at that very moment."

"She let you stay?" Delia whispered, her eyes open wide.

Ann laughed cheerlessly. "No. But what she did do would be considered generous by any member of her class. Saintly, even."

"What, then?"

"She packed me into a carriage within the hour and sent me to the orphanage from which I'd come."

"With the baby?"

"No. She took him from my arms the moment Dr. Shields left the room. It was the last time I saw him. Months later I heard her previously barren sister had given birth to a beautiful, blue-eyed boy."

"She gave away your baby?" Delia stared at the ground and shook her head from side to side.

Ann nodded. The pain from the retelling began to subside, and the familiar numbness around her heart returned.

"How could anyone do such a thing?"

"It could have been worse. Far worse. It was fortunate her sister desired a baby. I had no means of caring for him. And Mrs. Atherton was trying to impress Dr. Shields with her compassion when she placed me in that carriage. Otherwise, I would have been flung out of the house with only the clothes on my back."

Delia leaned forward and squeezed Ann in an embrace so tight she had to hold her breath.

"I'm so sorry for what happened to you, Ann. Do you miss him?"

Ann turned her gaze down. "He is with a family who can provide him more than I could ever imagine. I try not to think much more about him than that."

"What happened next?"

"The orphanage received me, despite my age. I suspect Mrs. Atherton paid them to take me in. I also suspect she knew the baby was her grandson."

"Oh, Ann! How horrible, to be surrounded by all those children after losing your own."

Ann shrugged. "I tried not to think about it. Two years passed and the orphanage asked me to leave to make room for another girl in a similar predicament.

By then all of London had heard the tale of Ann Cromwell—the servant who gave birth in the attic."

"Is that when you decided to find a husband through an agency?"

"What else could I do? I couldn't afford passage out of England, and no one would hire me."

"Couldn't you have left London and found work in another town? Somewhere no one had heard of you?"

Ann patted Delia's hand. "A maid is nothing without references from her previous employer. No one risks hiring a servant without them."

"What about work outside service? Your embroidery is exquisite. Aren't there apprenticeships in England?"

A sigh tickled Ann's throat. "Yes," she drew out slowly. "There are apprenticeships, but those are purchased, not bestowed, and I didn't have a pence to my name. I had only one avenue of employment available to me, and I was not about to take it."

"What was that?"

"Girls in my situation..." Ann searched for words delicate enough for Delia's ears. "Without references, a girl is left with little else but the body God gave her. Sometimes she is forced to sell even that."

Delia's hands flew to her mouth. Her eyes opened wide.

"So you see," Ann continued, "marrying a man I'd never met sounded quite appealing in comparison."

"Of course it did! Oh, Ann, I'm so glad you came to New Haven."

"And now I'm about to leave again."

"Why don't you stay here?"

Ann sighed. "I've had enough personal scandal to last ten lifetimes. I can't stay here and be known as the girl James McCann cast aside."

Delia pursed her lips. "I suppose you're right. Everyone knows you're a mail-order bride."

Ann threw up her hands. "Exactly. And though I thought I could find work as a maid somewhere, after speaking with Mr. Davis, I've learned I would need to cook as well as clean."

"You can cook a little, can't you?"

"Only if the results don't have to be edible."

Delia laughed.

"My cooking is positively dreadful," Ann assured her. "I considered purchasing a cookbook, but they might as well be written in French. I don't know mincing from dicing."

"I have an idea!" Delia announced. "I have a free day from time to time. What if I came out to James's farm and gave you a few cooking lessons? I'm certain your lace will be a tremendous success anywhere you go, so I don't worry about your making ends meet, but you should also learn to cook for yourself."

"I couldn't let you come on your day off."

"Nonsense." She patted Ann's hand. "It would be my pleasure. I'll even show you how to do a few things around the farm. Have you ever milked a cow?"

Ann snorted. "I'd never even seen a cow up close until I came to the farm."

"Well, you'll learn that, too."

Ann leaped to her feet and leaned down to wrap Delia in a firm hug. "Thank you so much for your kindness. I truly am a horrible cook, but with your help there may be hope for me yet."

Delia grinned. "That's the spirit. Mother always says the first step to success is deciding not to fail."

Ann giggled at the pithy observation, but it endeared her to Delia's mother all the more.

"If I do my job well, James may not want you to leave," Delia added.

Ann could tell Delia watched for her reaction to the comment. When Ann said nothing, Delia continued. "Is that something you would want?"

Ann gazed out at the courtyard lawn and thought of James. His patience with his Uncle Mac. His dedication to the farm. The way he teased her so. A spot in her middle twisted at the thought of him. She couldn't tell if she found the sensation pleasant or painful. "I don't know," she finally answered.

"Don't you like him?"

"He's lovely," Ann rushed out. "It's only that…" She pictured James on Sunday playing with the children at the church picnic. The twisting sensation persisted, but now she recognized it as pain. "I don't know how, but Mrs. Turner made two errors in sending me here. I'm in no part what he wants. Not in face…or in body. I know James would be happier with any other girl but me. And I'm afraid that may be true of any man."

"Listen to what you're saying, Ann! How could that be true?"

The sun grew suddenly brighter and the air much too hot. A bead of sweat tickled Ann's jaw.

"Girls at the agency are allowed to make requests of their matches, though they are only sometimes followed. Often they request to be sent to a home in New York or matched with a man who's only a little ugly or fat or old."

Delia giggled and Ann managed a weak smile.

"I only had one request. I assumed it was why I had

to wait so long. I asked to be matched with a man who did not desire children."

A wrinkle sprang up between Delia's brows. "You don't want children?"

Ann wiped at the tears streaming down her cheeks. "It's not a matter of what I want," she whispered. "My punishment for my transgressions has been manifold. Even if I were to desire children, I can never have another baby."

Chapter Nine

Ann had never told another soul of her barrenness, save for Mrs. Turner at the agency. Delia's expression morphed from shock to pity, the same as Mrs. Turner's had.

"Are you sure?" Delia whispered. "How could one really know such a thing?"

Ann drew a handkerchief from her pocket and twisted it in her hands. "I'm certain. When I arrived at the orphanage they had no knowledge of my giving birth just a few hours before, and I was too ashamed to tell them. They sent me to work straight away. My limbs were weak from blood loss, and every inch of me ached, but I feared I'd be cast out if I couldn't perform my duties. Within days I burned with fever and my body racked with a horrid pain. I collapsed in the midst of scrubbing the floor. A week passed before Mrs. Atherton could be persuaded by post to pay for a doctor. By the time he arrived, my fever had broken, but the damage was done. The doctor said the infection had taken away any chance of my becoming a mother again."

Delia's deep brown eyes glistened. Her lips parted

to speak, but she was interrupted by a bell chime. It chimed again and her eyes grew wide. "It's two o'clock!"

Ann's heart skipped a beat. Had her ramblings caused her friend to be late? "I'm so sorry, Delia. I never should have kept you! Will Mrs. Williams be cross?"

"No, no." Delia stood and squeezed Ann's shoulder in reassurance. "Mrs. Williams will likely not even notice. After her own lunch she often puts her feet up on a sofa in the dressing room and falls asleep."

Ann matched Delia's long strides across the court-house lawn. They passed Davis Mercantile, and Ann glanced at her reflection in the window and stopped short. Red, puffy eyes stared back.

"I look a fright!" She gasped and clapped her hands over her tearstained cheeks.

"No worries. We have a washroom in the back of the shop. And after you've freshened up, you can use the dressing room to work on your needle lace until James fetches you."

Ann gulped. She didn't want anyone to see her like this, but the thought of James seeing her in such a state tripped her heart. She shook off the thought. Why did she desire to look pretty for a man who wanted her to be anything but?

James strode toward New Haven Dressmakers with his heart in his throat. Frederick had been a good friend and not asked for an explanation as to why Ann wasn't staying. They'd talked business, though James had found it hard to concentrate. As Frederick walked him through the framed outline of the mill's new expansion, James couldn't stop wondering about Ann. What was she doing with her time in town? Were she and Delia getting along as well as it appeared? It was nice she'd been able to make a friend.

Why on earth are you still thinking about her? he scolded himself. He'd seen Ann only a few hours before. In a few weeks he would never see her again.

I'm worried about her working with Priscilla, that's all. Few could handle Priscilla Vollrath's temper or wrath. In fact, after meeting with Priscilla, Ann had likely declined the job even quicker than she'd accepted it.

The shop was empty when he arrived, but the clanging bell summoned Delia within seconds.

"Ann, James is here!" she called over her shoulder as she strode toward him. "How was your afternoon with my cousin?"

"The addition is coming along well. They should be able to double their business in a few years."

Ann appeared from the back of the shop. James began to grin but caught himself when he saw something was wrong. She smiled, but her normally bright eyes were dark with sorrow.

"Is everything alright?" He reached out to take her hand but caught himself again.

Ann's eyes widened, and she brought a hand to her cheek.

Delia stepped between them.

"Ann is fine!" she said, with far too much enthusiasm.

James craned to see around Delia. "Was it the meeting with Priscilla? Was she terrible?"

Delia glanced sideways at Ann. Did Delia wink?

"How would you expect it to go?" Delia asked, her eyes narrowed at James.

Something strange was going on, but James couldn't put his finger on it. Had Ann angered Priscilla in some way? Perhaps the whole thing had turned out even more poorly than he expected. He knew he should have stayed. Despite himself, he longed to shield Ann from conflict and discomfort.

Ann placed a hand on Delia's arm. Delia moved aside and Ann stepped forward.

"My meeting with Priscilla was a pleasure," Ann announced. "We agreed upon a pattern, and I believe she'll be quite pleased with the finished product."

"Really?" He couldn't imagine anything about dealing with Priscilla being described as a 'pleasure.' He studied Ann's sweet face. "I imagine Priscilla can be a difficult customer."

Ann shook her blond head. "I look forward to contributing something to her special day."

"Before she left, Priscilla even said she looked forward to working with Ann," Delia added.

Well, if that didn't beat all. Ann was a regular diplomat. James's chest swelled with pride, despite his attempts to squelch the feeling.

She'll make a fine shopkeeper's wife, he reminded himself. *Or maybe her true match is a politician or bank president. Someone in a position of influence over people, who seeks a canny and capable spouse.* Ann was proving herself to be a woman of many skills. Pity few of those skills were of use to a poor farmer. He had to remind himself of this every time her blue eyes looked his way.

"Ann, I must send you home with enough thread to keep occupied this week," Delia announced.

Ann and Delia excused themselves to the back of

the store and returned several minutes later, murmuring over the contents of a brown paper sack. They said their goodbyes, and Ann made arrangements to return the next week for her second meeting with Priscilla.

James stole glances at Ann as he drove home. She was normally so talkative during their trips, as if the silence had to be filled. But this time she drew a piece of lace from her pockets and lowered her head over her work. It was a wonder she could accomplish anything as the buggy jostled among the ruts of the dirt road. She remained so quiet, something had to be wrong. He couldn't shake the image of her emerging from the shop's back room. She almost looked as though she'd been crying.

A mile into the trip, he had to know.

"Did your meeting with Priscilla really go as well as you said?"

Ann lifted her golden head and gazed up at him. "She knows what she wants and has exquisite taste. It will be both a challenge and a pleasure to work with her."

"The challenge part you've got right."

Ann giggled but hurried to conceal the mirth behind her hand. "I don't know what you're talking about."

James leaned toward her and whispered, as if someone would hear and run off to tell Priscilla, "Tell me the truth. Didn't you find her to be a little… What's the word I'm looking for?"

"Arrogant?" she blurted, and covered her mouth again, but she couldn't disguise the smile in her eyes.

He laughed. "I was thinking *haughty, conceited* or maybe even *vain*."

"Surely some people must like her. Mrs. Williams said the whole town would come out for her wedding."

"Not because they care to see her get married. No one in New Haven is fool enough to turn down a free meal."

Ann's forehead creased. "I spent all afternoon with her and never inquired of her fiancé."

"Victor's not as bad as Priscilla, but he's caught up in all the excitement. I don't know if he realizes what he's committing himself to."

"You know him well?"

"No." James ran a hand through his hair. "Victor's only been in town a year. I can't say I've spoken to him more than twice, and only in passing. He works for Frederick at the mill."

"Really? A millworker?" There was no mistaking the surprise in Ann's voice.

"You expected Priscilla to choose someone a little more...exciting?"

Ann's expression softened. "I may have been mistaken about her."

James shook his head. "No, you've only underestimated her desire to be the first to possess anything new. It's why she's so keen on having your lace in her dress. And Victor isn't just a millworker. Frederick brought him on from Columbus to groom as foreman. He was the most eligible man in New Haven the moment he arrived. No girl in the county stood a chance once Priscilla set her eyes on him."

They were passing a squat white farmhouse sitting close to the road, and a plump woman in a red checked apron opened the front door and waved. James pulled back on the reins and Old Harriet slowed to a stop.

"Good afternoon, Mrs. Rausch," James called. "Any trouble?"

"Afternoon, James. No trouble at all. Wanted to let you know our cherry trees are plumb covered in ripe berries. I've been pitting and canning for days, but I'll never be able to get to them all before the birds do. Would you like some?"

James turned to Ann. "What do you think? Fancy some cherry pie?"

Her head bobbed. "I would adore some!"

James alighted from the buggy, and as always, Ann jumped to the ground before he could reach the other side to help her down. Mrs. Rausch lent them baskets, and they picked cherries from her laden trees until their lengthening shadows reminded him Uncle Mac still needed supper.

It wasn't until James took Ann's basket from her hands to place it on the floor of the buggy that he saw she'd picked almost double his bounty.

"How did you do that?" He marveled. Most of the remaining cherries had been high up on the tree. He'd strained and stretched and only managed to fill his basket halfway. Her cherries threatened to overflow.

"Hmm?" Ann looked up from her needle lace. "How did I do what?"

"Pick so many more cherries than me?"

Ann clucked her tongue. "You spent too much time hunting for clusters of cherries," she stated. "I picked the lone ones scattered throughout the branches. It's much more efficient."

It took a lot to surprise James. He scrutinized the petite girl beside him.

"I didn't realize you'd picked cherries before."

"I hadn't." She bent her head back over her work.

Her slim fingers moved over and over the rapidly growing lace.

Back at home they rinsed the berries at the well pump and poured them into a clean bucket. They set the cherries on the kitchen table and surveyed their bounty.

"What shall we do with them?" Ann asked.

James stroked the stubble on his chin. The cherries were so ripe, they'd spoil by morning. He looked at Ann. Her down-turned mouth and creased brow reflected his own feelings. He'd been so excited for the free fruit, he'd forgotten neither of them had any idea what to do with them.

"It would be a shame if they spoiled," Ann added, proving they were thinking the same thing.

A clap of recollection struck him. James shook his head and laughed. How could he have forgotten?

"I'll be right back," he called over his shoulder, and took the steps upstairs two at a time.

He returned to the kitchen a few minutes later with a shuffling, unhappy-looking Uncle Mac. The older man never liked leaving his room unless it was his own idea. But when Uncle Mac clapped eyes on the bucket of cherries, the gray haze behind his gaze was whisked away by a joyous light.

Uncle Mac jabbed a crooked pointer finger at the table in excitement. "Cherries!" he croaked.

"That's right," James said. "Cherries. We thought you could…"

"Cherry pie. Ch-cherry cobbler. Cherry jam!" The words tumbled forth faster than James had heard in over a year.

Ann's eyes grew wide and her mouth dropped open. "Uncle Mac used to win the blue ribbon at the county fair for preserves and pies every year." James explained. "Everyone made fun of him for entering the first few years, but that didn't stop him, did it, Uncle Mac?"

The older man grunted in the affirmative.

"Think you could give Ann and me a hand with these?"

Uncle Mac shuffled his feet and gazed at the ground.

Ann stepped forward and placed a slight hand on Uncle Mac's shoulder.

"You might not believe it, but I scarcely know how to begin pitting them. Would you show me?"

James's chest stirred.

Ann took Uncle Mac's arm and guided him to the table. "You must be so proud of your blue ribbons," she said as she helped Uncle Mac into his chair. A grin broke over the old man's face. Ann looked up at James and smiled just as wide.

James's stomach flipped over. He strode to the cabinets and retrieved two bowls, all the while taking deep, cleansing breaths. He stood in front of the kitchen window and stared into the barnyard.

I'm grateful she's so good with Uncle Mac while she's here—even if it won't be for long. Because she isn't staying. She doesn't want to stay. She can't stay.

He turned around after his stomach settled.

"Checked the post office today," he announced, far too loudly. "I received a telegram from Mrs. Turner."

Ann raised a brow. "Oh? What did it say?"

Had he imagined it, or was there an odd pitch to her voice?

"Not much one can say in a telegram without paying a fortune." He drew the paper from his pocket and unfolded it. Not that he needed to. He already had the short message memorized. "'Please await further instructions by post.'" An unnerving sense of relief washed over him every time he read it. A letter by ship and rail would take weeks. Ann would be—

Stop it, James! You should want her gone as soon as possible.

Ann chewed her lip. "What do you think it means?"

James snorted. "I think it means the agency is scrambling to contact your intended and to right their mistakes." He pointed to her hands. "Speaking of your intended. I hope he doesn't mind you arriving permanently stained with cherry juice."

Ann smirked. "My hands have seen far worse."

James took the empty chair across from Ann and tried to concentrate on the task before him. Within the hour the larger bowl brimmed with pitted cherries, and a large pile of yellow pits filled the other.

Uncle Mac gestured to the stove. Without hesitation, Ann stood and lit it.

She put her hands on her hips. "You're the cook tonight, Uncle Mac. Show me what to do and I shall do it."

James moved to help, but as the wordless directions began, he could only sit back and marvel. Uncle Mac would point and grunt, and Ann would place her hands on items around the room until she had the right one. Then Uncle Mac held up fingers to denote measurements, and Ann followed the rudimentary sign language as though she'd been doing so all her life. Soon a pot of sugar and cherries simmered into jam, and an adequate-looking cobbler bubbled in the oven.

When the flurry of production subsided, James stood and helped Ann prepare a platter of sandwiches. They ended their simple dinner with hot cherry cobbler and cream. James washed up the dishes and watched in wonder as Uncle Mac walked Ann through canning the cherry jam. By the end of the evening, six zinc-lidded pint jars cooled on the counter.

James excused himself to do his evening chores, and when he returned he found Ann at the kitchen table, working on her lace. All of the canning pots and utensils were already cleaned and put away, and the kitchen gleamed in the lamplight.

"You were wonderful with Uncle Mac tonight." The words spilled out before he could stop them.

Ann blushed. "I learned so much from him. It's a pity he stays in his room so often. If only he would give me cooking lessons every day."

James ran a hand through his hair. "I'm afraid we might not see this side of Uncle Mac again for a long while. I never know what's going to trigger his memory. It's like a flash of lightning. So strong and so fleeting. One day he'll forget how to lace his shoes, and the next he'll help me rebuild a broken wagon wheel." He sighed. "Those flashes are coming more and more seldom."

"But you knew the cherries would trigger his memory."

He raised a finger for emphasis. "I *guessed* they would trigger it. Some farmers whittle as a hobby or take up fishing. Uncle Mac canned blue-ribbon-winning preserves."

Ann chuckled. "He must have been quite the catch in his day. Handy on the farm and in the kitchen."

James had never noticed how genuinely she laughed. Deep and from the belly. No forced mirth like some people he knew. He found himself taking a seat in front of her when he knew he should wash up and ready his hammock on the porch for bed.

"How's your lace coming along?"

She glanced up long enough from her work to flash him a quick smile.

"Quite well, thank you."

The cherry pitting had flecked her porcelain skin with specks of cherry juice, which had darkened to a deep brown. His fingers ached to wipe away a large splotch on her neck. Was her skin as soft as he imagined?

He shook his head and dragged both hands through his hair.

"What will you do if we hear from Mrs. Turner before the lace is complete?" he asked her.

Did he detect a shudder in her shoulders? Ann didn't look up from her work.

"I must pray I finish in time—for Priscilla's sake."

James chuckled. "I think you mean *Mrs. Williams's* sake." He could already picture the magnitude of Priscilla's wrath if she didn't get exactly what she wanted, when she wanted it. And if Ann was gone, the weight of that wrath would fall on the dressmaker's shoulders.

Ann kept her head down, but a smile played on her lips. "For all of our sakes."

Chapter Ten

Ann sat up in her bed with a start. The room was still dark, but she'd meant to wake before five. A quick squint at the wall clock told her it was already a quarter past six. No matter how hard Ann tried, she was never up before James. Her entire life in service, both at the Athertons and the orphanage, she'd awoken at half past four. Now she desired to rise that early, but her body rebelled. It was as if her soul knew her wages would not be garnished or her position threatened if she rested a little longer.

Downstairs, the kitchen was dark and cold, but it would soon be too warm a day to start a fire. Ann put on some coffee and prayed it would turn out better than it had every other day. When James entered the kitchen ten minutes later, he stopped in the doorway and drew in a deep breath.

"It smells good in here," he said with a smile.

Ann placed a warm cup of coffee in his hand. His smile dissolved into a grimace at the first sip.

"Tell me what I'm doing wrong," she pleaded.

"Hmm?" He took another sip and sputtered out a cough.

"The coffee. I know it's always terrible but I don't know why. I watch you make it and think I'm doing it exactly the same. Obviously, I'm not."

James took yet another sip, and stared into its inky depths. "You know, I think this is growing on me. Uncle Mac sure seems to like it."

Ann put her hands on her hips and bit her lip to hold back her temper. "Please don't patronize me. Tell me what I'm doing wrong."

If she was going to learn as much as she needed about cooking in a few short weeks, she needed more than help from Delia on the rare days that she had time and the occasional surprise tutorial from Uncle Mac.

James's eyes widened, but his cool demeanor didn't change. He took a long slurp. "I'm not patronizing you. It's doesn't have grounds in it anymore, so it's already much better than your first attempts. It's stronger than I'm used to, but some people like strong coffee."

Ann turned her back to James and directed her attention to the skillet.

"Let me do that," James offered and moved to her side. She wondered if he was going to take her hand and show her again the way he had when she first arrived. Her middle quivered at the thought. Instead, he took the egg from the basket and cracked it over the skillet.

"I should do it. I need the practice."

James shook his head back and forth as the egg sizzled. "I feel bad for asking you to learn to do this when you'll probably never have to cook another meal in your life after you leave. You should work on Priscilla's lace. I'll take care of breakfast."

Ann backed away from the stove and watched James work. He whistled as he plated the eggs and added cold squares of leftover cherry cobbler. Uncle Mac's eyes shone with excitement when she brought him his tray.

After breakfast Ann washed the dishes, checked on Uncle Mac and hurried outside to join James.

"What's wrong?" he asked as she approached, his blade coming to a halt over the weeds in midswing.

"Nothing. I thought now that your house is clean, you could use my help."

"What about Priscilla's lace?"

"Needle lace is tedious work. I can only work on it for so many hours before my hands begin to ache. Anyway, I can work on the lace by lamplight. We must make hay while the sun shines."

James threw back his head and laughed.

Ann's cheeks warmed. "Is that not something farmers say in America?"

He shook his head and continued to smile. "No, we say it alright. It just sounded funny coming from you."

"Well..." She drew her shoulders back and tried to sound confident. She suddenly felt ridiculous. "Would you like to show me what to do?"

"Are you sure Uncle Mac doesn't need anything?"

"He came to the door when I knocked and waved me away when I asked if he needed anything."

"Alright." He placed his hands on his trim hips. "Have you ever weeded a field before?"

She pursed her lips. "No, but don't you think I can learn?"

James smirked. "I suppose so—though I thought you'd learn to cook an egg without crumbling the shell by now."

Ann let out a huff. His teasing always quickened her pulse. Sometimes in excitement, occasionally in annoyance. The former was pleasantly unnerving. The latter was infuriating.

This time was the latter.

"It can't be very hard if you can do it," she threw back.

Ann knelt down and grasped a weed.

"Stop!"

Every muscle in Ann's body tensed. Her fingers gripped the base of the plant, but she didn't move an inch. Ann held her breath as James knelt beside her and wrapped his hand around hers. He smelled of sweat and earth, and his hands were hot but dry. He pried back Ann's fingertips, and guided her hand from the straggly plant she'd almost pulled to a robust green shoot topped with feathery leaves.

"What you were about to pull is our crop—corn. This—" he squeezed her fingers together around the base of the green leaves "—is a weed."

Ann's heart sank. "I—I'm sorry," she stammered. "It's the same height as the corn."

"That's why we're weeding. See these leaves?" He ran his fingers over the feathery top. "These leaves are shading out our corn and drawing nutrients from the soil. Our corn is being choked and starved by the invasion. Once the weeds are gone, the corn won't have to fight anything for water and sun. It can grow healthy and strong."

She tried to follow what he said, but his nearness was so distracting, she could scarcely hear her own thoughts. What should have been a methodical lesson grew suffocatingly intimate as James's patient voice caressed her ear. They both crouched near the ground, their faces inches from one another.

When he took her hand again to demonstrate the best way to pull a weed, she held her breath. His large hands and calloused fingers were steady and gentle. The brim of his hat obscured his hazel eyes, and so Ann kept her eyes on his mouth, hoping it would help her focus on his words. Instead, she found herself admiring his perfectly formed lips and the line of his masculine jaw.

"Do you understand?"

Ann shook away the fog of attraction and nodded.

Please, Lord, help me guard my fragile heart. I can't let it break again.

He continued on, "Think you can tell the difference now?"

"That's corn." She pointed to several plants marching in a drunken row. "And those are weeds."

He smiled. "I'll be going down each row with a hoe to break up the roots. You follow behind me and pull the ones near the corn's base that I can't reach without damaging the crop."

Ann pointed to some tiny weeds, not more than a few inches tall. "Am I to pull these, too? They certainly aren't going to shade out the corn."

"Get them early. You'd be surprised how fast they can grow. Besides, they're still using soil and water."

Ann eyed the enormous expanse in front of them. "I never imagined there could be so much work involved."

James laughed. "You have no idea. This is the third time I've cultivated the soil this season, and if we do it right, it may be my last."

He dropped his head and dug into the soft soil with the blade of his hoe. Ann crouched behind and plucked the tiny seedlings that were sure to grow as green and tall as their brethren. At first, he stopped every few minutes to check on her progress, and each time she was right there behind him. Soon his checks became less and less frequent, and each time the smile on his face grew wider and wider.

Two hours later they were within a few yards of the woods at the back of the property, and the house stood a quarter mile away. Ann pushed the wide-brimmed straw hat back from her forehead and looked heavenward. The sun beat down from its highest point in the sky.

"Are your knees sore? Does your back hurt?" he asked as they came to the end of a row.

"Not at all," she answered.

He squinted through the sweat slipping off his brow. "Are you sure? You've been kneeling for hours."

"I'm fine. This soil is soft compared to the floors I used to scrub."

James chuckled and shook his head from side to side. "I know you were a maid, but I always pictured you helping ladies get dressed, even after you cleaned my house so well."

"You're thinking of a lady's maid. I was a chambermaid. The two are very, very different."

He held out his hand and pulled Ann to her feet. "They must be."

James held fast to her hands as she gained footing on the uneven ground. She found a small clear spot to stand on a mound of dirt and noted that the elevation raised her height several inches. Ann let go of his hands and immediately teetered forward on her perch. His hands darted out and grasped her by the waist, and Ann's grasp found his shoulders.

In an instant she became keenly aware of every part of James McCann. The warmth of his cotton shirt and the firm muscles beneath. The way he smelled like earth and clean sweat. How perspiration on his brow had curled the locks of hair on his forehead. Despite the firm grip he had on her, Ann's head spun and her legs wobbled. She wrapped an arm around his neck to steady herself. His hazel eyes were so close, she was certain she could count each one of his dark lashes. Had his breath grown faster, or was it her own?

"Can you forgive me?" he murmured.

She shook her head, not in response, but to push away the fuzzy feeling that left her dazed. "Forgive you for what?" she finally managed.

"You once told me you could work as hard as anyone, and I laughed at you." He stared down at her with half-lidded eyes. She'd never seen such attractive eyes on a man.

Stop looking at him! Protect your heart.

She wrenched her arm from his neck and took several steps back, nearly tripping herself in the process. Once steady, she glanced about for some other topic of conversation. The next field over had grown quite near.

"No one is outside at the Schneiders."

James followed her gaze. His soft eyes narrowed and his jaw tightened. "No, they're not." He removed the dusty hat from his head and beat it fiercely against his leg, sending waves of dirt off the brim. "And I don't expect they will be anytime soon. It's a wonder Hal Schneider got his crop in the ground."

"Why?"

"See there?" He pointed to several spots bare of corn, but teeming with healthy weeds. "Sometimes he was so drunk when he planted, he missed entire sections of his field. I doubt he'll harvest enough to make it through winter without help."

Ann's heart ached for the two raven-haired children she'd seen playing with James on Sunday. Both had gorged themselves each time as if it was their only decent meal in a week. "The family—they'll have enough to eat, won't they?"

James sighed. "Right now the children aren't neglected, but just barely."

"Do you ever visit them?"

"I tried once. Even had some food with me. Hal saw me coming and waved me off with his shotgun. He'll only accept Margaret Ludlow's charity. The rest of us keep our distance."

"I hope they aren't too hungry."

"They're alright. If the time comes when people in this town think Hal can't care for them, they'll go to Judge Vollrath."

Ann's heart quickened. "The judge wouldn't send them to an orphanage?"

James must have sensed her panic. He placed a warm hand on her shoulder.

"The children will be fine. I heard they have family in Pittsburgh."

"What about Mr. Schneider? Can't someone talk to him?"

"You can't make a grown man take responsibility. All we can do is pray he wakes up and realizes his wife isn't at the bottom of a bottle."

James's voice was hard but matter-of-fact. Ann still knew so little about James, but *matter-of-fact* seemed a good way to describe how he saw most situations.

Find a problem—fix it. Need work done on a farm? Get an ugly wife.

They took a break for lunch, and then returned to the fields.

Halfway down the next row, James stopped.

"What's wrong?" Ann asked.

"Nothing's wrong. In fact, I hate to admit it, but I think having you work behind me is slowing you down. I can tell you're waiting on me."

Ann shrugged and bit back a smirk. She couldn't lie. Weeding was an easy day's work compared to many of the tasks she'd done for years.

James shook his sandy head and chuckled.

"You'd be fifty yards ahead of me if I let you go on ahead, wouldn't you?"

Ann couldn't suppress her smile.

"Fifty yards at least. Perhaps one hundred."

James snorted. "That's what I thought. Why don't you move on ahead at your own pace?"

Ann hesitated.

"Might I work over there?"

She pointed to the westernmost point of the field. She enjoyed working near James, which was exactly why she knew she shouldn't any longer. Her heart wasn't safe. Taut muscles on his back moved with every thrust of the hoe, and she pictured his strong forearms wrapped around her once more. It drove her to distraction.

James raised a brow. "Of course."

Ann shook the dust from her skirts and strode toward the edge of the property. She didn't stop until she reached the wooden fence separating McCann land from Hal Schneider's, and a clump of trees in the middle of the field blocked her view of James. Better not to be tempted to look back and admire him as he moved through his field.

The Schneider house was close, but it looked no more inviting than it had from the road. All the shades were drawn and no signs of life stirred. A vision of Sadie Schneider sitting on James's shoulders flashed before her. Ann's stomach tightened. The fence separating the two fields was little more than a property marker. She had no trouble climbing over.

Now on Schneider land, she looked back toward James to see if he'd witnessed her trespass. A voice from behind startled her.

"What are you doing in my field?"

Ann's heart raced, and her legs itched to run. The voice belonged to a child, but the sharp shadow cast over her included the silhouette of something long and lean in the boy's hands.

Surely a child wouldn't shoot me.

She'd heard stories of wildness and violence in America, but had yet to see a hint of it. Today might be the first.

"What are you doing in *my* field?" The voice was insistent now, and when the shadow stomped his foot it sent up a billow of dust over her skirts.

"Please put the gun down." She tried to keep her voice steady, but it quavered.

"Gun?" The shadow moved toward her and a child's laugh moved with it. "Ma'am, I don't have any gun."

Ann turned by inches. The child stood barefoot and clad only in a dirty pair of overalls with no shirt beneath. She laughed out loud in relief at the object in his hand. Nothing more than one half of a pair of stilts.

"I'm sorry." She pointed to the crudely made stilt. "I thought you had a gun." Ann's heart slowed. "So silly of me. Of course you wouldn't have a gun. You're just a child."

The boy cocked his head to one side. "My gun's in the house," he stated matter-of-factly.

"Oh," she croaked.

"What are you doing on my Pa's land?"

"I'm staying next door. I'm Miss—"

"Miss Cromwell. I know who you are. Mr. McCann sent away for you 'cause he doesn't have time for nonsense."

"I—I'm sorry. Nonsense?"

"You know. Courtin' nonsense. Daddy says Mr. McCann's the only sane man in the county. Instead of courtin' he just wrote a letter and they sent him a wife."

She giggled at the boy's surprisingly accurate version of events. "I think I've seen you at church on Sunday. Are you George?"

The boy straightened his shoulders. "Yes, ma'am. George Schneider."

"How old are you, George?" She knew this was every child's favorite question.

"Seven. I'll be eight before Christmas."

"Very nice to meet you."

"So what are you doing in our field?"

She hesitated. Anything she told this child would surely make it back to his father's ears. "I came to meet you," she answered finally.

George's face broke out in a grin that framed his missing front teeth. "Really?"

"Yes. I saw you and Sadie at church and have been meaning to introduce myself."

"Sadie's in there." The boy pointed to a curtained window. A slender hand poked through the fabric and mustered a timid wave. "Pa's still asleep."

She seized the opportunity. "Then I'd better get going. I wouldn't want to wake him."

George shrugged. "You can't wake Pa. We've tried."

Her stomach quivered. "You can't wake your father?"

"Not without a big cup o' cold water, and why would I do that? I'm not keen on a whippin'."

An uneasy feeling gripped her middle. "Who looks after you while your father sleeps?"

George cocked his brow. "Why would I need lookin' after?"

Ann's thoughts turned to the dozens of children at the orphanage. All had needed help with their hair, their clothes and their washing. And all before breakfast. At the time she'd found each task to be agony. Each child's face reminded her so much of the baby she'd had no choice but to forget. But now, with George staring up at her through a heavy shock of tangled, dirty hair, something tugged at her heart.

"Are you hungry, George?"

The boy shrugged. "I don't know." He rubbed his stomach.

"Would you like me to bring you something to eat?"

His eyes lit up before he frowned and looked at the ground. "Sadie might be hungry. I'm fine," he said and kicked at the dirt.

"Wonderful. I'll be right back with something."

She returned to the fence line with the last of the cherry cobbler and a bottle of fresh milk. George was waiting where she'd left him, and Sadie had joined him. She too had a stilt, and Ann laughed out loud to see how charmingly the set had been reunited. Each child perched on their own stilt, and they remained aloft by wrapping their free arms around one another. When Ann held out the food, the children jumped from the stilts and ran at her at full tilt.

Both children ate as if they were starving, shoving cobbler into their mouths and gulping great mouthfuls of milk. Soon the food was gone. Sadie wrapped her arms around Ann's waist and squeezed tight.

"Will you bring us more?"

Ann crouched down so she was nose to nose with the girl.

"I'd be happy to."

"Pa doesn't like us to have visitors. Says no one should be trespassing. Doesn't like charity neither," George interjected.

Ann paused to consider how to address his concern. She remembered Delia's mother.

"Doesn't Mrs. Ludlow come to visit? And she brings you things, doesn't she?" Surely the woman who had been so quick to offer an apple to a complete stranger would bring food along when visiting these poor, neglected children.

"Sometimes, but she's been gone awhile. Won't be back another week or two, I think."

"And I'm here now, and it's alright."

The little boy's shoulders stiffened.

"Probably shouldn't be here, but Pa drank from his dark bottle this morning. He won't be up for hours."

Pity clawed at Ann's heart.

"How about this? I'll leave a pail for you every morning in the shade by this fence post with something to eat inside. I won't step on your land, so it won't be trespassing, and it's not charity either. Simply a gift from one neighbor to another." Her lack of cooking skills would limit the offerings, but judging by how quickly they'd eaten, Ann guessed the children wouldn't turn their noses up at hard-boiled eggs and vegetables from James's garden.

George screwed up his mouth in a thoughtful expression. "Sounds alright to me."

"Splendid!"

Ann said her goodbyes to the children and climbed back over the fence. For the rest of the afternoon and evening, her thoughts were consumed with only one thing.

What would become of these children?

Chapter Eleven

James studied Ann over their supper of fried potatoes and salt pork. She'd spent over two weeks weeding the entirety of the fields with him without complaint and looked more beautiful every day, as if hard work itself fed her body and soul. But something was wrong tonight. Melancholy languished behind her usually bright eyes. She speared a potato and swirled it about her plate.

"You look worried," he commented.

"I have much weighing on my mind."

"It'll all be sorted out in the end. Mrs. Turner will see to it."

"It's not that." She added a slice of pork to her fork but still didn't bring it to her mouth. "I was thinking of the Schneiders. Of George and Sadie."

James exhaled. "They're easy to worry about."

His hand rested on the table across from hers. It itched to move forward.

"Is that all?"

She pursed her rosebud lips. "I'm anxious over finishing the wedding lace. Last week, Priscilla requested

additions that will take longer than I originally antici-
pated. I'm also worried Mrs. Williams will never sell
one of my handkerchiefs and…"

She paused and the creases on her forehead deepened. Why was she always so concerned about money?
He could only guess how wealthy she'd find herself
soon enough.

"Go on."

"I worry I'm becoming more and more of a burden. You've boarded me for several weeks, and still no
word from Mrs. Turner. I'm sure you're growing quite
tired of me."

His heart leaped, and his hand slid over the worn
wooden surface of the oak table to grasp her fingers.

"You aren't a burden. In fact, I've been feeling guilty,
working you so hard. When you leave, I'll likely owe
you wages for labor."

Her eyes narrowed. "You're winding me up."

Did she mean he was teasing her? For once, he
wasn't. "I'm being serious."

"So am I."

His grip tightened. "I'm not sorry I met you. Only
that all of this ever happened—to you, I mean. I wish
you'd been matched to the right person from the beginning so you could already be living the fine life
you deserve."

She forced a smile. "And I wish the same for you. I
imagine you'd like to move on with your life. Move on
with building your family."

His chest tightened. His plain match—how could he
forget her so easily? He never forgot the world held a
better match for Ann.

"Mrs. Turner's reply will come, and soon after

you'll be in some opulent house, making needle lace as a hobby."

Ann laughed. It sounded forced. "And my servants will prepare the meals."

He laughed and released her hand. He had to remember she wasn't meant for him. Emptiness welled in his chest.

"The eggs. Don't forget about the eggs," he added.

"Yes, of course. No one will ever be forced to eat any of my cooking again."

"Now, now. It isn't all bad. I told you I'm growing fond of your coffee."

A door upstairs creaked open, and Uncle Mac appeared a few moments later.

"Coffee… Porch." His tone was resolute.

James winked at Ann.

"See? I'm not the only one. Uncle Mac used to drink coffee on the porch after dinner almost every night."

He turned to his uncle. "Why don't you persuade Ann to get the coffee started, and I'll get the old rocking chairs?"

Ten minutes later, Ann and Uncle Mac joined him on the front porch with a tray and coffeepot.

"Got these out of the shed. We used to keep them here all the time." He gestured to the high-back wooden rockers that had seen better days. "Once Uncle Mac decided he liked the company of books more than me, I put them away. I never felt like sitting on the porch alone." He'd kept the porch swing well oiled in case Uncle Mac changed his mind, but the bench seat felt too intimate for Ann and James to share.

As if on cue, Uncle Mac took his cup of coffee and stepped off the porch and shuffled toward the barnyard.

"Figures." He snorted. "At least he made it outside today."

James took a seat, and Ann fixed him a cup of coffee before sitting beside him.

"If I may ask, when exactly did your parents pass away?" she asked.

James took a long draft of the strong liquid. His chest still tightened to think of them.

"Five years ago this December."

"Were they ill?"

He nodded. "It was very sudden. A fever swept through this whole area."

"Did you become ill?"

James bent his head and looked into his coffee cup. "No, I wasn't here."

"You weren't?" Her eyes widened in surprise.

"I was away at medical school in Columbus."

She stared at him, her mouth agape. He knew she'd never have thought him capable of such a thing.

"You don't believe me?"

Ann closed her mouth and cocked her head to one side. "No, I do believe you. You would have made a fine doctor."

He raked a hand through his hair. "Why do you say that?"

She dipped her head down and gazed into her cup. "The way you were with me that first day when I burned my hand. I've not known many doctors in my life, but they were all rather brusque. All business with no regard for the patient. You were so…gentle."

James's cheeks flamed at the memory, and her recollection of it.

"Did you ever finish?"

Regret doused James's embarrassment. "I made it halfway through."

"Did you return because your parents died?"

"Not right away. Uncle Mac came at first. He owned a small farm a few miles from here. He sold it and took over things so I could stay at school."

"What happened?"

James waved his hand toward the barnyard. "Uncle Mac's problems happened. At first it was letters from neighbors, commenting about how he never came to visit them anymore. Then Doc Henderson said Uncle Mac had a hard time finding the right words in a conversation. Still, I ignored the signs for as long as I could." His voice cracked and he coughed to disguise it.

"It must have been hard to come back."

"Medical school was something I'd looked forward to all my life. Leaving was almost as hard as losing my parents."

James surveyed Ann's exquisite face. So like Emily's. Only Ann's face creased with worry and concern, not disappointment and disgust.

"If I hadn't returned, the farm would have been sold. My father worked so hard to clear this land. I knew I could never let that happen," he added.

"I'm sorry you've been working alone so long."

James shook his head from side to side and laughed. "Funny thing is, when I left school I didn't think I was coming back here to do this all by myself."

Ann cocked her head at him. "You didn't?"

James shrugged. Why was he telling her this?

"I thought I'd be bringing my wife home with me from Columbus."

"Your wife?" The coffee cup danced from Ann's

hands. She fumbled for it and caught it an inch from the ground. "You were married?"

James's heart skipped a beat and he waved his hands back and forth. Why was he always saying the wrong thing in her presence? "No, no. That's not what I meant. I courted a girl who I thought would return with me to the farm as my wife."

"Oh." Ann shot him a scolding look, as if he'd meant to mislead her. "Who was she?"

His hand worked double time on his hair. It wasn't an easy matter to discuss. He'd spent years pushing the memories down deep.

"Her mother ran the boardinghouse where I lived. Her name was Emily."

"You were going to marry her?"

"I thought so. I was young and smitten. She was very beautiful." The words bubbled forth, like water from the well pump.

"What happened?"

He spread his arms out toward the expanse of land in front of them. "This happened. When I realized I had to come back, I asked her to join me. She came—for a visit at first. From the moment she set eyes on the farm, she couldn't hide her disappointment."

And her disgust. His stomach turned at the memory. How her dainty nose had wrinkled in disdain at the simple farmhouse and the scent of animals in the air. And that was after he'd spent a week readying it for her.

"She was disappointed? With all of this?" Ann's cheeks flushed pink and her ladylike repose dissolved. She stood and strode to the edge of the porch. "You have a lovely farm, James. Beautiful."

She nodded her head to punctuate the last word. As if it was the first and last word anyone could ever use to describe his farm. The only word.

"She said she'd agreed to marry a future doctor, not a farmer."

"Where is this Emily?" Ann's shoulders drew back and she clasped her hands in front of her. "I believe I would like to give her a piece of my mind."

James burst into laughter as he longed to wrap Ann in his arms. She was a bewildering contradiction of English elegance and country spitfire. Both facets pulled at his emotions with equal fervor.

Be strong. Emily had seemed equally charming, at least at first. And did he have to remind himself every moment of the day this woman was intended for another?

"It's not her fault, really," he said.

"Not her fault?" Her voice rose an octave. "What does it matter that your profession changed? She said she would marry you. She should have honored her promise."

The angrier Ann became, the lovelier she grew. Her rosebud mouth pinched tight and her cheeks flushed even brighter. Her anger on his behalf plucked at his heart. He had to turn this conversation in a different direction.

"The heart wants what it wants—isn't that the saying?"

He couldn't believe he was actually defending Emily. But he'd do anything to cool the fire burning in Ann's cheeks and his own chest.

Ann dropped into the rocking chair with a huff. "I can't imagine it was her heart that guided her."

He cringed at Ann's words, knowing full well she was right. After the pain of losing Emily had diffused enough for him to see straight, he'd begun praying for her every night. Emily needed a light for her path, and he asked God to open her eyes to it.

"The last I heard, she'd met and married a young man about to inherit his father's banking business."

"And now a rich banker is waiting for me, as you like to say. Or a doctor or a barrister or a shopkeeper. You say you only know it's someone who requested a beautiful bride," she said.

"Someone who holds a woman's beauty above all other virtues," James added.

Ann's warm blue eyes widened in sorrow and her lip quivered.

He'd said the wrong thing again! His words hung in the air like a poison as he mentally grasped for the antidote. A tear slid down her cheek and his heart shattered. He stood and moved toward her, but was torn between the need to comfort her, and the certainty that he couldn't touch her. He shouldn't touch her.

"I'm sorry. That didn't come out how I meant. I pray your true match is a wise and honorable man."

She shook her head and wiped the tear away with her fingertips. "It's not that. It's only… I was thinking of a man quite like what you just described. He was…" She paused and stared out over the front yard.

Reluctantly, he admitted, "I've known a man like that, too, I'm afraid."

She turned to him. "You have?"

He put his back to her. He couldn't let her see the shame in his face. "Five years ago, that man was me."

"You're teasing."

"After Uncle Mac took over the farm, it was a matter of months before others wrote to me with their concerns about him. But I ignored them. Uncle Mac's letters finally convinced me something was wrong. I'd receive two or three scribbled lines when he used to write pages and pages. I knew I had to return, but I couldn't bring myself to tell Emily. As I grew to know her, I realized she'd never be happy here. So I stayed in medical school."

"Yet you did quit, and you did return."

He nodded. "I did, but not for another six months. For six long months I told myself I could find some other way to make everything work. I'd always planned to return to New Haven and open a small practice. It soon became apparent even that life wouldn't suit Emily. She expected me to be a successful doctor in a large city. So still I tried to avoid coming home. I used what little savings I had to hire workers for the farm, and someone to check in on Uncle Mac."

"She must have been very beautiful."

His shoulders slouched at the memory of her. He'd burned her photograph, but the image of her would never leave his mind. "She was one of the most beautiful women I had ever seen, and also one of the ugliest."

"What did she look like?"

He turned around and surveyed the beauty in front of him. He had to choose his words carefully. "You don't possess the same heart, but she looked remarkably like you."

Ann gasped. "She looked like me?"

"Yes, only her hair was dark, and her eyes were different."

Emily's eyes were cruel. Conniving, even—though it had taken him months to step far enough back to see them. Once he had, he knew he could never pass on her eyes or her heart to his children. Not as a farmer, or as a rich doctor.

He took several steps and closed the space between them. The muggy night air hummed, and Ann shivered despite the heat.

"I know you never understood why I didn't speak up sooner that first day—when I knew there had been a mistake. But it was as if I was looking at Emily all over again. Your beauty blinded me in the same way Emily's did."

He bit back the rest. He'd also seen the kindness in Ann's eyes and longed for it. Longed to have everything he'd thought he'd find in Emily and more.

His words hung in the air between them. A force pulled him toward her. Hadn't he been several feet away a moment ago? He stood so close her cool breath washed over him.

She backed away and bumped into the porch post. The force sent her off balance and she tumbled into a cluster of zinnias below.

His heart jumped to his throat. In an instant James was crouched beside her. She gasped for breath and struggled to get up.

"Stay calm and stay down. You've had the wind knocked out of you. Breath will come—give it time."

Her blue eyes watered and James saw the terror behind them. She opened her mouth but no sound emanated. He had to find a way to reassure her.

James cupped her face in his hands. He caressed her satin-soft skin and her pulse raced against his fingertips.

"Look straight at me. You'll be alright."

Her eyes locked with his, and James's own heartbeat raced to match hers.

She sucked in a shallow breath. Then another. She moved to get up.

"Not just yet."

He pressed her shoulders to the ground. She frowned in protest, but remained still.

James moved through his assessment as quickly as he could, testing her limbs for tenderness and abrasions. When his fingers traced over her silky golden hair to check her head for bumps, he held his breath and recited a now-familiar prayer.

Lord, give me strength.

"Will I survive, Dr. McCann?"

Her breath tickled his ear and his heart jumped.

"I think you'll be fine. I've fallen off that porch more times than I could count. Really ought to put a railing up one of these days."

He helped Ann to her feet. She shook dirt from her skirt and plucked blades of grass from her hair.

"You've fallen?"

"Certainly. Of course, I think the last time I was eight or nine years old."

Her eyes narrowed and he scolded himself for the comment.

"Don't put up a railing on my account."

He opened his mouth to apologize, but a figure at the edge of the field caught his eye.

"Sadie, sweetheart, you must go home," he called out as he jogged toward the tiny girl climbing under the fence. Rather than turning toward home, she dashed forward. James stopped and waited. Her little legs pumped furiously until she was close enough to leap into his arms. He swung her into his chest and held her tight.

"Little one, you need to go home right now. This instant." His tone was firm, but he didn't put her down. Instead, he stroked the back of her hair as her thin arms wrapped around his neck. After a brief embrace, Sadie leaned back and took his face in her small hands. The fading light reflected off her tearstained cheeks.

"I know. But it's Papa. We can't wake him."

Chapter Twelve

Ann dashed to James's side, her stomach in knots. Had Mr. Schneider learned of the food she left for the children? Was he angry?

"Sadie? Where is George?" She'd never seen the tiny girl without her older brother. Her protector. The knots in her stomach twisted.

"With Papa. George said not to come here, but I got scared when Papa never woke for meals today."

The sun sat above the horizon, but it was well into evening. James's face fell and he reached for Ann's hand. She squeezed his fingers and took Sadie from his arms.

"Sadie, we have some bread and jam inside that needs to be eaten. Could you help?"

She nodded vigorously. "I could!"

Ann forced the corners of her mouth into a smile. "Splendid. I'm going to fix a snack for you, and you can stay inside until we return."

James placed a hand on Ann's arm. "You're staying here."

Ann set Sadie on the ground. "Why don't you try those new rocking chairs on the porch? I'll join you in a moment." She watched until Sadie skipped out of earshot before turning to James. "I'm going with you. You said Mr. Schneider has waved a shotgun at you. If he's alive, having a woman with you may be your only protection."

"If Hal Schneider is alive, he's likely so drunk he'll shoot at anything."

"Then we'll both have to keep our wits about us, won't we?"

She hoped that if she treated the conversation as done, he'd stop arguing.

"Don't you dare leave without me, James." She wagged a finger in his direction, then grasped her skirts and ran back to the house. Uncle Mac had joined Sadie on the porch, and within a minute, Ann set bread and jam for two on the kitchen table. Uncle Mac raised a quizzical brow, but she had no time to pull him aside and explain.

"Sadie? Uncle Mac is going to…" Her mind raced. He couldn't read to her or tell her a story.

"Dr-draw," he croaked.

Ann exhaled. "Yes! You're going to draw." She scrounged up paper and pencil and hurried out the door.

Her heart and mind raced as she dashed back to James.

Please, Lord, grant us wisdom to deal with whatever we may find at the Schneider farm.

James remained where she'd left him and they hurried together to the Schneider's front lawn. Or what must have been the front lawn. Thorny weeds grasped at her skirt, and she stopped to wrench them away. When she sidestepped a wild blackberry bush growing directly in the path of the front porch steps, Ann tripped over an upturned paving stone. James's strong hands caught her by the waist and steadied her. His hand remained on the small of her back, steady and comforting, as they picked their way over the broken path.

The front porch was in a miserable state. Several floorboards were missing, and the roof sagged precariously overhead. James forged ahead and gingerly tested the remaining boards with his weight until he reached the front door. Ann followed close behind him.

"You should stay here. I'll call for you if you're needed."

Ann shook her head. "I'm coming inside. My presence is no protection for you if Mr. Schneider can't see me."

James pursed his lips and sighed. "Fine. But no matter what happens, stay behind me. Even when he's sober, Hal can be a mean old cuss."

She stepped behind him. James raised a fist before the door, but left it to hover an inch from the peeling blue paint. His trepidation was obvious. "I'll knock," he announced, before letting his knuckles softly fall.

"If he's dead drunk, you'll have to do better." Ann winced at her poor choice of words, but James only nodded.

"Of course." This time, when his fist fell against the heavy oak door, he rapped hard and long.

Floorboards creaked, followed by a clang, like tin cans striking together. Ann sucked in a breath and held it as the door creaked open. Ann peered around James's back. A filthy George Schneider stood a few steps inside.

George's clothes were rumpled and gray with grime, and his hair matted down on one side. A dark streak of dirt trailed down his left cheek. Ann dashed past James and into the hall.

"George, are you alright?" She knelt down and grasped the boy by both arms. George let out a strangled sob and placed his head on her shoulder. Something wet and sticky clung to her cheek. She stroked the boy's hair and found an oozing wound. What she'd thought was dirt on George's face proved to be a trickle of congealing blood. "You're bleeding!"

George lifted his head. "Don't mind me. Just a scratch. You have to check on Pa. He's real sick."

James brushed past them and into the next room. It appeared he'd been in the house before, because the piles of refuse littering the floor didn't deter him from his path. He strode straight through what appeared to be the sitting room, and opened a door which revealed a flight of stairs.

"Is he in his room?" he asked, pointing upward.

The boy shook his head. "When Pa walks funny, he can't get up the steps. He's in there." George gestured to a closed room to their left.

James hesitated. His normally broad shoulders sagged, and his chest heaved with several deep breaths.

"Shall I go in with you?" Ann asked.

"No." His voice was firm. "And I really mean it this time, so don't go charging in anyway. Stay here with him."

Behind them squatted a worn sofa piled with dirty clothes. Ann cleared a cushion and sat down. "Come, George. Let me look at that head of yours."

The boy sat dutifully in front of Ann on the floor, and she made a feeble attempt to examine the wound in the dark room. Not only were there no lights lit, but curtains were drawn tight over all the windows. The lamp on the side table proved empty of oil.

"I haven't seen you in several days. How have you been?" Ann's hands shook as they grazed the child's head. What waited for James in that room? Was Mr. Schneider dead? If so, for how long? What did he look like? She'd never seen a dead body. At the orphanage, several children had died of diphtheria, but their bodies were whisked away in the dark of night.

George didn't answer, but he winced as her hand probed his scalp. Ann stopped her examination. Without any way to see what she was doing, she might do more harm than good to his wound. She pulled the boy to his feet and into her lap.

"How did you hurt your head?"

"Will my Pa be alright?" His eyes glistened in the feeble light.

Ann wrapped her arms tightly around him. "Right now, I'm fretting over you. How did this cut come to be?"

He chewed on his lip and shrugged. "I fell."

"You fell? You must have fallen into something to receive this horrid gash."

George opened his mouth to speak, but they both started as the parlor door squeaked. James burst forth, his eyes wide with worry.

"George, run to my house and stay with your sister," he commanded. The little boy remained on Ann's lap.

She took George by the hand. The little fingers were as cold as ice. "Sadie is there with Uncle Mac and a plate of jam and bread, but I forgot to pour them milk. Will you do that? And then stay there and make sure they have everything they need until one of us comes to get you?"

"What about my Pa?"

"We'll be along shortly, George. Right now we need you to help Sadie and Uncle Mac."

He hesitated one more time before nodding and dashing out the door without closing it. His dark head bobbed across the barnyard and toward James's farm.

Once George was safely out of earshot, Ann grasped for James's hand in the dim room.

"Is it horrible?" she whispered. She grew dizzy at the thought of what might lie in the next room.

James didn't answer. Instead, he gripped her hand and pulled her toward the parlor door. He pushed his shoulder into it and sent it swinging open.

"No, James, no! I can't look!" James still had a tight hold on her hand, and she used her free arm to shield her eyes. "I can't look at him, I just can't!"

James moved her arm away from her face and released her hand.

"You'll have to look if you're going to help me save him. Or at least try to."

She opened one eye. "Save him? He's alive?"

She would have thought it impossible, but the parlor proved even darker and messier than the sitting room. James was already across the room and hovering over a figure reclining on a tattered horsehair sofa. Her eyes adjusted to the stray bits of light trickling under the curtains. James's fingers prodded the man's wrist and neck.

"He's alive, but just barely. His pulse is very weak, and growing weaker by the minute."

"What's wrong with him?"

"Drank himself into a stupor, most likely, and now his own body doesn't know it's supposed to keep his heart beating. He'll be dead soon if we don't get help."

The knot of fear that had held her back now unwound like a spring and sent her running across the room. She didn't want to see this man die. She didn't want to see anyone die.

"Is there something you can do?"

James continued to move over Mr. Schneider's body, loosening his shirt and removing his boots. He didn't look up as he answered, "Yes. I can stay here and try to keep him breathing while you go to the Zwebels'."

"The Zwebels?" Ann's head fogged. James had pointed out so many neighbors, and she remembered so few names.

"The closest neighbors as you're headed toward town. They live in the yellow house about a mile from here. Take Hal's horse, and tell Jed Zwebel you need Doc Henderson."

"James, I can't."

He stopped his movements over the body. "You can't?"

"Oh, I wish I could, but I can't. I don't ride— remember?"

James raked his hands through his hair.

"I shouldn't have sent George away. He could have gone, but there's no time now. I'll ride and you'll stay here."

Ann grasped James's wrist as he passed by.

"W-what should I do?"

He bent his head so his hazel eyes were inches from hers.

"Just keep Hal alive."

Then he was gone. No chance to protest or beg for

more instructions. The front door slammed and she was alone.

The setting sun sent fingers of light through slits in the tattered curtains and cast the dark room in a sickly orange glow. A sudden chill traipsed over Ann's back despite the heat, and she hastened to the nearest window and threw back the heavy fabric. A cloud of dust billowed from the curtains and Ann coughed and choked on the thick air. She yanked at the window frame, but it had been haphazardly painted shut. Covering her mouth with a handkerchief would have to suffice until the dust cloud settled.

A gagging cough arose from the corner.

Ann's heart raced.

"Mr. Schneider, are you alright?"

She wished she could stay as far away from the man as possible until James returned, but she only had one task—to keep him alive. He coughed again. What if he was choking? She tiptoed to the corner. The cough continued, growing into a strangled wheeze. His head lay on a tattered gray pillow, but his slouched posture on the sofa pushed his chin into his chest. Ann gingerly slipped her hand behind his greasy head and removed the pillow. His head flopped back and the sound stopped.

With reluctance, Ann placed her head on his chest. *Please let me hear something. Anything*, she prayed.

Her own heart beat deafeningly in her ears and threatened to drown out any other sounds. His shirt stood up stiff with grime, and the once-soft cotton scratched her cheek. She held her breath and pressed her ear even more firmly against his chest.

Nothing.

I've killed him.

The stench of alcohol and unwashed body set her eyes to water. She held her breath and quieted the room like a grave. After a moment, a slow, irregular thump pulsed against her ear.

Ann sank to the floor. She hadn't killed him. Not yet anyway. She stood and crossed the room to a dusty lamp sitting on the sideboard. Only a quarter inch of oil remained, and she didn't know where to find more. She would light it only when the room became too dark to see. The cluttered space was crowded with odds and ends, but it held little furniture, save for the sofa, a worn leather trunk and a bare wooden rocker tossed on its side. Ann drew the rocker next to Mr. Schneider and dropped into it.

The grit clinging to her hands proved the rocker, too, was shrouded in filth. Muffled scratches and scurries telegraphed countless mice in the walls. How on earth did George and Sadie live in a place like this?

Ann scooted to the edge of the rocker and listened to each now-raspy breath. They were shallow and infrequent, and she began counting between each one. No clock was in the room, and she marked time by the space between each ragged intake of air. Despite the stench of man and dirt in the air, the heat and the counting soon drew Ann into a stupor. Her eyes grew heavy, and she rocked the chair to rouse herself. But the rhythmic movement only added to the trance.

She continued to slowly count, even as her eyelids grew heavy. *One…two…three…four…five…six…seven… eight…nine. Wait, nine seconds between breaths?* Her eyes fluttered open. In hundreds of breaths, she'd never reached nine in her count. She lit the lamp and thrust it over Hal Schneider's face.

His pale, waxy skin stood out against the dark fabric of the sofa. Perspiration beaded on his forehead. She grasped his hand and found it cold and clammy. No signs of life. Ann reluctantly placed her head against his chest again, but heard nothing except the stiff scratch of dirty flannel. She moved her ear to his mouth, and prayed to feel hot, foul breath against her cheek.

Nothing.

She had to do something, but what? A dim memory sent her racing outside. The well pump was rusty but in working order, and a pail hung from the handle.

She raced back to the room and the pail sloshed water onto the floor as she heaved it into her arms and up-ended it over Mr. Schneider's head.

With a tremendous gasp, he bolted upright. The shock sent Ann stumbling backward into the leather trunk, the pail flying across the room and clanging against the wall. The man's eyes were still closed. Water streamed over his face and soaked his clothes and the horsehair sofa beneath him.

"Mr. Schneider? Mr. Schneider?" She crept toward him, a hand outstretched to block any blows he might try to land in his stupor. He turned in the direction of her voice, mumbled something indecipherable, and promptly retched on the floor. Then he fell back against the sofa in the same posture as before, and commenced to snore violently. His eyes never opened.

Ann collapsed against the trunk. Her heart raced, only now in exhilaration. She hadn't let him die. At least not yet. She moved to clean up the mess, but the sound of horses and men's voices floated in from the yard. Relief washed over her. James had returned.

Chapter Thirteen

Please let him still be alive, James prayed as he crossed Hal Schneider's threshold. His stomach knotted. He'd been gone far too long. And he'd left a large, obscenely drunk and dying man with a tiny woman with no medical training. What had he expected her to do? The fear in her eyes when he'd left was unmistakable. He wouldn't blame her if she'd fled back to his farm.

Doc Henderson entered the parlor first and darted straight to the stricken man. James's heart jumped at the scene. Hal Schneider looked as if he had barely moved on the sofa, but now his hair and shirt were soaking wet. Fresh vomit soiled a spot on the floor. What could possibly have happened?

"I'm so sorry. I made such a mess, but I didn't know what else to do." Ann appeared next to him and sank into his side. He wrapped an arm around her shaking shoulders and drew her close. She shivered despite the stifling heat of the room.

Doc Henderson looked up from his patient. "No need to be sorry." He nodded to James. "She's done right by him. His pulse is better than you described."

The doctor turned to Ann. "Did he vomit before or after you roused him with the water?"

"A-af-after," she stammered. Her delicate arms clutched James's waist and he struggled to focus on anything else in the room. He wanted to scoop her in his arms and take her far from this horrible scene. "The water was the only thing I could think of to do. I thought he'd stopped breathing."

"He likely did. You did the right thing, young lady. A man can be in such a stupor he can't rouse himself. If he'd vomited on his back, he very well might have drowned."

James's stomach flipped. Ann's heartbeat thudded against his ribs.

"In London," Ann explained, "I once saw a constable perform the same service for a man passed out in an alley, though I doubt his intentions were the same as mine."

"Best thing you could have done," the doctor continued, "given the circumstances." He drew a small glass vial from his bag and plunged a syringe into the clear liquid. "If you two hadn't found him, Hal Schneider would have likely—" he paused to administer the injection "—been dead by morning," he finished.

James gazed down at her. "Thank you, Ann. And forgive me. You never should have been left with Hal for so long."

"How long were you gone?"

"Over an hour. I intended for Jed Zwebel to fetch Doc, but found no one at home. Hal's horse threw a shoe half a mile later. I ran to the next nearest house— the Winters'—and by the grace of God, Doc was there delivering a baby."

"A fine baby boy," the doctor called over his shoulder.

Doc Henderson stood and replaced the items he'd withdrawn from his bag. "I believe the worst is over, but I don't think he should be left alone tonight."

"I can stay," James offered.

"No, you can't!" Ann pushed away from him and cast him a scolding look. "If he aimed a gun at you for being on his property, imagine what he could do if he awakes and finds you in his house!"

The doctor peered over his glasses. "Is this true?"

James saw no sense in lying, and he'd be a fool to argue his way into staying the night in a filthy house with a drunk who might wish him harm.

"More or less." He shrugged.

Doc Henderson removed his glasses and rubbed his eyes. "I suppose that leaves me to do the job. Very well."

Ann stepped forward. "George—Hal's son—has a terrible cut on his head I believe needs tending."

"Of course, of course. Is the boy upstairs?"

"He and his sister are next door at my house," James interjected. "I can tend to his wound."

The doctor straightened his shoulders and shook his head. "Nonsense. If you stay with Hal awhile longer, I'll see to the boy. Should I return with the children?"

James glanced at Ann. Her brows were arched and her eyes wide in concern.

"Given the circumstances, they can stay at my house this evening," he answered.

Ann's countenance relaxed and she squeezed his upper arm in thanks.

"I'll fetch the children some clean clothes and leave with James when you return, Doctor," Ann added.

Together, they scrounged another lantern with some

oil from the kitchen and Ann disappeared with it upstairs. She returned at the same time as the doctor, carrying an enormous bundle. "I couldn't find any clean
clothes but plenty of dirty ones. I'll wash these tomorrow," she explained.

"How is he?" Doc Henderson asked James.

James swung the lantern over the drunken man's
face. "Breathing is deep and regular now."

"I imagine he'll awake in the morning with a powerful headache. If he has any food in the house, I'll try
to get him to eat."

The two men shook hands, and James and Ann left.

The clock struck eleven as they entered the front
hall. The kitchen was still ablaze with lamplight and
they found both children there with Uncle Mac. Draw-
ings of every kind littered the table.

The eyes of all three brightened when they entered,
but none more than Uncle Mac's. He creaked to his feet
and let out a heavy sigh.

"Bed," he announced.

James patted him on the back as he passed, his chest
expanding with pride. It was a wonder he'd entertained
the children as long as he had.

Ann leaned into James and murmured in his ear.

"We need to bathe these children before bed."

Ann was right. The doctor had wiped George's forehead clean to tend to his wound, but grime plastered his
hair to his head, and dirt streaked his arms and throat.
Sadie didn't appear much cleaner. How could he have
missed the decline in their care? Though their clothes
were often rumpled and soiled, they had at least appeared freshly bathed at church each Sunday. Was Hal

Schneider getting worse than before? How long had these children been so totally neglected?

James fetched the large washtub from outside, and Ann put on the kettle. With startling efficiency, Ann prepared the bath and scrubbed the children from head to toe. Her scrubbing was gentle but thorough. George protested at first that he was too old for her to bathe him, but quickly settled into the warm water and brisk scrub with a contented look on his face. Sadie splashed and giggled, and cried piteously when Ann announced it was time to emerge from the warm water and Pears' soap bubbles.

James marveled as Ann moved through the motions of readying the children for bed. Her voice was simultaneously soothing and firm, and they followed her about like kittens. If she stood still too long, they wrapped their thin arms around her and held on tight until she gently pried them off. His heart panged. With each touch, Ann likely showed them more love and affection than they'd received in a year.

Ann repurposed two of James's old work shirts as nightclothes and put Sadie's wet hair into two long braids. James sloshed out the wash basin and wiped up the dribbles of water on the floor. Ann walked them to the privy, and when they returned, George and Sadie stood in the middle of the kitchen like two tiny soldiers awaiting instructions.

"Could they both sleep in your bed?" Ann suggested.

"As good a place as any."

The four of them climbed the stairs, and with each step James felt the day's stress weigh on him more heavily than he ever had in all his twenty-five years. His legs ached. His back cramped. He didn't look forward to sleeping in the hammock tonight.

Ann set the lamp on the dresser and tucked both children into James's bed.

"You two will be staying here tonight in Mr. Mc-Cann's room. Isn't that exciting?"

For the first time that evening, Sadie's obedience wavered. She jumped up from the bed and threw herself into Ann's arms.

"Don't leave me. Please, don't leave me!" Sadie sobbed.

"Shh, shh. It's alright," Ann whispered against the girl's cheek. "You're safe here."

Sadie's arms tightened. "Let me sleep with you."

Ann looked up at James with wide, soulful eyes. "What do I do?" she mouthed.

George remained on the bed, but there was no mistaking the longing in his eye or his faintly quivering lip. George didn't want to be left alone any more than Sadie did, but he was too proud to say it. The last year had taken so much of the little boy out of him.

James bent his lips to Ann's ear. "I was thinking of staying in here with George, if that's alright with you."

"Does that mean I can stay with you?" Sadie exclaimed, clearly having overheard.

"Alright, then. Come along."

Ann sounded exasperated, but James could see it was only a show. She hugged the little girl tight and smiled.

James caught Ann's eye as she squeezed past him in the doorway.

"Thank you," he whispered. "Thank you for everything tonight. I don't know what I would have done without you." He stroked Sadie's back and his fingers brushed Ann's. A tingle raced over his skin, and his hand lingered. Her fingers twined with his and heat traced up his arm.

"I haffa use the privy again," Sadie mumbled into Ann's shoulder.

They both chuckled and James slipped his hand free from her grasp.

James rolled over and was struck with a blinding light. Sun streamed through the window and warmed his face. What time was it? He hadn't slept past dawn since he was a boy, but his own bed had been like a balm to his body after weeks of sleeping on the back porch. So much so, he'd slept harder and deeper than he had in years. He moved to get up, but George Schneider lay draped over his chest on top of the covers.

It all came back to him. Hal's drunkenness. Fetching the doctor. Ann surprising him yet again with her strength and resourcefulness. His face warmed as he recalled last evening. It was a good thing George and Sadie stayed. Without them in the room, he would have swept Ann into his arms and kissed her in gratitude and admiration.

Light knuckles rapped on his bedroom door.

"Come in," he whispered.

The door slit open, and Ann's blue eyes peered through the crack.

"Are you alright? Can I get you anything?"

Her lilting accent tumbled his heart.

He tilted his head to George. "Should I wake him?" James whispered back.

George stirred and flopped off James. His face was slack and his mouth hung open, the picture of exhaustion.

Ann cracked the door farther and craned her neck inside. Her lips curled into a pitying smile.

"We must let him rest. Yesterday was a trial for such a wee one."

"Right, right." His legs itched to move. He'd never been comfortable staying in bed when the room was this bright, even when he'd suffered from influenza. "What time is it?"

"Noon."

"Noon!"

James cringed as his shout reverberated off the walls. Fortunately, it didn't wake George, who began to snore.

"Shh… Shh!" Ann moved her hands about as if she could grasp any further exclamations from the air. "I'm joking. A quarter past seven, I think."

James sighed. "Better, but not much."

Ann closed the door, and he extricated himself from the bed as stealthily as possible. Someone rapped on the front door as he came down the stairs. He opened it to find Doc Henderson.

"Morning, James," the doctor greeted him.

"Morning, Doc. How's Hal?"

"Fine, fine. Nothing time won't cure at this point."

"May I offer you some breakfast?"

"A good cup of coffee would be wonderful."

James stifled a laugh. "I'll see what I can do."

Three sets of eyes turned as James and the doctor entered the kitchen. Ann stood at the stove and Sadie sat on Uncle Mac's lap while she tucked into a plate of eggs.

Ann wiped her hands on her apron and hurried toward them.

"Everything alright?" she whispered, her alabaster forehead creased with worry.

"Doc says Hal's going to be okay. Would you get him some coffee?"

Ann faltered, and rightly so. Her coffee was like nothing he'd ever tasted. Maybe it had killed all his taste buds because he was actually starting to like it.

"Ann makes a mighty strong cup of coffee, Doc," he warned.

The doctor took a seat at the table and Ann poured him a cup. James held his breath as the older man sipped.

Doc Henderson smiled.

"Very good, Miss Cromwell. And much needed after last night."

The doctor was either a tremendous liar or had a taste for strong coffee, quite like the one James was developing.

"Sadie, dear. Please take the basket and fetch more eggs." Ann shooed the little girl out the door.

The doctor glanced back distractedly as the screen door banged behind Sadie. "I'll check on Hal one more time before I head back to town. James, may I assume you can keep these children a few more hours?"

"A few more hours!" Ann stood with her hands on her hips. "You're not suggesting they return to their father today?"

"We'll bring them on home around suppertime," James offered.

"Good, good." The doctor nodded into his cup.

Ann crossed her arms and huffed. Uncle Mac patted her shoulder, and James longed to do the same. His heart ached for both the children and for Ann's concern, but what could he do? Hal Schneider's pride wouldn't allow him to relinquish his children, any more than he could put down the bottle. The doctor slurped two more cups of coffee while Ann stomped about the kitchen, her lips pursed and her cheeks a deep crimson.

When all the coffee was drunk, the doctor pushed away from the table and James walked him to the door.

"Hey, Doc? Can I ask you for a favor?"

"Certainly."

"Hal keeps a shotgun above his front door. Any chance you could unload it while you're there?"

The doctor laughed and shook his head.

"You must think I'm fresh out of medical school. I unloaded every gun in the house the second you left. Hid the bullets, too. I told Hal he could have them back when he comes into town to see me."

"How did that go over?"

"About as you'd expect."

The doctor paused and rubbed at his thinning hair.

"I understand Miss Cromwell's concern about the children. But medically speaking, I see no reason why they can't be returned today."

James nodded grimly.

"I understand. I imagine he'd want to see them straight away."

The doctor's shoulders slouched.

"You'd think that, wouldn't you? But he didn't ask for them this morning. Only for the bottle."

Disgust shot through James. How could a man love anything more than his own children?

"Is that so?" Despite his best effort, the vitriol in his voice was obvious even to his own ears.

"I mixed a draft to help him sleep off his headache. When he wakes, I imagine he'll find one of the many bottles he likely has hidden throughout his house. I emptied as many as I could find, but I assure you he has more tucked away somewhere."

Blood roared in James's ears. He pictured George and Sadie fending for themselves as their father slept yet another day away.

"Hal Schneider will be drunk again. Drunk for days. The presence of two small children will not make a difference. He will be drunk regardless."

The doctor spoke slowly and methodically. James understood his meaning immediately.

"When might Hal notice his children are gone?"

"I know the two of you aren't on the best terms. I'll stop by Jed Zwebel's and ask if he can check in on Hal tonight and again in the morning. As soon as he asks after the children, you must send them over directly."

James thanked the doctor again and returned inside. As he entered the foyer, a blur of blue cotton flew into his arms.

"Thank you, thank you," Ann murmured into his chest, her arms wrapped tight around his waist. She jumped back quick as a jackrabbit before he could return the embrace, flushed scarlet from her hair to the bodice of her dress.

"I was eavesdropping," she explained.

James's heart thudded. The blush of embarrassment only enhanced Ann's beauty.

"They must return the moment their father asks for them," James gruffed, though he felt exactly as Ann looked. Excited and relieved at the thought of giving George and Sadie some proper care. Anxious for what the future held for the children.

She clasped her hands in front of her. "What shall we do with them until then?"

"Don't you have a meeting with Priscilla Vollrath this afternoon?"

Ann clapped a hand to her forehead. "I'd completely forgotten! Will the children be much trouble for you? I can't ask them to walk all the way to town with me."

"Now you'll get to ride. I'm sure George can handle Old Harriet."

"George? Are you certain?" She raised a brow.

A voice echoed down the front stairs and George's dark head peered over the railing? "Certain of what?"

"Can you drive a horse and buggy, George?"

The young boy screwed up his mouth, as if the question was the greatest insult of his short life.

"Of course I can! Who can't?"

And so it was settled.

Chapter Fourteen

Ann's hands were already sweating. A seven-year-old boy driving a horse and wagon. Though James had insisted it was completely normal—*a farm boy is born with the reins in his hands*—her heart still thudded.

"What if the horse spooks?" Ann whispered to James. She didn't want to offend George with her doubts in him.

"Old Harriet is the least spookable horse God put on this earth. She's stepped over every kind of snake and critter without so much as a whinny." He cupped his hand around his mouth, as if sharing a secret, and Ann leaned in. "I think she's a mite blind."

Ann stifled a laugh. "Is that supposed to make me feel better? To put my life in the hands of a blind horse and a little boy?"

"In the hooves of a blind horse. And I was only kidding. Her eyesight is fine. It's her hearing that's going. Come now, I'll get her hitched."

Ann smothered another laugh and followed him to the barn, with the children following close behind, both dressed in clean clothes she'd washed before dawn and dried under a hot iron. Despite her name, Old Harriet was still beautiful, with a shiny, lustrous coat that only came from good care. Her steps were steady and careful, as James had said, and she quickly and dutifully followed each of his commands as he hitched her to the wagon.

"She'll need water when you get there, but George knows that. Don't you, George?"

George nodded vigorously. The bandage on his forehead stood fast.

"Any questions?"

"Just one."

James stopped stroking the horse's nose and gave Ann his full attention. "What is that?"

"Was she ever New Harriet or Young Harriet?"

James chuckled and shook his head. "She was simply Harriet for many years, but as the old girl got older, I began to think of her as Old Harriet. Soon that name was coming out of my mouth." He turned to the horse and scratched behind her ears. "Have any other questions—Annoying Ann?"

He hadn't teased Ann in more than a day. She tried very hard to be annoyed rather than pleased at the return.

"No, I don't...Juvenile James."

James slapped his leg, and threw back his head with a laugh. He leaned forward again—still laughing—so far that his hat tumbled off his head and into his hands.

She could never pass up an opportunity to make him laugh, as she'd never met anyone who laughed with his whole body as James did. Making him laugh felt like she owned a special key that could unlock his joviality. It made her feel special.

James hoisted Sadie onto the buggy seat, but made a show of standing back so George could pull himself up. Ann moved to mount the buggy, but James grasped her arm and guided her back into the barn, out of earshot of the children.

"I still haven't properly acknowledged what you did last night, Ann, or apologized for what I did. I left you alone with a gravely ill man. You could have refused. Instead, you saved his life."

The warmth of his fingers spread to her fingertips. And with each word, his grip drew her closer. "I—I didn't do anything. It was stupid, really. If I saved his life, it was completely by accident."

He released her arm and removed his hat so he could run a hand through his mop of hair. She now recognized this motion as a precursor to a nervous speech. "This isn't only about the life you saved." He licked his lips. "You were brave. So brave. You entered Hal's house even though you knew the danger. You never hesitated."

His hands kneaded at his hat brim. She wanted very much for him to place his hand back around her arm. "I wasn't brave. I was terrified."

He smiled and shook his head. "Bravery is facing danger even when you're scared."

Ann grasped for words, but her thoughts were jumbled and hazy. Instead, she stared at his hands, going over and over the hat brim. How many times had he touched her? Had there ever been a time her heart hadn't tripped in response?

Before she could think, he crossed the space between them and pressed his lips to her forehead. "Thank you, Ann," he murmured against her skin.

He stepped back as quickly as he'd stepped forward, and replaced his hat on his head. "I'd best get to the chores, and you don't want to keep Priscilla waiting."

Ann waved at him dumbly and watched as he strode quickly away and toward the nearest field. She'd arrived in America in a gloom of uncertainty. She was now certain of so very many things, but the uncertainty hadn't lifted.

James McCann was an honest, hardworking, decent man. He cared for others as himself and desired a family more than any man she'd ever met. He would make someone a fine husband.

And I'm certain that someone can never be me.

On their return trip from town, a handsome buggy turned onto Mud Pike from a side road and the driver drew along beside them. It was Frederick Renner.

"Good afternoon, Miss Cromwell. Hello, George! Hi, Sadie!"

"Hello!" the children chorused.

"What has this trio been up to?" Frederick was dressed much as he had been at their first meeting. Drab, ill-fitting shirt and pants that did little to indicate the wealth she now knew he possessed.

"I had an appointment in town," Ann replied. "With Priscilla Vollrath." *How to explain the children's presence?* "George and Sadie were kind enough to accompany me. I've never driven a buggy."

"You're kidding."

"I'm afraid not. But George is an excellent driver."

Frederick nodded in acknowledgment. "I'm certain he is." George beamed with pride but kept his eyes dutifully forward.

"Are you on your way to see James?" Ann asked.

"I was, but now you can save me the trip. The mill will be running overtime beginning tonight and for the next few weeks. If he can lend a hand, we're desperate for the help."

"I'll let him know."

He tipped his cap. "Much obliged."

Frederick expertly turned his buggy around on the narrow road, and headed back toward New Haven.

When they passed the Schneider farm, both children strained for signs of their father, but the house appeared as quiet and neglected as it did every other day. She scowled as she pictured them returning to that filthy house. Returning to the bare cupboards and the grime, their father lying prostrate with a bottle in his hand.

A few minutes more and they were back in the barnyard. James's sandy head appeared from behind the barn door. Her heart tripped at the sight of him. The memory of his lips on her forehead had replayed over and over these last few hours.

"Mr. McCann!" Sadie's tiny voice screeched in delight. "We missed you!" She threw herself from the wagon with abandon into James's waiting arms, fully trusting he would catch her.

"Have a successful trip?" James croaked, his voice strangled by Sadie's tight grip around his neck. Sadie giggled and loosened her arms but didn't relinquish her hold.

"Priscilla should be pleased with her dress."

He smirked. "If she is, it'll be the first time that girl is pleased with anything." He paused and ran his free hand through his hair. "That wasn't an insult to Mrs. Williams—or you. I'm sure it's a fine dress."

"I'm used to your teasing, James. I wasn't offended."

He ducked his head. "I've been trying to keep the teasing in check."

Please don't.

"Will you be in soon for supper?"

"Shortly. I need to muck out this stall first."

Ann led the children to the water pump to wash up and fashioned a game out of empty thread spools at the kitchen table. Once they were occupied, she joined James in the barn. He was spreading fresh-cut hay for the horse when she entered.

"We can't delay the children's return home much more than a day, can we?" she asked.

James turned, startled, and struck his head against a low beam. Ann gasped and ran toward him, but he held out a hand to signal he was alright.

"You're not the only one with a clumsy streak around here. At least I have a little padding." He pointed to the shock of wavy hair hanging over his brow.

Ann lifted the locks away from the injury, her fingers grazing his forehead. The skin was intact but painted with a rosy red mark that grew darker by the moment. She bit her lip. "It doesn't look very good." He winced as her fingertips traced along the mark's border.

"Comes with the territory." He reached up and slapped a hand on the offending beam. "My father built this barn, and he was a head shorter than me. Guess he never figured on having a tall son."

The thought of James's diminutive father moving back and forth beneath the beam without impediment struck Ann as funny. She laughed, and James stuck out his lower lip in mock offense. Her hand still lingered on his brow. She mussed at his hair to dislodge dust from the day's work, as if it was always her intention. A cloud of dust motes and hay caught the light. "It's a good thing the skin didn't break. You're filthy." She darted her hand back to her side.

His lips upturned ever so slightly, and she was filled with the sudden wish for him to lean down and kiss her again. Instead, he turned and passed Old Harriet one last handful of alfalfa and sweetgrass. "The children have to go home tomorrow. I don't think we can avoid it much longer than that. If we wait until Jed Zwebel says Hal's asking for them, Hal will probably have already worked himself into a lather. I'll take them back after breakfast."

"What about Hal?"

"Doc said he took all his bullets."

"Still, I'm coming with you."

James made no argument, unlike the night before. He simply nodded.

At supper, everyone marveled over the bountiful spread Delia had been kind enough to send home with them. Ann's mouth watered at the sight of foods she might have some hope of recreating if her cooking lessons were as successful as Delia seemed certain they'd be.

"You'll be able to make all of this and more," she'd promised. But Ann had her doubts. Lattice-topped apple pies were Delia's specialty. An item that Ann knew, from her examination of cookbooks, required multiple steps and recipes. Multiple opportunities to ruin the final product.

Ann surveyed James as he ate. He closed his eyes after each bite, savoring each morsel. And little wonder—it could be months before he'd eat this well again. When James's desired match finally arrived.

Her stomach turned and a savory bite of roast beef caught in her throat. She hadn't wanted to stop by the post office while in town, but not doing so would only delay the inevitable. Her limbs had nearly gone limp in relief when the postmaster announced no mail for James McCann. But one day there would be, and it was all Ann could think about.

The children dived into the offerings with both hands until she shooed them away and filled their plates for them, and one for Uncle Mac. They no longer ate like they were starving, but she glimpsed George pocket two split-top rolls, and Sadie meekly requested seconds, thirds and fourths.

After supper, Ann helped the children wash up, and carried a food-stupored Sadie upstairs. The girl dived under the covers in Ann's bed and curled herself into a ball against the wall. Ann undressed and hurried quietly through her toilet before gingerly peeling back the covers and climbing into bed.

Before the previous night, it had been months since Ann had slept next to anyone. While working in the orphanage, despite being afforded a semiprivate room in the attic with the other maid, most nights she stumbled to bed and found a small girl nestled there, waiting to cuddle with her. Ann never understood why. The little children shared one large room with dozens of other girls—all willing and eager to share a bed on a cold night. They had no need to creep up two flights of stairs.

The attic grew cold and drafty in the winter, and on those nights part of Ann welcomed the warm body. It was in the heat of the summer, when the attic held on to every bit of moisture the house had belched forth during the day and every ounce of heat, that she was bewildered by the discovery of a small child eager to be snuggled. Each would wrap her thin arms around Ann until the stifling warmth drove them apart.

The one tiny attic window could never hope to release the choking humidity. The girls' own bedrooms were flanked by comparatively luxurious long windows that opened out into the night and sucked cool air over their beds. And yet a child appeared each evening. Sometimes, the same girl curled next to her for subsequent nights. Other times, someone new arrived each evening.

Never mind that they would be swatted and scolded if they were discovered by the orphanage's senior staff. Entry by the children into the servants' quarters was strictly prohibited. But they had no night nurse and no bed checks, and so their visits continued.

She could have stopped them. She could have reported the behavior and looked on as they were whipped for it. Nellie, the chambermaid with whom she shared a room, was jealous on those cold winter nights, and she tried to persuade the girls to join her instead. But it was Ann's company they wanted. Her bed for which they were willing to risk a beating.

The pain of having a child in her arms was as acute the first time as it was the last. Every moment reminded her of the child she should have had in her arms. Or rather, all the children she could have had in her arms, had she not thrown her honor and her future away. Perhaps that was why she braved the pain each night, letting the girls sleep beside her without a word of objection. It was her penance.

Most peculiar of all, was why these girls were drawn to her. The absurdity of it all made it clear this was God's punishment for her. During the day, Ann never cast smiles at these girls or gave them pats on the arm in encouragement. She didn't pass them the occasional sweet like the cook or turn her worn-out uniforms into dolls like Nellie. Instead she did her best to avoid them at every turn. She cleaned their vacated rooms and side-stepped their outreached arms in the corridor. Yet still each night they found her.

Sadie hadn't moved from her tucked position against the wall. She had lain the same way the night before, and Ann had fallen into a deep sleep of exhaustion after the stress of the day, thankful to be only mildly aware of the girl's presence. Ann was keenly aware of her tiny body tonight. Sadie's deep, steady breathing reminded Ann another soul curled beside her. She closed her eyes.

It's only the wind, she lied to herself.

A thin arm snaked over her chest and wrapped itself around Ann's neck. She held her breath and dared not move as Sadie's body nestled into her side, and her head tucked against Ann's shoulder. She couldn't breathe without taking in a mixture of little girl scents. Pears' soap. Hay. Spicy, sweet cinnamon apples. Her heart skipped a beat. Sadie's breath was sweet on her cheek, which felt surprisingly cool. The strange chillness that only comes when your cheeks are wet with tears.

She did something she'd never done in the orphan-age. Not in all those many nights. She lifted her free arm from the bed and wrapped it around the waist of the tiny girl. Ann's fingers traced a slow, soft pattern on Sadie's back, and she let the tears flow. She cried as silently as she could, but was not quiet enough. Sadie stirred and raised her head.

"Why are you crying?" she whispered.

In the dark Ann could make out nothing of her face, but the empathy in the girl's voice was unmistakable. Ann's heart ached.

"It's nothing, sweetheart. Go back to sleep."

Sadie's head descended and her lips landed a soft kiss on Ann's teary cheek.

"Kisses make it better," she announced resolutely before nuzzling her head back into Ann's shoulder.

The pain in Ann's heart intensified and she gripped the girl tighter.

Dear God, I can't wait for the letter from Mrs. Turner. I must get away from this place.

Chapter Fifteen

"I'll walk with you to the edge of the property and wait there until you return. It's probably best if I hunker down in the weeds a bit, in case Hal's bent the wrong way, but you'll know I'm there."

James's heart pounded in his chest. Tiny Ann Cromwell was about to confront Hal Schneider. The man whose life she'd saved. He'd thought her as fragile as a china doll mere weeks ago. Now he knew just how strong and determined she was as she strode in lockstep next to him in the barnyard, far out of earshot of the children.

"What do I say?" Her voice quavered, despite the confidence in her stride.

"This is where that accent and charm of yours are going to serve you well. Introduce yourself. Act like a new neighbor coming for a visit. Tell him the children had a nice time, but don't bring up why they were with us in the first place. If he thinks he agreed to let them visit, he might even go along with it. If he's in a particularly foul mood, apologize."

"Apologize for what?"

"I don't know. For not introducing yourself sooner. For not bringing the children back until after breakfast. Whatever you do, pretend that night where he nearly died never happened. Hal's a prideful man, and if he ever found out you saw him in that condition, let alone saved his life, there's no telling how he'd take it."

She licked her lips and drew in a deep breath. "We should go now. Before I have too much time to think about it."

The children screamed and shrieked as they chased each other around the barnyard.

"George? Sadie? Time to go home."

Both children stopped short. Sadie's eyes lit, but George cast his head down and kicked the dirt.

"Is Papa okay now? Is he better?" Sadie implored.

What could he say? He was going to live—for now, at least—but he was far from healed. "He misses you very much," James finally answered.

"When will we see you again?" George asked. The boy had been even more serious and quiet the last two days. He sidled up to Ann and slipped his hand into hers.

"We'll be at church this Sunday." She knelt down until she was eye level with the boy.

Had Emily even liked children? The thought bobbed up like a bubble in a pond. Sudden and incongruous. He ignored it.

"Will you visit us?" George's dark eyes were wide and serious.

"I'll try. I'll try as hard as I can." Ann pulled George into a hug and pressed her fair cheek against the boy's thin shoulder. A knot grew in James's throat.

The sun danced high in the sky as midday approached. It was a five-minute walk to the Schneiders', and they couldn't delay the children's departure any longer. Sadie pleaded with James to ride on his shoulders, and he obliged. George kept his grip on Ann, and the two walked hand in hand. In her other hand she carried a neatly folded bundle containing the children's clean clothes.

When they arrived at the line between the two properties, James plucked Sadie from his shoulders and squeezed her tight. The little girl clung to him like a briar. He patted George on the back. A firm, manly clap of the hand so as not to embarrass the boy, but to let him know he wasn't alone. The knot in his throat grew larger. He couldn't cry in front of the children.

I can't cry in front of Ann.

Emily's unwelcome face flashed before him. *I despise a man who cries*, she'd said more than once. *Such a sign of weakness*. At the time he'd agreed. He'd actually been proud to agree until his parents died, and he cried like a baby. The unmistakable disgust on Emily's perfect face twisted the knife of his sorrow.

An ancient oak tree near the fence provided convenient cover, and James shooed the trio onward before ducking under the massive limbs.

"Go on. Be safe," he called, hoping a fortuitous breeze carried his words.

He observed the scene from the safety of the tree's cloaking shadow. The children didn't skip along or giggle or chatter at Ann. Instead, the three walked in a solemn line. James breathed a silent prayer. A petition for safety for Ann today, and the children for all of their days.

As James watched, the barn door slid open and a figure emerged, swift and surefooted. It ran toward the children. Hal Schneider was upright and alive.

The children hugged their father, but when Ann's yellow head bent down to them, they gripped her long and tight. Within minutes it was done. George and Sadie followed Hal into the barn with Sadie now carrying the stack of clean clothing.

He expected Ann to hurry back over the field. Instead, she walked slow as molasses, frequently turning to look back at the children, as if she expected them to race to her at any moment. One glance. Two glances. Three. It was plain to see how much she cared for those children. Just as she cared for Uncle Mac. For the past day, he'd been guilty of enjoying having them all together, like a real family—a family he could scarcely imagine with anyone but Ann at his side.

James's heart seized. How could he have been so wrong about Ann? So quick to judge her that first day? What would have happened if he'd waited a few days before sending the letter to Mrs. Turner?

You'd still want her to stay and she'd still want to leave.

He could try to rewrite the past few weeks, but it wouldn't change that simple truth. An English rose may thrive in an Ohio cornfield, but that doesn't mean it belongs there. Ann deserved a private garden. She deserved so many wonderful things he couldn't give her.

Tears streamed down Ann's cheeks by the time she reached the oak tree. James was at her side at once. "Are you alright? Did he say something to upset you?" The exchange had appeared quick and easy from afar, but Hal could have landed any number of verbal wounds.

"I know it's not one of your fancy ones, but it's clean," he said, offering a handkerchief. She took it without a word, and halted long enough to dab her nose and eyes. Then she was off, walking double time toward the farmhouse.

James stumbled along beside her, unsure of what to do or say. He never should have let her go alone. One moment she stomped ahead of him. The next moment her foot caught a bit of rough terrain and she dived headlong toward the ground. He caught her around the waist mid–free fall and his arms stayed tight around her as she found her footing.

She turned toward him, his arms still encircling her, and tilted her chin up to meet his gaze. Her blue eyes were already red and swollen. "How could we do that to those children?" she sobbed. She pressed her cheek to his chest and his cotton work shirt soaked up her tears.

"Do what?" His fingers grazed over her silken hair. "We fed them, bathed them and returned them to their father. What else could we do?"

"But they'll surely starve."

"Ann, they aren't going to starve. Hal doesn't feed them well, but he does feed them."

"Didn't you see the house? Absolutely filthy! I can only imagine what's crawling over those poor children when they go to sleep at night." She shuddered and he pulled her closer.

"Mrs. Ludlow—Delia's mother—is due to return tomorrow. I imagine she'll be there first thing in the morning."

"James McCann, how could you not tell me?" She pummeled his chest with soft, closed-fist blows of frustration. He chuckled and held her tighter.

"I'm sorry, I'm sorry!" He laughed. "I thought I'd told you!"

"I've been positively frantic over letting those children return home. The last few hours have aged me a year." She pressed on his chest with her palms and pushed herself free from his embrace while he fought the urge to draw her back into his arms. She stepped back from him, and stutter-stepped over a gopher hole. He caught her by the arms before she could fall back. Ann might not only be the most beautiful woman he'd ever seen, but also the clumsiest.

"I assumed Delia had mentioned something about her mother returning," he said. "The two of you have become such fast friends."

"We were busy yesterday. It must have slipped her mind."

"I guess it slipped mine, as well. Life has been much busier lately than I'm used to."

"You're right." Her voice grew soft and she dipped her head. "The last few weeks have been a bit overwhelming. The strain has affected me, but I shouldn't have taken my frustrations out on you. I'm sorry."

His chest panged with guilt. She was the one who'd offered to help him in the fields these last few weeks, but he didn't have to accept. *Soon you'll be with your rightful match, away from all this stress and work.* His attempts at hospitality had been a colossal failure. He had to remember to treat her more as a guest in the future, and not a hired hand.

"You really care for those children, don't you?" he asked, and she nodded. He would arrange for letters to be exchanged with them after she left. Something to ease her mind while she reclined on richly upholstered sofas and produced needle lace for leisure. Not as an excuse to distract her from life with him, as she did now.

"Thank you for letting them stay here these past two days. I know it was an added burden."

"No trouble at all. In fact, it only made me wish more for a few of my own."

Ann's shoulders stiffened beneath his fingers, and she turned and quick stepped toward the house. What had he said? He stood stock-still, mentally fumbling over what might have offended her before he gave up and hurried to catch her.

"I saw Frederick Renner on my way back from town yesterday," she said when he finally reached her side. "He says there's work at the mill."

"Work? Did he say when?"

"Beginning last night, but lasting several weeks. I'm sorry I forgot to tell you."

James had always dismissed Frederick's offers, though that never stopped his friend from continuing to ask. The mill often had extra work, but James could rarely find time to pick it up. He'd once told Ann he would speak with Frederick about work, but it had really been an excuse to drive her into town so she wouldn't have to walk to meet Mrs. Williams.

He surveyed the crops stretched out around him on three sides. Healthy green corn stalks stretched toward the sky with nary a weed to be seen. Waves of rippling wheat danced in the wind. If only he had some help in the barn, it would be easy to make a little extra money at the mill. Money he could use for… He shook his head to jar the thought from his brain. He couldn't let himself even think it. No sense hoping for something that could never be.

"I truly am sorry. With everything going on with the children…it slipped my mind."

James crooked his neck to observe Ann's furrowed brow on her exquisite face. She must have mistaken his silence for anger at not receiving the message.

"I suppose we've both forgotten to tell the other something now."

Her countenance softened. "So will you be going?"

"No. I couldn't leave you here alone with Uncle Mac. Too many things to do."

"You said the crops didn't need attention until harvest. I'll be alright."

James stopped short and she halted beside him. They'd both been walking so fast it might have been easier to run, but Ann wasn't flushed or breathing hard. Ann Cromwell, who appeared more delicate and vulnerable than a wild rose growing in the middle of a field about to be plowed, but who was as stubborn and strong as an oak tree with deep roots. Everything he'd thrown at her, she'd handled.

"The cow needs milking. The garden needs tending. The animals need to be fed."

"Delia Ludlow is coming first thing in the morning to help me learn everything you just described."

"She is?" He tried to control the shock and hope in his voice. The hope that Ann's interest in learning farm skills was more than a way to pass the time. That maybe she actually liked life here, with him. This didn't change anything. She was still intended for another. Hadn't he just promised himself he'd treat Ann more as the guest she deserved to be?

"Don't think I'm naive enough to believe I can learn everything in one day, but I think between the two of us, we'll make out alright."

"It's not that. It's just…" He searched for the right

words. He was forever offending Ann. He could only guess he'd offended her before when he'd mentioned his desire for children. It must have reminded her of the other woman who would replace her someday. Not that he believed she was jealous. James couldn't even let himself imagine she might want to stay. No, her reaction was likely one of annoyance. No doubt Ann Cromwell had never experienced a man's rejection. No matter how humble Ann showed herself to be, it had to carry a sting. "I want you to enjoy the rest of your time here. I don't want you to look back on this time and find it unpleasant."

If she ever thinks of her time here at all.

Ann threw her shoulders back. "Delia is coming first thing in the morning and I have no way of reaching her to cancel our plans, short of walking five miles into town or having you take me there."

"Fine. I'm sure both of you will have a lovely visit when she arrives. You can use the parlor."

She crossed her arms over her chest. "I would like Delia to give me cooking lessons. And show me how to perform chores in the barn. We won't be spending our day in the parlor."

It wasn't a request. It was a statement. Ann appeared to realize this. Her cheeks colored and her hands dropped to her side. "If you don't mind."

Even angry, her fine English manners were not long behind any outburst she might make. James pushed down the desire to press his lips against the pink in her cheeks.

"Does Delia know of your plans to leave New Haven?"

The pink in her cheeks blanched to white. "W-why do you ask?"

"She's a busy woman. I wouldn't want her to spend her one free day here showing you skills you'll never need."

Ann's color returned. "She knows I'll be leaving as soon as we receive word from Mrs. Turner, and she'd like to teach me a few things before I go."

"Very well. Have your lessons then."

Ann clapped her hands in excitement and regained her composure just as quickly. He marveled at her enthusiasm. She would no doubt be living in a fine home by Christmas, but now she was excited to learn skills she would never need. Hadn't he once read Marie Antoinette had a working farm built on the grounds of Versailles for her amusement? Maybe it was something like that. One last frolic in working-class life before embracing a life of luxury. It was a good thing Ann was leaving, because he would never understand her.

At least that's what he told himself as her blond hair caught the sun. And he repeated it again to himself at lunch when she coaxed Uncle Mac from his room for the fifth time in as many days—a feat he hadn't matched in months. He repeated it a third time when she joined him on the porch after supper, and she laughed at his stories. A lilting, genuine laugh that swelled his chest and sent him chasing through his memory for other stories to entertain her.

That night, before he headed off to the back porch for a night of fitful slumber, he stared at her in the darkness. The bright, full moon cast its glow over them and lit up her eyes like two stars. That was when he allowed himself to think about what he'd tried to push out of his mind and his heart these past few weeks. What was more, he let himself say it.

"What do you think would have happened that first day if I hadn't told you there'd been a mistake?"

The rocking chair beside him grew silent. An inconvenient cloud passed over the moon, plunging the porch into darkness. Had she even heard what he'd said? The silence continued. A swirl of hope eased over him. Maybe she really hadn't heard, despite the hushed quiet of the farm. Maybe it wasn't too late to take his words back.

"What I mean is…"

"I don't know," she interrupted.

His heart clamored double time. Her chair resumed creaking. Slow and steady. Back and forth. Minutes passed and a strong breeze whisked the cloud across the moon's face. Moonlight illuminated her face once again, but he couldn't discern a single emotion. Her face was a mask.

"What do you think would have happened?" she asked finally.

This was his chance. He could share the emotions that had been building inside of him these last weeks. Ask her to stay a little longer and get to know him. What was the worst that could happen? Rejection? It would be no different than the path they currently walked. And as for the *best* that could happen… His middle tightened at the thought of her feelings matching his budding ones.

The letter. The telegram.

His heart sank to his boots. He could tell Ann anything he wanted, but it didn't take away the fact that he'd already brought the mistake to the agency's attention. They had likely contacted her true match by now.

Contacted his match, as well. He couldn't take back that letter.

He cleared his throat. "I think if I hadn't said anything, you would have figured out quickly our match was in error."

Her rocker stopped creaking again. "What do you mean?" Her voice had an edge. She sounded…nervous?

"I mean…you'd have known as soon as you got here that this wasn't a castle and I wasn't a prince. You would have hightailed it right out of here. Since you can't drive a wagon, you would have dashed down that road back to town and to the train station as fast your legs could carry you."

She stifled what sounded like a nervous laugh. "Then what would have happened?" she asked.

"Let's see. I wouldn't have developed a taste for coffee that can be eaten with a spoon. Priscilla Vollrath would be wearing a completely average dress on the day of her wedding and having an absolute fit about it. Abner Milholland wouldn't have a bump on his head from walking straight into a door while watching you at church on Sunday."

Ann's giggles had turned into full belly laughs. He could listen to that laugh forever.

"I wouldn't have thirteen mosquito bites from sleeping on the back porch. Hal Schneider would probably be dead…"

He froze. Why had he said that? Though true, it was a heartless comment.

"Y-y-you're right," she stammered out of the darkness. "I'm very glad to have been here, even if I saved his life by accident."

He had to choose his next words carefully. No more slipups that would expose his heart.

"So I guess it could be a good thing you were sent here by mistake. I hope you look back on your time here as an adventurous detour on your journey to the life you deserve."

Ann grew silent again. He raked his hands through his hair. He was a fool to have even broached this subject. He wished he knew more about how to divine a woman's emotions. Emily had had only three: smug, irritated and incensed.

"I'll look back on my time here with great fondness," she whispered into the darkness. Did he detect a catch in her voice? It must be wishful thinking.

"I'm glad to hear it," he answered. "I feel the same way."

If only she knew it was the biggest understatement of his life.

Chapter Sixteen

The coffee was just beginning to boil the next morning when there came a sharp knock at the door. Uncle Mac, in one of his sociable moods, which had become more common, had chosen to begin the day by reading on the porch. When Ann reached the foyer, he was already wordlessly greeting their guest and ushering her in.

"Delia!" Ann moved to embrace her friend, only to discover Delia's arms laden with bundles. "How did you arrive here so early?"

Delia expertly balanced her packages, despite Ann's jostling, and stepped into the front hall. "Mother arrived from Columbus yesterday, and she wanted to visit the Schneiders as soon as she could. We hitched the wagon long before daybreak."

She placed her packages on the hall side table and unpinned her hat. "Will you be able to visit the shop again soon? Mrs. Williams has been raving about you to everyone, and Priscilla, too—in her own way. I wouldn't be surprised if girls in town start pressing their beaus for a proposal, just so they can order some of your lace."

Ann waved away the compliment. "No one's seen the dress yet."

"It doesn't matter. Priscilla Vollrath's praise is as good as gold. Besides, they've seen your handkerchiefs. We sold the first two yesterday."

Ann's heart drummed. "Two?"

"Mmm-hmm. At the very least you'll have to come into town so Mrs. Williams can pay your share. Twelve dollars."

Ann's head spun. She grasped for something to catch herself, but found nothing but smooth plaster walls.

"Let's get you a chair." Delia grasped her under the arms and walked her like a marionette to the kitchen. Her head floated while her legs felt as heavy as lead. She made it to a chair and pressed her hands to her temples as Delia poured her a cup of coffee. She took a sip and the room stopped spinning.

"I'm sorry, I don't know what came over me," Ann apologized.

Delia grinned. "It is an obscene amount of money, isn't it? And to think, you'll receive five times that when you finish Priscilla's lace."

The payment for Priscilla's dress had always felt ephemeral. Dreamlike. An amount so absurd she would never really possess it. The news of her first handkerchief sales made it all the more real. She would soon have enough money to pay James back and to support herself.

And you can leave…him. Ann's head spun again, and she slurped her coffee as if it were a reviving elixir.

"That must be delicious coffee," Delia observed, as Ann took another long draft. She poured herself a cup and took a sip. "We'll work on your coffee first."

"I knew it!" Ann exclaimed.

"Knew what?"

"James keeps telling me he actually likes it. I started to believe him."

She giggled. "Maybe he does. Where is James?"

"In the barnyard."

Delia lifted the coffee cup to her lips again but stopped short, as if she remembered the contents. "By the day's end, we'll have everything in order."

"Is your mother next door?"

She nodded. "I still can't believe you were there alone with Hal Schneider, Ann. He doesn't like anyone in his house. Not even Mother. She said he rarely lets her past the sitting room."

"He wasn't in a condition to protest."

Delia lifted the cup of coffee again, only this time she took a sip. She was polite enough to suppress her grimace. "I suppose we ought to get started." Out of her pile of packages, she produced a thick sheaf of paper and extended it to Ann. "Mother's best recipes," she explained. "All of them are fantastic, of course, but I only copied the ones easiest to learn and reproduce."

Ann accepted the stack of recipes and thumbed through each page. They were grouped by breakfast, dinner, supper and desserts, and all in Delia's neatly flowing script. "This must have taken you forever to copy," Ann marveled.

Delia shrugged. "It was no time at all. Besides, it gave me an excuse to review them. I'd forgotten all about her Apple Brown Betty, and James has some of the best summer apple trees in the county. I already helped myself to some this morning."

"What's Apple Brown Betty?"

One of Delia's packages was a burlap sack, and she lifted a corner and sent plump red-and-yellow apples skidding across the tabletop. "The perfect recipe for a beginner."

They spent the next hour in the kitchen, first reviewing the proper method for brewing coffee, followed by a lesson in dessert. Ann peeled, chopped and seasoned the apples, while Delia cracked walnuts she produced from yet another package. At the end of the hour, Ann had sliced her finger with the knife, and spilled precious cinnamon on the floor, but the Apple Brown Betty was also in the oven, bubbling away.

Delia nodded in approval while Ann wrapped her thumb with a clean bandage. "Only one cut. I'm pronouncing this lesson a success."

Next they ventured into the barnyard, where the cow lowed pitifully. "She's overdue for her milking," Delia announced, puzzled.

"Oh no!" Ann exclaimed. "I asked James to save the first milking for me and completely forgot!" She stroked Bessie's side and the cow turned her pitiful brown eyes toward Ann. "She must be terribly uncomfortable."

"It's nothing you can't fix," Delia said.

Ann abandoned all decorum as she squatted on the milk stool, and Delia showed her the easiest way to fill the bucket full to the top with creamy milk. Then they moved through lessons on how to properly hitch and unhitch a horse. Old Harriet waited patiently despite Ann's fumblings.

In the next stall stood James's plow mule. Delia laughed until she doubled over as Ann ran forward with a pitchfork full of hay just far enough to deposit it in the feed trough and dashed back again just as quickly.

"She's not going to bite!" Delia called out between laughing fits.

Ann stopped in midthrust, bewildered, her pitchfork ready with a fresh slice of hay. "I thought mules were stubborn and they kicked?" James had even referred to Hal Schneider as "more stubborn than my mule" on at least two occasions.

Delia straightened and wiped the tears from her eyes. "Even if she wanted to kick you, she couldn't do it from inside her pen. Here—" She took Ann by the hand and led her forward. "She seems really sweet."

Delia placed her hand on the mule's nose and stroked downward. After confirming Delia still had all her fingers, Ann followed her example. Her fingertips glided over the short silvery hair and onto the mule's velvety nose. Her flank was speckled white, as if she'd been spattered with paint.

"What's her name?" Delia asked, as the mule nosed her muzzle into Ann's palm.

A deep voice resonated behind them. "Her name is Mildred."

Ann jumped at the sound of James's voice but didn't turn. She was certain her cheeks were flushed and she waited for them to cool. She hadn't spoken to him since last night but had observed him ambling about the barnyard that morning from the relative safety of the kitchen window. Even her request to save the first milking had been in the form of a note left on the kitchen table where she was sure he'd find it. She chided herself for avoiding him. He'd only been making conversation when he'd asked her those questions last night—wasn't he? Why did thinking about it make her so flustered?

James sidled up beside her and added his sun-darkened hand to the donkey's nose. "She likes to be scratched right here." As if on cue, Mildred snorted and closed her eyes in mule contentment.

"So, Delia, I heard the two of you have lots of plans today." He didn't stop stroking Mildred's muzzle. His fingertips brushed the back of Ann's hand and a shiver raced up her arm.

"Oh, a few odd lessons," Delia replied. "Ann's a natural once she sees something done once. We'll likely run out of things to do."

Ann disguised a snort as a delicate cough. She knew Delia exaggerated for effect, but the idea that she could learn everything in less than a year was ludicrous. She had *only* cut herself once during the first cooking lesson. How would they count success next time? Singeing off her eyebrows but not burning down the kitchen?

James bent down and whispered in Ann's ear, his warm breath on her neck, quiet enough so only she could hear. "I couldn't agree more. I've seen the evidence myself."

Her stomach tumbled. "I'm sorry?"

James straightened and moved to the mule's flank. She couldn't avoid his gaze now. His hazel eyes twinkled. He addressed both women. "Ann's proving to be a natural around the farm."

Ann couldn't disguise her snort this time. "Don't tease!" she scolded.

James ducked his head and raced a hand through his hair. "It's true. I have to admit, I was in the hay mow when you milked the cow. I'd have never guessed it was your first time."

"It's true," Delia chimed in.

"Maybe you can have a hobby farm at your new home," he added. "A cow in the back for fresh milk. A few chickens and a rooster milling around for ambiance. Rich people do that, don't they?"

Ann's belly quivered. If only he knew the truth. At least she could say she'd prepared the way for whomever came after her. Whether bland featured or beautiful, James McCann was unlikely to ever judge a book by its cover again. And no bride of any appearance could possibly be a worse cook. Anything would be a step up for James and Uncle Mac.

Delia was by her side now and gave her arm a quick squeeze. "I think it's time for us to move on to something new."

"Of course, of course." James backed up, ducking a moment before his head struck the low beam. "I have some things to get in order if I'm going to take work at the mill." He stood there awkwardly a few more moments, with both hands thrust into his pockets, as if waiting for something more to be said.

"Come in for lunch. Ann will be preparing all of it," Delia said as she shooed James out the barn door. Even under Delia's questioning eye, it was difficult for Ann not to watch him until he was out of sight.

The two women fed the hens and waited for them to scurry off their nests before gathering the eggs. Then they ducked inside for a moment to remove the Apple Brown Betty from the oven—it was perfectly browned on the top and had filled the kitchen with a sweet and spicy aroma. Delia placed it on the windowsill to cool and they were back to Ann's lessons.

The last task before lunch was the garden. Ann had

already had lessons on weeding the field from James, but the scraggly green tops before her looked nothing like the corn or wheat she'd hoed before. Delia walked Ann through the differences between radish tops and beet greens, and showed her how to plumb the soil around carrots to determine their size and ripeness.

"We'll do some canning and drying of the garden bounty next time," Delia said as they tucked into their lunch of boiled beets, fried beet greens and Apple Brown Betty a few hours later. They'd rung the great iron bell in the barnyard to signal the meal, but James had yet to arrive. Uncle Mac had appeared, eaten lunch with his eyes rolled back in approval and returned to his book on the front porch.

Ann ate her lunch in relative silence. Her head spun with new knowledge, and her palms sweat to think about everything she still had to learn. But every new skill increased her chances of finding work later. She said a silent prayer of thanks to God for the sale of her handkerchiefs but knew she couldn't count on selling them outside New Haven. The fact that she'd been able to place them in even one shop—and at such a high price—could only have been divine providence. She only hoped the money from her lace would be enough to support herself as she sought out a job with some permanence.

"You're so good at all of this," Ann moaned around her first mouthful of warm apples and spice. "I don't know how I could ever learn enough to earn a proper position."

Delia reached across the table and patted Ann's hand. "You're doing a wonderful job. Besides, you only need to know the basics for now. The rest can be learned on the job."

Ann groaned as she imagined the master of a fine house eating burned rack of lamb while she experimented in the kitchen. "I don't think I could subject someone to any more of my practice."

"James seems to be doing just fine. Which reminds me—have you heard yet from the agency?"

"No, Mrs. Turner hasn't responded. I imagine she's at a loss for what to do."

"You could always stay," Delia said quietly.

Ann's heart fluttered. "You know why I can't," she said firmly.

Delia sighed. "It will all work out in the end, you'll see." She paused and chewed her lip. "I should have told you this sooner—but James and I...we almost courted once."

A flood of jealousy and confusion stole across Ann's chest. "You said you didn't know him well."

Delia colored crimson. "I said I didn't know him well now. It's all so silly in retrospect, but I should have told you."

Ann squinted at her friend across the table. Tall, beautiful, kindhearted and talented beyond measure. The perfect farmer's wife. The jealousy twisted a little deeper. "Even your mother told me on the train she barely knew him."

"She doesn't, Ann. That's how insignificant the whole thing was. It was years ago."

"How serious was it?"

Delia flashed her a sheepish smile. "So very not serious. I was fourteen, and he was eighteen. We'd shared a schoolhouse for years, but barely spoke. One day, the summer before he was to go to medical school, he began walking me home from school. We spoke of his desire to be a doctor, and I told him of how I wanted to become a dressmaker. After a few talks, it sounded as if he planned to court me once he returned home from school."

"So what happened?"

"He met someone else. I heard he brought her home once, but no one ever saw her again. When he returned to take care of Uncle Mac and the farm, he came alone."

The jealousy squeezed Ann in a vise. "Why didn't he court you then?"

Delia shrugged. "He'd dreamed of becoming a doctor but became a farmer instead. My dreams remained the same. He asked me once in passing if I hoped to take over Mrs. Williams's shop one day. I told him I wanted to leave sleepy New Haven and strike out on my own. We both saw how far our paths were destined to diverge."

Ann's heart quivered. "So you believe a husband and wife must complement each other...for their marriage to work?"

"Yes, I do. But Mother also taught us marriage is about sacrifice. If you each hold something dear, and those two things are in conflict, love means you'll sacrifice your own desire to fulfill theirs."

Ann's heart sank to her shoes. "But what if you can't simply choose to sacrifice? What if it's something you can't change?"

Delia pursed her lips, and her eyes filled with tears. She knew what Ann referred to. "Ann, God can always make a way," she whispered.

The front door creaked, and a vaguely familiar voice carried down the hall.

"So nice to see you out and enjoying yourself, Mr. McCann. Take care." The next moment Mrs. Ludlow strode through the kitchen door frame.

"Miss Cromwell, how delightful to see—"

Ann stood and cut off her words with a tight embrace. Somehow, seeing Delia's mother reminded Ann of all the good she'd experienced since coming to New Haven.

Embarrassment washed over her as she realized she had met this woman exactly once, and it had been many weeks before. She released her hold. "I'm so sorry, I don't know what came over me. We barely know one another."

"Nonsense," Mrs. Ludlow replied, before pulling Ann into another hug. "Sometimes people are friends in their hearts before they've even met."

Ann smiled. She had a feeling Mrs. Ludlow had a wealth of pithy sayings.

Delia stood close behind Ann, and stepped in to give her mother a quick peck on the cheek. "Tell me, Mother. Was the Schneider's home as bad as everyone is saying?"

"Worse." Mrs. Ludlow pursed her lips. "But it was nothing I couldn't handle. Mr. Schneider wasn't particularly pleased when I began to clean, but I wasn't going to let that stop me. Sadie and George are working on the wash right now, and their father is looking for his bottle. Without it, he should be well enough for work by this evening."

"What if he finds it?" Ann asked.

"That's doubtful—unless he has a habit of looking for things at the bottom of his privy. How did the two of you get along?"

"Ann proved herself a quick study." Delia gestured to the leftovers from their lunch on the table and began to fix a plate for her mother, but Mrs. Ludlow waved it away.

"All this work today has suppressed my appetite." She patted her ample stomach and winked. "If only I could say that more often."

"Mother, if you're ready, I think Ann has had enough of me today."

This was far from true, but Ann knew it would be selfish to monopolize any more of Delia's time on her free day from work.

"Anything else?" Delia asked.

"I only hope I can survive without you until your next day off."

"We'll see each other before then. Write down any questions you have and I'll try to answer them." Delia's eyes opened wide. "I completely forgot—Mrs. Williams asked if you could come to town tomorrow with the lace you've completed. She has a fitting with Priscilla this week but needs to attach the bodice lace first."

"If she needs me, I'll be there."

"Excellent!"

With no more excuses to detain them, Ann accompanied her guests to the barnyard.

"Will you be visiting the Schneiders every week, Mrs. Ludlow?" Ann asked.

Delia's mother frowned. "I'm afraid not. That's why I was working with the children on some lessons today, rather than doing all the work myself."

"Lessons?" Ann asked.

"Cooking, laundry and gardening. Very quick learners those two, like you. They should do fine the next few weeks while I'm away. I'd always planned to teach them these things eventually, but when I last visited, Hal appeared to have things in hand."

From their position in the barnyard, Ann could make out tiny white dots dancing between the Schneider's evergreens. Freshly washed linens and clothing hung out to dry. She swallowed hard. "I thought you were back for good."

Mrs. Ludlow smiled weakly. "I thought so, too." She sighed. "It's my dear sister. After this last baby, she hasn't been herself. Doesn't want to hold the sweet child or even look upon her face. Frankly, I don't know what's the trouble. All I know is she needs me. I'll be returning to Pittsburgh in a few days."

"What about the Schneider children? Who will watch after them?"

Her mouth turned down. "I truly wish it were me. I suggested to Hal a few who'd be happy to drop in and help. The Zwebels' daughter, Zelda, Mrs. Gibbons down the lane—even you, dear! He said no to them all. We'll have to trust and pray God is watching over them."

After the Ludlows left, Ann turned toward the Schneiders' house. If she squinted, she could make out the children in the yard, and she guessed by their movements they were checking the wash to see if it was dry. Mr. Schneider was nowhere to be seen. In the fields if he knew what was good for him and his family. The pulling on her heart returned, but she forced it down. Whether Mrs. Ludlow was here to check on them or not, she soon wouldn't be.

Mrs. Ludlow was right—she could only pray.

Chapter Seventeen

James entered the kitchen and was greeted with a scent of sweetness and spice that made his heart ache. The house hadn't smelled like this since Uncle Mac stopped baking and shut himself in his room. Uncle Mac now sat at the table, his head thrown back with snores emanating from his open mouth.

Ann stood at the wash basin and smiled sheepishly. "He ate four servings of Apple Brown Betty and fell promptly asleep. I didn't have the heart to wake him."

"Who would?" James agreed. It was nice to find his uncle in the kitchen or on the front porch more often than not these last few weeks. His wan cheeks had gained color, and he no longer resembled a wizened old man awaiting death. It was as if Ann's arrival had sparked something inside him, even if he couldn't give a voice to it.

"We missed you at lunch."

"I heard the bell, but I was in the middle of something at the time. I suppose there's no chance of leftovers."

He'd hardly said the words before Ann uncovered a nearby plate with a flourish.

"It wasn't too hard to keep Uncle Mac away from the beets and greens. But I'm afraid you'll have to wait until the next Apple Brown Betty is out of the oven before you can have a piece. Uncle Mac even licked the dish clean."

"You made another?" Ann was responsible for this delicious smell…after one lesson? He should have known she'd be a natural with a little guidance.

"And Delia showed me the proper way to make coffee."

She poured a cup and set it before him. He took a sip. It was good, like the kind of coffee he was used to, but something was off.

Ann's eyes widened expectantly. "What do you think?"

"Truthfully?" He paused and considered his answer. He was sure he was going to mess this up. "I like your old coffee better."

Ann raised a slim brow. "Don't tease me, James," she scolded.

"I'm not, I'm not!" He raised his hands in protest. In surrender. "I prefer the way you made it before. And Doc Henderson did, too, remember?"

Ann's brow dropped, but her delicate face remained contorted in suspicion. "If you're serious," she said slowly, "I'll make it the old way in the morning."

Ann left the room and returned with a large roll of lace. "Mrs. Williams wants this by tomorrow," she explained. "Would you be able to take me into town?"

James nodded. "I had plans to go there myself. I'm going to ask Frederick a bit more about the extra work at the mill."

Uncle Mac startled awake. "Mill?" he grunted.

"Yes, I'm going to Renner's Millwork tomorrow. Would you like to join me?"

The older man screwed up his mouth in thought, but then shook his head. "More books," he demanded, pointing a stern finger in James's direction.

"Absolutely, Uncle Mac. I'll bring home a bundle for you."

James sipped his coffee and observed Ann over the rim. Her slight fingers moved over the lace so quickly his eye barely followed the movements. She chewed her lip in concentration.

"Are you working on a difficult section?" he asked.

"A little. Priscilla specifically requested dozens of these rosettes. I've made so many these last weeks, I may choose to never make one again." She looked up and winked, her fingers neither halting nor stuttering as she maintained her fluid pace before looking down again. Either rosettes weren't all that difficult, or Ann truly was a master lace maker.

He leaned forward on his elbows, mesmerized by her work. Despite the speed at which her hands flew, the lace grew at a snail's pace. "Will you finish it all by tomorrow?"

"She doesn't need all of it by tomorrow, but I've decided to finish it anyway. Mrs. Turner's letter is already overdue."

His heart skipped at the reminder. "But can you—really?" he pressed.

Ann's shoulders dropped a hair. "Yes, even if I have to stay up all night." She paused and drew a deep breath. "I must confess, I'll likely be awake until dawn."

So Ann had spent all morning and much of the afternoon learning how to do chores around his farm, all the while needing time to do this. He would never understand her motivations for keeping herself occupied the way she did, or for learning tasks she would soon have no use for, but he would always admire her work ethic.

"What can I do to help?" he offered.

Ann's head snapped up, startled. "What do you mean?"

"How can I help you finish this lace, save for doing it myself?"

She shook her blond head. "Nothing, I'm afraid."

He would try a different tack. "How about this? First I'll make supper. Then I'll sit here with you until you're done. I can make coffee. I can tell stories. I can jump up and down or moo like a cow. Anything to keep you awake."

Ann stifled a laugh. "I appreciate the offer of supper, though I can manage without everything else."

"Supper it is." James slapped a hand on the table, hard enough to jar a nodding Uncle Mac awake.

"More books!" he ordered, before dozing again.

The next morning, before the sun had crested the horizon, James awoke to the aroma of coffee wafting from the kitchen window and onto the back porch. He stumbled groggily into the house to find Ann hovering over a table strewn with lace.

"Good morning," she called cheerfully when he entered. No hair on her perfect head was out of place, but her rosy cheeks were a bit less pink, and faint shadows creased under both eyes.

"Were you up all night? What time is it?" Ann had never risen earlier than him. That fact, coupled with the fog of receding sleep in his head, gave the scene a dreamlike quality. He clod stomped across the floor and poured himself a cup of coffee. Its inky, almost mud-like properties proved Ann was a woman of her word. A sip confirmed it. Thick and bitter. Who could have guessed he'd ever grow to not only like Ann's coffee, but prefer it?

"Not all night. I retired at two and was up again at four. Oh, and it's almost five o'clock."

The sun wasn't due to rise for another half hour. No wonder his mind felt so thick. As thick as his coffee, which needed a healthy glug of milk.

"You didn't milk the cow by chance?"

Ann smirked. "I'm afraid I hadn't gotten that far. But no worries…" She began exaggerating her movements as she stitched. "Four…three…two…done!" Ann laid the lace on the table and mimed wiping sweat from her brow. She stood and stretched her slender arms toward the ceiling.

"Congratulations!" James stepped forward to pat Ann on the shoulder, but his toe caught the edge of the rug. In an instant he was falling forward. Time slowed as his cup of coffee sailed from his hand and toward the table. Not even a second could have passed, but for James it was a lifetime.

In the same moment, Ann saw what was to happen and her eyes widened in horror. Her body lurched forward and she flung herself between the lace and his cup. It collided with her skirt and sent droplets scattering everywhere in a cloudburst of coffee.

Time returned to normal, and James's heart sank to the cellar. He lunged for Ann's coffee-soaked hand and assessed it.

"Are you burned?" Her fingers looked fine, but it was hard to assess everything while blood pounded in his ears.

She wrenched her hand free and turned toward the table. He reached for her to continue his assessment, but she pushed him away.

"Ann, that coffee might have seriously burned you! It may *still* be burning you."

"I'm fine, I'm fine." She waved a dismissive hand. "My skirt took the brunt of it." She wiped her hands on a nearby dish towel and tentatively held a long piece of lace to the light.

James sucked in a breath. How many hours had she toiled over that lace last night? How many other nights had she stayed up working by lamplight? And he had ruined it all in seconds. His chest tightened and his head grew light. Minutes passed like hours.

"Two drops," she announced finally.

"Are you sure?" He craned his neck to see for himself from the safety of several feet away. There was no telling what more damage he could do if he got too close again.

"Yes. Two tiny drops. And this pattern is the same on both sides, so we can simply affix this piece with the stains facing down. Here, see for yourself." She held the lace out toward him but James backed away. From now on, he would treat the lace like a bundle of dynamite.

James surveyed the young woman in front of him. Her light blue dress was stained brown down the front. "Ann, I am so, so sorry."

She narrowed her eyes at him and bestowed on him a half smile. "It's alright. No permanent harm done.

Though I'll admit, I would have had to ask the good Lord's help in forgiving you if more of the coffee had landed on the lace."

"Now that we're certain the lace is okay, please let me check you." He reached for her hand, and this time she acquiesced.

James unbuttoned her right sleeve at the wrist and pushed the material up to her elbow. The coffee had painted her forearms with splotches and spatters of pink.

Ann's head snapped up and her blue eyes widened as she gazed into his. "Will I be alright?" she whispered.

Her skin was warm to the touch as he traced over the evidence of his clumsiness. He broke their gaze. "You have some first-degree burns. Nothing the McCann family salve won't soothe by tomorrow. Oh, Ann, I'm so sorry."

"You said that already."

He left the room and returned with the familiar salve container. How odd to have applied it to Ann on her first full day here, and now again as they neared her last. Every sensation from that first day flooded over him, mixed with guilt at having been the cause of her injury. Even her hair smelled the same. Lavender and rose petals.

She wrinkled her dainty nose as he opened the tin. "I'm not looking forward to the odor."

"Mother said, 'Take out the odor, and you take out the medicine.'"

Ann cocked her head and gazed upward in thought. "I suppose that makes sense."

"Really? Because Mother never said that. I just made it up."

Ann gave him a playful shove, but he held steadfast to her hand. His heart thudded. *So much like that first day.*

He pushed through the flood of memories and the odd squeezing sensation in his chest, and focused on her minor wound. It didn't even require bandaging, and within moments the salve had already soothed much of the redness.

She excused herself to her room to wash up and change, and James escaped to the barnyard to do his morning chores before their trip into town. When he returned his heart tripped again. Ann stood at the stove wearing the same dark green traveling dress she had worn on her first day.

"Will you be ready to leave soon?" she asked cheerfully as she plated two perfect eggs.

James groaned inwardly. Why did he feel as if they were repeating their first days together, only running in reverse? Though he was certain they'd return that evening, it felt as if he were taking Ann to town to send her away. He tried to shake the feeling as he washed and changed for the trip but it clung to him, heavy and inescapable.

James accompanied Ann into Mrs. Williams's shop. Though he knew the stains on the lace were almost imperceptible, he wanted to be there to take full responsibility.

"Did Delia tell you about the sale?" were the first words out of the dressmaker's mouth when they entered. Ann beamed and nodded. Delia squeezed Ann's shoulders.

Sale? What sale?

The plump woman turned to James. "I'm sure you were so proud of Ann."

James nodded dumbly. If Ann had sold one of her handkerchiefs, why hadn't she told him?

Mrs. Williams pulled an envelope from the pocket of her half apron and pressed it into Ann's hand. "And what Delia couldn't have told you yesterday, was that we sold a third in her absence."

Ann's hand trembled as she grasped the envelope. James had been in the shop when they'd set the prices. She'd likely just been paid almost twenty dollars. Or was Mrs. Williams also paying her for Priscilla's lace? In that case, Ann no longer had a reason to stay at his farm while they awaited Mrs. Turner's letter. She could repay him for her passage and move into Donahue's Hotel while they awaited word of her true intended.

Or a hotel in any other town...or city.

His stomach twisted. She was always going to leave, but now it felt as though her departure was becoming real. He'd never considered he might grow fond of Ann Cromwell during her stay. He'd only worried he wouldn't be able to resist her beauty. Now he barely noticed it. Not when her numerous other qualities shone even brighter.

The room grew strangely quiet. All three women were staring pointedly at him.

"I'm sorry. I didn't catch that," he said, hoping someone had spoken to him.

Mrs. Williams pursed her lips. "I said you must make sure Ann sees Mr. Davis while you're in town. He stopped in the other day and was so impressed with Ann's handkerchiefs. He said he wished to speak with her."

"Of course, of course." The grocer likely wanted to commission something special for his wife.

A few minutes later, James stumbled outside into the blistering August heat with Ann close at his side. Her cheeks had flushed rose pink when Mrs. Williams handed her the envelope, and the color hadn't diffused.

"Where to next?" she chirped.

His head was thick with indecision. Hadn't he said he was going to the mill to accept the extra work? Until now he hadn't realized how much that decision hinged on Ann staying with him awhile longer. The millwork would mean extra money to help buy Ann a few nice things. He hadn't even realized he'd planned to do that until now. A ridiculous thought. He should be saving money for his new wife—whoever that would be.

"Did you want to come in with me?" Ann had stopped in front of Davis Mercantile.

"If it's alright, I think I'll run a few errands." What errands, he didn't know. He needed time away from Ann. Time to get a hold of himself. To think rationally.

If Ann thought he acted strangely, she didn't let on. Her full lips spread wide, turning a smile into a grin. "Of course. I'll wait by the wagon until you're done."

The New Haven Library sat across the square, and James hurried into it, grateful to have a true errand to complete. The librarian promised to put together a selection of books Uncle Mac would enjoy, and asked him to return in a few minutes.

He stepped back into the blinding sun on the street and considered going to the mill after all. It would be good to see Frederick, and Ann's help in the fields meant he did still have time to take on the extra work before the harvest needed his attention. His head began to clear as he strode purposefully down the sidewalk. No matter how much his heart had tried to persuade him these last few weeks, he had to imagine a future without Ann Cromwell.

A storefront on his left reminded him of another errand, and he stepped inside. Writing to Mrs. Turner had used the last of his envelopes, and he'd forgotten to purchase more.

"James McCann, just the man I wanted to see!" announced the pimply young postal clerk behind the counter. "I have a letter for you!"

James's heart pounded. "You do?"

"Yep," the young man said, flourishing a slim envelope. "And it's all the way from England."

Chapter Eighteen

Ann stepped from the stifling sidewalk into the pungent heat of Davis Mercantile. Coffee and leather aromas tickled her nose. A young man behind the counter coughed and colored scarlet at the sight of her.

"May I help you, miss?" he squeaked as he hurried toward her.

Ann's beauty had elicited this reaction more times than she could count. It generally garnered her prompt service in the shops, even when they knew she was a maid. An extra scoop of horehound candy from the confectionery if she batted her eyelashes just so. She'd always considered her beauty an asset. Now, as the young clerk rushed to her side, even as an older woman waited ahead of her at the counter to be served, irritation twinged her.

What else had her beauty brought her? Had it ever gained her anything of value? Would William Atherton have taken notice of her if she had been as plain as the bride James pined for? She had known the value of hard work for as long as she could remember, but as she grew older, she'd expected her beauty to bring her something more. Hadn't she even imagined the agency had garnered more for her match than others? Young, sweet girls she'd deemed not as attractive as herself. The twinge of irritation devolved into nausea.

Dear Lord, please forgive my prideful nature.

The prayer settled her stomach like warm chamomile tea. She smiled at the clerk waiting patiently by her side. "Would you please assist that woman at the counter? I believe she was waiting before me."

"Of course, of course. Let me know when you're ready," he said before returning to the counter at half the pace he'd used to reach Ann's side.

"Miss Cromwell?" A man's deep voice echoed from the dark rear of the store.

"I'm here, Mr. Davis. Mrs. Williams said you wanted to see me."

The store owner emerged from behind a man-sized display of canned green beans and potatoes. His thick mustache turned up at the corners when he saw her. "I did want to see you. I stepped into Mrs. Williams's shop the other day to see if she had anything new. Your lace greatly impressed me. It's simply exquisite."

As Ann's cheeks warmed, she prayed again to be released from her pride. "Thank you. I'm glad you liked it."

"May I take a few moments of your time?"

Ann nodded and followed him into a small back office. He took a seat beside a tiny walnut desk piled high with papers, while she perched on a nearby chair.

"I'm obviously not the only one who likes your work, Miss Cromwell. I'd already heard Priscilla Vollrath put much of her wedding dress into your obviously capable hands. Two of your handkerchiefs were sold during my time in the shop, and to local women. I can only imagine how well they'd sell in a larger city."

The reminder of the sales and the money in her pocket filled her with excitement and trepidation. She had enough money to give her some security when she was on her own again, after Mrs. Turner's letter arrived.

After James asks me to leave.

"Did you want me to create something for your wife, Mr. Davis?" Even with the tremendous sum in her pocket, she would take any additional income offered. Only the Lord knew if or when she'd ever find success outside New Haven.

Mr. Davis laughed. "Yes, I'm sure she would love me to commission something for her, but that wasn't why I wanted to speak with you. Miss Cromwell, have you heard of the city of Indianapolis?"

"*In-dee-uh...* I'm sorry, what was the rest?"

He chuckled. "It doesn't matter. I have the opportunity to open a brand-new department store there with my brother, and I'm taking it. Four stories high in the best part of the city. My nephew Leroy, the one behind the counter today, will be taking over this store."

"Congratulations, Mr. Davis," she said, puzzling over what this had to do with her.

"We'll have a large women's department, covering all of the second floor. We want to offer our customers the finest goods in the city, and I think your handkerchiefs would be the perfect addition."

Ann's heart stopped. She'd certainly misheard. "Excuse me?"

He paused, clearly trying to figure out what she hadn't understood. "They have department stores in England, don't they?"

"Of course." She'd walked by Harrods numerous times, always wishing she could afford more than a stick of candy if she stepped inside. Would she ever have dreamed her work might be offered for sale in a store such as that? The heat in the room grew stifling. "We have Harrods."

"Ah, yes, I'm somewhat familiar. This store won't be on near as grand a scale, but it will be the largest in Indianapolis. Which is why I want to offer certain goods that can't be had from any other shop. If you'd like to do business with me, I'll need a large selection of handkerchiefs ready when we open eight months from now. Multiple copies of at least a dozen styles to start. Does this interest you?"

Ann's mouth filled with cotton. Dozens of handkerchiefs, for sale in a large city where wealthy women would acquire them. She glanced about for a pitcher of water but found only papers and empty crates.

Mr. Davis took her silence as hesitation. "I can only advance you a small percentage to pay for supplies, but we can make the terms of the sale the same as you have with Mrs. Williams. I hope you don't mind that we discussed your arrangement."

"You'll pay sixty percent?" she choked out.

His mustache screwed up at the corner and he stared at her long and hard. "Alright, seventy percent. But not until the sale. You can bring them to me until I leave New Haven, but then you'll need to cover transportation fees for the goods themselves."

Ann swallowed hard. "Where is Indianapolis?"

"Why, it's just one state over. If you took the train in the morning, you'd be there by evening. A package can arrive in as little as a few days."

Her head spun. So much had happened today. Was God guiding her path as she'd prayed for? She stood and offered her hand. "Mr. Davis, I believe I'd like to do business with you."

Ann's heart thudded against her ribs and her hands trembled as she waited for James in the wagon. She had no reason to be so nervous, she reminded herself. She'd learned within hours of her arrival in New Haven that her time there was finite. For weeks she'd fretted and worried over how she could support herself when she left, and God had opened door after door. She did the math in her head. With the money from Mrs. Williams, there was no reason she couldn't be on a departing train within days. Indianapolis was as good a place to live as any, and she'd be close to the store to deliver her handkerchiefs as often as Mr. Davis wanted them.

She still might have to seek employment as a maid for a short time. The Indianapolis store wasn't open for business yet, and because she'd delivered the lace early, Mrs. Williams couldn't pay her the full amount until the dress was complete and Priscilla approved it. She'd take any job she could until then. But Mr. Davis had gone on to describe his store in detail, including the custom dressmakers he planned to employ, and Ann's future rose up in front her. Indianapolis was a large city and close enough for her to afford passage there. All she needed was a little more of God's help, and the next stage of her life could be a bright one.

If this was God's will for her life, why did she feel something tugging her back with an invisible string? She should be elated at the prospect of what was to come, not filled with trepidation. Ann chided herself for hesitating. Nothing held her here. Nothing but—

"James!" When he appeared across the square, she called out his name in spite of herself. Did he blush when she called to him? His cheeks must be flushed from the summer heat.

"I'm sorry to have kept you waiting so long," he apologized. He passed her a stack of library books when he approached, and his muscular arms swung his body into the wagon even faster than usual. He removed his hat and mussed his hair with both hands. Ann found the habit both telling and endearing. What did he have to be nervous about? That he'd left her waiting so long? No, it had to be something more than that. All of his movements carried a sense of frenetic energy.

"How was your afternoon?" she asked.

"Very good," he answered, and gave her a peculiar half smile.

"Were you able to see Frederick at the mill?" Perhaps she could keep up this small talk forever. Anything to put off the inevitable task of announcing her departure. If only she had followed God's clear path for her life years ago, she could be the wife James deserved—one who could give him children.

"Mmm-hmm," he murmured before glancing her way. The shadow cast from his hat brim brought out the green in his hazel eyes. Her stomach tumbled. If she told him now, while they rode side by side in the wagon, she might not have to gaze deeply into those eyes.

James's hand darted to hers and gave it an unexpected squeeze before grasping the reins again. Ann's heart leaped, and she fiddled with the envelope of money in her pocket. She didn't have to say something right away. James was in a good mood, likely because of the work he got at the mill. She could stay a few extra days, couldn't she? There were the needed goodbyes to Delia and Mrs. Williams, and the matter of Priscilla's dress. One stray snip of the scissors, and they might be in need of her services. It would be best that she stay at least until the final fitting.

As they drove alongside the Schneider farm, Ann thought about how Mrs. Ludlow's absence meant that Sadie and George needed her close to keep an eye on them. She mentally tacked on more and more days to her departure date. It was easy to think of reasons to stay a little longer. It would be nice to watch Priscilla walk down the aisle, and Ann had been invited along with the rest of the town. Soon it would be harvest time, and James could always use an extra hand, no matter how inexperienced.

"I'd like to try to take the Schneiders something this evening," she announced.

James nodded in agreement. "Please be careful. I have something I'd like to talk to you about when you get back." His voice was warm like fresh honey. She shivered in the stifling heat.

"And I have something I'd like to speak with you about," she replied.

James furrowed his brow. "I'd like to go first, if that's alright."

Ann agreed, and at that same moment Old Harriet turned down the lane toward the house. Uncle Mac sat in a rocker on the porch, and jumped up to greet them. Ann passed the library books down to him and he shuffled them between work-worn hands. "G-good, good," he murmured in approval.

James leaned in, closing the distance between them on the wagon seat. "I thought you might take the Schneiders the rest of the Apple Brown Betty and some cream. Maybe a few of the extra vegetables from the garden. If you're still up to it, of course."

"Of course I am!" she said, a bit too forcefully. Was it always this hard to breathe when he was so near?

Ann jumped from the wagon and made straight for the garden. She'd left the children food by the fence row for weeks before Hal's accident, but never more than they could eat before returning home. A glass of milk and a bowl of wild blackberries, or two hard boiled eggs and some bread and butter. She'd worried more would raise both Hal's suspicion and ire. Half an hour later she set out for the Schneiders' laden with enough food to last the children a few days. James had never accompanied her before, but as she passed by him in the barnyard, he fell in lockstep beside her. He remained by her side until they reached the great oak by the property line where he'd watched over her when she'd returned the children.

"If you see him, remember to say it's from you, not me. I think he liked you when you met."

Ann rolled her eyes. "How could you possibly know that?"

James squeezed the fingers of her free hand. "Because everyone likes you."

Ann bit the insides of her cheeks to keep from smiling. This was exactly why she should have told him her news on the wagon ride rather than making excuses for staying longer. It was so hard to concentrate looking into those eyes.

He patted her on the back. "Go on—it'll be fine."

Ann climbed over the fence row before she could think more about it. Last time the children had given her a measure of protection. This time, what was to stop Hal Schneider from leveling his shotgun at her head? Sweat beaded on her forehead as she neared. She prayed for courage. She only had to leave the basket at the door, knock and dash back as fast as her legs could carry her.

She ran-walked across the barnyard and was feet from the front porch when Mr. Schneider appeared from around the corner of the house. Ann jumped at the sight of him and thrust the basket out in the air toward him.

"Mr. Schneider, I have a bounty I'm hoping you could help with." Something told her it was better if she spoke first. She rambled on. "I've begun cooking lessons, and my practicing has produced an abundance of Apple Brown Betty. And my garden is yielding a fair amount more than I need at the moment. I thought you and the children might help me not waste all this food." Her hands trembled as she continued holding the basket out in front of her body.

He took three long strides forward and peered in the basket. "Can't say I've ever heard of a grown woman needing cooking lessons."

Ann laughed nervously. "I agree, I'm a rather old pupil, but I can assure you it's quite good. I made it from Mrs. Ludlow's recipe."

He cocked a brow and rubbed a hand over his chin. He hadn't shaved in several days. "Is that so?"

"Where are the children?"

As if on cue, George emerged from the barn, carrying a bucket full to the brim with milk. Sadie followed close behind clutching a crude wooden object to her chest.

"Miss Cromwell," she cried when she saw Ann, and dashed into her arms. The object she carried was sharp and uncomfortable, and it pressed into Ann's skin as she embraced the girl. "Look what Papa made me!" Sadie cradled the object lovingly in her arms. Now Ann could see it had a head, arms and legs, and was wrapped in a scrap of burlap. A homemade doll.

"It's lovely." Ann stroked the doll's blank face.

"Her name is Ann," Sadie said. She blushed and buried her face into Ann's shoulder.

"George, come get this basket," Mr. Schneider barked.

The boy carried himself in a stoic way that showed how he'd shouldered far too many burdens at a young age. But his bandage appeared to be fresh, and his hair was combed. He flashed Ann a quick smile but didn't say a word as he hefted both the milk pail and now her food offering.

"I should let you children get back to your chores." Sadie still had a firm grip around Ann's neck, and it only tightened as she tried to leave.

"Don't go," she whispered into Ann's ear. "We miss you."

Ann's heart tripped. Within a week she would never see these children again. She swallowed hard. "You'll see me at church in a few days." She looked pointedly at Mr. Schneider, and he nodded in agreement.

Sadie eased her grip, and Ann slipped the girl's arms from her neck. She knelt to hug her. George had already set off for the house, so Ann called out a goodbye. He stopped long enough to glance over his shoulder and nod. Ann left the Schneider house and didn't allow herself to look back.

* * *

James held his hands out expectantly as she approached, as if awaiting an answer. He cupped his hands around his mouth as she grew closer and called out, "Well?"

She found his concern, as always, endearing. Ann waited until she didn't have to shout her reply. There was no telling how well their conversation would carry on the wind. "He didn't point a shotgun at me, if that's what you want to know."

James's shoulders dipped in relief. "And the food. Did he take it? Was he offended?"

"He didn't appear to be." She didn't feel like talking about the Schneiders.

He placed a warm hand on her shoulder. Her skin tingled. "I told you he liked you."

Ann forced a smile. The task she had just accomplished was nothing compared to what she was about to do. But it was for the best—for both of them.

"James, I have something I need to tell you."

He grasped her hand and placed it on his arm. "You said I could share my news first, if it's still alright."

Her heart would break regardless. What was a few more minutes until he'd said what he needed to say? She nodded.

James patted her hand. "Let's get some dinner first. Uncle Mac must be starving."

He was right. Uncle Mac waited for them on the front porch, tapping his foot impatiently. They hadn't been gone more than twenty minutes, but like the trains, Uncle Mac's appetite ran on a schedule.

They supped on a light meal of late-summer vegetables and smokehouse ham, though Ann found it difficult to eat more than a few bites. *You have no reason to be nervous*, she reminded herself. But it wasn't nerves that tickled her belly. She stole glances at James across the table. He looked at everything in the room but her, though a hint of a smile played on his face throughout the meal.

After supper, James performed his evening chores while she washed the dishes. She watched him through the window, as she often did. He was so tall and trim, one would never guess his immense strength without seeing the way he hefted hay bales, and dragged his reluctant milk cow back into the barn. She pulled the cotton draperies closed. She should not be admiring a man who was not to be her husband.

James came in from the barnyard glowing with a fine sheen of perspiration, and still possessing a strange smile Ann was at a loss to interpret. Had he guessed she planned to leave soon? Was he relieved? She pushed her own questions out of her mind and prayed for courage to say what must be said. To do what must be done.

"Come, sit with me on the porch." James offered his hand and she accepted. He'd washed up at the well pump, and his shirtsleeves were pushed up and damp. His calloused hands held hers as gently as one might cradle a china cup or a baby.

Tears welled in her eyes. Though she longed to stay, she must leave before her heart fell any deeper. James deserved so much more than she could give. Staying any longer would only delay the start of the life he desired.

Ann took a seat next to James on the worn wooden rocking chair. She drew a deep breath and summoned some courage. She knew she'd said he could share his news first, but she was afraid if she didn't speak now, she'd never be able to.

"James, despite the mistake that brought me here, I want you to know how much I've enjoyed staying on your farm."

James leaned forward with his elbows on his knees, his eyes locked with hers. A trickle of perspiration trailed down her neck.

"I'm glad to hear you say that, Ann. I feel much the same way."

Her mouth was like cotton again as she looked into his eyes. She should have brought a glass of water with her.

"James, I know we were waiting on a letter from Mrs. Turner, but…"

He lifted a finger to interrupt her. Slowly, from his breast pocket, he withdrew a slim envelope.

"That's why I wanted to speak first, Ann. Mrs. Turner's letter arrived today."

Ann's heart dropped. So this was why James hadn't stopped smiling, and why he'd been acting so strangely. Mrs. Turner had no doubt found him another match. Her pulse quickened. Was this woman coming soon? She had to leave. She had to leave at once!

"I'll leave tomorrow," she announced. Tears welled in her eyes and she looked away from James to hide them.

"Ann, you don't need to leave if you don't want to." He must have leaned even farther forward in his chair, because his warm voice was now inches from her shoulder. "The letter from Mrs. Turner says this wasn't a mistake at all."

Chapter Nineteen

James held his breath and waited. Ann continued to stare out over the south field.

"What did you say?" she asked, her voice not more than a whisper.

He pressed the letter into her hands. "There was no mistake—at least not in Mrs. Turner's eyes. She was more than aware of my request for a plain bride, which is exactly why she sent you to me. Here, read for yourself."

She turned slowly toward him, her blue eyes wider than he had ever seen. She stared back at him, the envelope trembling in the breeze on her palm. "Would you please read it?"

He took the envelope back and retrieved the crisp ivory sheets inside. He skimmed through the polite formalities until his gaze alighted on the paragraphs that had sent his own heart racing hours before. He cleared the catch in his throat and drew a deep breath.

"Though Ann Cromwell is not a plain girl, it was never my intention to ignore your request. Instead, it is always the utmost desire of the Transatlantic

Agency to ensure happy matches. I have it upon excellent authority that Ann is as hard a worker as they come, and I believe she would be well suited to the labors of farm life.

"I must admit, Mr. McCann, there was something beyond Miss Cromwell's impeccable work ethic that compelled me to make this match. You see, it is a certain type of gentleman who requests a beautiful bride. I've grown quite fond of Miss Cromwell, which is why I could never match her with such a man. Your request was the first of its kind in our office. It certainly gave us pause. But what is more, it gave me hope Miss Cromwell could be matched with a man who would look beyond her beauty. She has a rare heart, and I prayed it would find a match with yours.

"It is my greatest hope that in the time it has taken for this letter to reach you, Miss Cromwell's other great beauties of heart and character have become evident. If you still desire a new match, please telegraph our office at once. If you do not, we will interpret your silence as blessed news."

James didn't want to look up from the letter, but he had to gauge Ann's reaction. If only she'd read the letter herself, and he could have surveyed her face for some clue to her feelings. Like any other mail-order bride, she was under no obligation to stay. Ever since reading the letter, he'd mulled over his many missteps and chastised himself for each one. All because he'd thought she was intended for another.

He slowly raised his eyes to her face. She was staring

down at her lap, and her face held no elation. His heart seized. She glanced up and gave him a weak smile.

"I spoke with Mr. Davis today. Did you know he's opening a new store in Indianapolis?"

James head spun with the abrupt change in topic. "I heard mention of it, yes."

She looked down again. "He wants to sell my hand-kerchiefs there."

"That's wonderful." He grasped for more words. "You have a great talent."

Her porcelain skin tinged pink. "Thank you. It means much to hear you say that."

The letter burned like fire between his fingers. Had she heard its contents, and simply ignored them? Was she disappointed she wasn't meant to be matched with a wealthy man after all? Was she waiting for him to express his feelings before she revealed her own? He'd spent the summer reminding himself another woman would one day arrive to take Ann's place, and reminded Ann often of the better life he thought she had waiting for her. She must think he wanted nothing to do with her.

What are my feelings? He'd slipped up often, hurting her feelings unintentionally. The letter gave him permission to admire Ann. To woo her. But was it too late? There was only one way to find out.

"Ann, would you like to stay at the farm awhile longer—with me?"

Her cheeks colored a deeper pink that only made her more beautiful. Her lips trembled as she opened them to speak. "I'm afraid that's what I was going to tell you tonight. I have enough money to pay you back for my passage. Mrs. Williams paid me half today for the wedding lace, plus the money for the handkerchiefs, and I'll receive the other half upon Priscilla's approval of my work. Now Mr. Davis has asked for my handkerchiefs for his store, and I believe I can support myself. I thought I might leave on Monday, but I'll understand if you'd like me to go sooner."

Her words were a knife to his heart. His mind flashed to Emily and the night she'd broken their engagement. It had been on this very porch, though she hadn't been nearly as gentle as Ann was being now.

"I see." He should have known the letter would make no difference. Just because Ann proved she could hold her own on the farm as well as anyone didn't mean she wanted that life. And it didn't mean she wanted a life with him.

A tear slid down Ann's cheek. "I wish I could say yes, I truly do."

His heart tripped. "Then *say yes.*"

Fresh tears trickled down and he reached out to wipe them away. She didn't stop him. "You don't have to say yes to forever, or even to staying here," he told her, his voice as soft and persuasive as he could make it. "We'll find you somewhere to stay. I'm sure the Ludlows have some extra room." Words tumbled out faster than they ever had before. He reached for her hands and she gripped his in return. "I'll give you as long as you like to make a decision. I'll wait years if I have to. Please, give me a chance to win your heart."

"I can't, James. I can't." She released his hands and stepped to the edge of the porch, putting her back to him. His words had not been a comfort. Instead, he'd upset her all the more. Befuddled, he walked tentatively to her side and placed a hand on her shoulder. She tensed but didn't turn.

"What's wrong, Ann? Why can't you stay?"

Her shoulders heaved with deep, irregular breaths. "You should write to the agency. They should be able to send you the right match," she exhaled.

Confused, he turned her to face him. "Didn't you hear the letter? Mrs. Turner said there was no mistake. She meant to send you here."

Ann blinked slowly. Her lashes were dark and wet with tears. "She sent me here because she thought you might overlook my...shortcomings. But I know you, James. I know how important this farm is to you. How important *family* is to you. Even if you could accept me, I'm not the woman you deserve."

James drew her to his chest and she sank against him. "I know God didn't make you for farm life, and I'm sorry I ever thought less of you for it. Which is why I'll never ask you to lift a finger on the farm again, if you'll only stay with me."

She sucked in a breath. "James... I can't. I could never ask you to—would never ask you to..."

"Give up the farm?" he finished. "I don't have to. I've arranged everything. Frederick always said there was a job for me at the mill if I wanted it. Now I do. His business is growing, and he wants me to assist Victor in the management when I'm not working the land. If I work both jobs, I can hire a farmhand and you'll have plenty of time to work on your lace. To work on anything you want."

"No, this isn't right." She lifted her hands to his chest and pushed against him, but he pulled her gently back.

"What isn't right? That I want us to get to know

one another? That I want to give you everything you deserve? That I… That I'm falling in love with you?"

"You want to give me so much," she hiccuped through sobs. Then, as if she'd finally surrendered to his embrace, she buried her face into his chest. His hands rose up and tentatively stroked her soft, golden hair. "You want to give me so much, and I can give you nothing in return," she continued.

His right hand cradled the back of her head, while the other lifted her chin to face him. His mouth pressed to her cheek and hovered over her lips. She exhaled and pushed up to meet him. Their lips met in a searing kiss. She pulled away and he drew her back to him.

"You can give me everything," he murmured into her hair.

"James, I can't," she protested.

"Why can't you? I know you feel something for me, too." He stroked a tender line along her jaw, and his fingers ached to tilt her face up for another kiss.

Ann kept her head down, speaking into his chest. "You want children, don't you? I know you do. You've said so more than once."

"Of course I want children."

She stole a glance upward and their eyes locked. "And that was how I knew our match was a horrible mistake from the first day we met. You had only one request of the agency—a plain bride. I also asked for one thing in my match. A man who would be content not to have children with me."

James laughed nervously. "I don't believe you. I know you want children. I see the way you are with Sadie and George."

Ann's face remained as unreadable as stone. "And I

didn't believe you wanted an ugly bride, but it was true. You want children, and no matter how terribly I might desire them, it can never be." She paused and looked down at the porch floor. "You see—I can never give anyone children."

His heart skipped. "You can't know that. You're so young. Why, you'll only be nineteen next month."

Ann pushed against him, and James relaxed his grip, though only enough for her to take a half step back. He tipped her chin up so she would meet his eyes again.

"When I was in service, I fell in love—or at least I thought I was in love. He was charming and handsome, and I believed all of his lies of loving me in return, of planning to marry me. I allowed myself to be seduced, and the result was a baby."

His heart dropped. "You had a child?"

"A boy. He's with a fine family now, but yes, he was mine once—for a moment."

She stepped toward him but something pushed James back. His hands grew numb and he dropped them to his side.

"There were…complications afterward. When I finally saw the doctor, he said the damage was too extensive to heal. I would never bear another child."

James's mind was a blank. Of all the responses he'd imagined she might have—all the objections—he could never have imagined this.

"Please, James. Say something."

The screen door banged open, startling them both. Uncle Mac rushed out, pointing to the road. A horse and rider headed their way at breakneck speed. James stepped off the porch as the horse turned down his lane.

"It's Jed Zwebel."

James's neighbor was red faced and gasping and gal-
loping straight toward them. He pulled on the reins
and the horse skidded to a stop inches from the porch.
"James, we need you quick. Delmar Winter has gone for
the doctor, but the accident is only a mile from here."

"Who's hurt?"

"It's Hal Schneider. We could smell the liquor before
we saw the body. Don't know rightly what happened,
but his wagon flipped right off Mud Pike and into my
field. If Delmar hadn't been coming over to borrow my
old saddle, who knows when he'd have been found."

Ann was at James's side in an instant. Her fingers
gripped his arm and squeezed so tightly he winced.

"The children. Were the children with him?" Her
eyes were wide and terrified.

"No, miss. Thank the good Lord. No one's checked
on them though…"

Before Hal could finish, Ann had dashed off the
porch and through the field toward the Schneiders'.

Jed turned his horse around and headed back to the
accident. James saddled Old Harriet and followed close
behind. Old Harriet could no longer manage a gallop,
and the ride gave James time to dread what he would
find. He'd never performed more than minor proce-
dures, and always with the close guidance of a physi-
cian.

*Please, Lord, give me wisdom. Please guide my
hand.*

By the time he reached the wagon, all of the nearest neighbors had received word and gathered around.
James dismounted his horse and handed the reins to
one of Jed's many children. The crowd parted as James
approached.

His stomach clenched as he took in the scene. Hal's horse had already been put out of its misery. A body lay prone some thirty feet away. A half dozen men and women crouched around it.

"Is he breathing?" James asked. The shake in his voice was obvious but no one appeared to take notice.

Jed's wife, Gertrude, turned and shook her graying head. "We're not sure. The wagon was on top of him when Jed and Delmar found him. When some of the other men arrived, they pulled him out before we could stop them."

James drew a deep breath and knelt beside Hal. His neighbor's waxy pallor could only mean one thing, though he hoped he was wrong. James moved his hands over Hal's wrist and neck to make sure, probing and praying as he examined the stricken man. After several minutes he sat back on his haunches and exhaled. He couldn't find a pulse.

Jed Zwebel crouched down beside him and kept his voice low. "Hal's dead, isn't he?"

During his examination the men in the crowd had turned their attention to righting the wagon, but their wives stood only a few feet away, murmuring and praying among themselves. James nodded slightly, so as not to alarm them. He stood and addressed those nearest him. "Alright, folks, if you could give Hal some room. We don't want anything hindering the doctor when he gets here."

His words sent the assemblage scattering. Gertrude Zwebel announced she was serving coffee in her kitchen, and the crowd was welcome to sit a spell. James could guess why when everyone politely declined and turned toward home, their heads hanging low. No one was fooled by his playacting.

Doc Henderson arrived a short while later. "I wish I could have done something more for the man" was all he said as he looked over the body.

"We all do," James replied.

The doctor stood and shook his balding head. "But we can only help those who are willing to accept our help. A man can change, but you can't make him *want* to change."

Jed and James transferred the body to the doctor's wagon and the doctor set off back to town. Jed ran to fetch Old Harriet, and for a moment James was alone in the field. The sun had set since he arrived and he dropped exhausted onto the ground among the summer wheat and buried his head in his hands. Never had he experienced a more exhausting day in his life. Not even when his parents died had he experienced such emotional turmoil. It was as if he'd climbed a mountain only to stumble off a cliff. Hours ago he'd been full of hope. Now his heart seized with despair.

He retrieved his pocket watch and squinted at its face. Not even an hour had passed since Jed had first arrived at his farm.

A frantic voice pierced the quiet. The new moon meant the earth was cast in shadow, and he strained to see in the inky dark. The voice grew closer, and he recognized the lilt long before he saw its owner. He stood just in time for Ann to stumble headlong into his chest.

"Oh, James! Is he alright? Is Hal…alright?"

She was clearly out of breath and paused often to draw great lungfuls of air. Despite the dark he could see Ann's golden hair had fallen from its tidy bun and spilled over her shoulders.

"He was crushed when the wagon overturned. He's gone."

Ann gasped and pressed against him. He gripped her tightly in his arms. The tragedy with Hal had given him no time to even think of Ann's confession. As he held her, all the events of the evening rushed back to him, but he pushed them to the back of his mind. He could only concentrate on one thing at a time.

"Did you find the children? Are they safe?"

"Yes. They were both at home, already asleep in their beds. I had to climb through an open window to check on them. They're at your house with Uncle Mac."

"And you ran all the way here? In the dark?"

Ann shivered in the chilled night air. "I couldn't sit at home. I had to see if I could help."

"I'm afraid there was nothing anyone could do."

A bobbing lantern approached in the distance. James called out to guide Jed and Old Harriet to their spot in the pitch-black field.

Jed looked surprised to find Ann there with James. "Did you find the children, Miss Cromwell?"

Ann had stepped away from James's arms as soon as they'd spotted the lantern. She nodded. "They said their father had sent them straight to bed after supper. They hadn't even known he was gone. Where do you think he was headed?"

Jed sighed. "I can only guess he wanted to visit the saloon in town. About the only place to buy liquor this time of night, though I guess we'll never know for sure."

James sensed Ann shudder in the dark.

"We should get home," he said, and took the horse's reins.

Ann moved to follow him but stopped short. "Mr. Zwebel? Will you be heading into town soon?"

"Tomorrow morning, as a matter of fact."

"If I meet you at your farm, will you give me a ride the rest of the way?"

James's heart quickened.

"Certainly, though I'm leaving as soon as the cows are milked," Jed said.

"I'll make certain I'm here long before," Ann answered.

The trio exchanged goodbyes, and Jed headed for home. James helped Ann mount Old Harriet and swung himself up in front of her.

"Will you be able to hold on to me?"

Ann wrapped her arms around his waist and pressed tight against his back. "I'm ashamed to admit I may have trouble staying awake."

James turned the horse toward home and let the reins go slack. The farm was straight down the road, but on a moonless night he trusted the horse's sight better than his own.

When they trotted into the barnyard, James turned to find Ann nodding off. He wrapped an arm around her shoulders to help her down, and she drew her own arms around his neck. He lifted her from the horse. She weighed no more than a feather.

James carried her through the front door and set her in the foyer.

"Both children are asleep in your bed," she said. They were the first words she'd spoken since they'd left the field.

He nodded. "I'll tell the children about their father in the morning. Unless you think it would be better if you did."

She dipped her head. "I'll be leaving at first light. I wouldn't want to wake them."

"Will you be back in the evening?"

Ann exhaled and shook her head.

His heart screamed at him to say something. Anything. But her revelation was too fresh, and the many traumas of the evening had overwhelmed his senses. He couldn't think.

"When will I see you again?"

She looked up at him, but without a light he couldn't make out her expression. Tentatively, he reached out and touched his fingertips to her cheeks. They came back wet with tears.

"I don't know if we'll ever see one another again. I think this should be goodbye."

James opened his mouth to speak, but no words came out. Her slim form disappeared up the dark stairs and he watched from the foyer, still grasping for what to say and coming back empty-handed.

Chapter Twenty

James turned Old Harriet onto the Zwebels' lane almost without thinking. It had been a week since he'd seen George and Sadie, who were staying with the family until permanent arrangements could be made. More than a week since the worst night of his life.

No. He pushed the memories down before they could grab hold and draw him back in. The anguish would be with him every waking moment if he let it. He already relived the pain countless times a day. How he could have done things differently. If he *should* have done things differently. If it was really too late.

Sadie was off like a shot from the Zwebels' front porch before the wagon came to a stop. He jumped down in time to catch her as she threw herself into his arms.

"Why weren't you at church on Sunday?" she scolded, wagging a tiny finger at him.

"I was working at the mill until very late on Saturday. I attended church in town."

Her bottom lip pushed out and she dipped her chin. "We thought we'd see you there," she said softly. She wrapped her slim arms around his neck and squeezed tight. "I missed you."

Guilt nipped at his heart. He hadn't meant to stay away from the children so long, but he didn't think they'd notice his absence. Not with loss of their father so fresh, and the large Zwebel clan always ready with comfort and distractions.

Mrs. Zwebel emerged from the house with George in tow. The boy stood at her side until she nudged him gently. He trudged reluctantly forward with his arms slack at his sides, his eyes downcast. James carried Sadie and met the boy at the bottom of the porch steps.

"How are you getting on, George?"

The boy shrugged. "Alright."

Mrs. Zwebel gave James a half smile. "George has proved a great help around the farm. He does as much work as my Jesse and at only half the age."

A tiny flicker of pride stole over the boy's face, but disappeared just as quickly. James grasped for something else to say to cheer or encourage George. He'd lost his own parents as an adult. He couldn't fathom how that kind of loss affected a child. He'd already spoken with Jed Zwebel several times, and knew the children cried themselves to sleep, though a little less each night.

Without warning, George stepped forward and wrapped his arms around James's waist. "Are you here to take us home with you?"

"Yes, please!" Sadie cheered and clapped her hands.

James's heart tore. He set Sadie down and knelt so he was eye level with both children. "No, I'm sorry. You'll be staying with the Zwebels awhile longer. Until we find your relatives."

Sadie's dark eyes teared and George set his jaw, though it didn't stop his lips from trembling.

"We don't even know our relatives. We want to live with you," the little boy pleaded.

"Yes, with you and Ann!" Sadie chimed, her tiny arms around his neck again.

James blinked hard to keep the tears at bay. Mercifully, Mrs. Zwebel joined the children and drew them into her skirts. He stood and took the opportunity to wipe his eyes under the guise of mopping the sweat from his brow.

"Now, children," Mrs. Zwebel said. "We've told you many times. You have uncles and aunties somewhere, and they love you very much."

"But we love James," George stated simply. Sadie nodded vigorously.

Mrs. Zwebel sighed and leaned in close. "It's all they talk about," she whispered. "Going to live with you."

James gave the children each one last hug, and promised to visit again. As Old Harriet pulled the wagon back down the lane toward Mud Pike, he stole one last glance. George and Sadie stood arm and arm, tears streaming down their cheeks.

Please, Lord, provide them with the loving home they deserve.

Ann awoke and stretched, wincing as the blood flowed back into her cramped legs. Even with her petite stature, she was still a head too tall to be sleeping on the Ludlow's worn velvet sofa. One or two nights would have been tolerable, but it had been more than two weeks, and the furniture tested the elasticity of her limbs.

A knock rapped on the parlor door.

"Come in," Ann called, knowing full well it was Delia on the other side. None of the other Ludlows dared to even peek into the parlor where Ann made her bed each night until she indicated she was awake. They'd insisted she have the privacy of her own room, rather than sharing the largest bedroom with Delia and three of her sisters, which only added to her guilt over the arrangement.

Despite her desire to flee New Haven as quickly as possible, Delia asserted it would be a mistake to leave for a strange new city in haste and the Ludlows insisted Ann stay with them as plans were put into place. Delia's father wrote to a distant cousin in Indianapolis to arrange respectable lodging, and Ann spent a week writing up advertisements for her services as a maid, to be telegraphed ahead to Indianapolis and placed in the paper.

Delia poked her dark head through the doorway. "Today's the day!" she crowed.

Ann's stomach turned. Indeed, today was the day. The last tenuous thread holding her to New Haven was about to be broken. It was the day of Priscilla's final dress fitting, and the day she'd receive final payment. She'd never expected to remain in New Haven so long, especially after Mrs. Williams completed the dress early, but Priscilla had insisted Ann be at the final fitting and then postponed the appointment numerous times in favor of trips to Columbus to peruse china patterns for her new home.

It didn't matter. By the evening she'd have enough money to both repay James in full, purchase a train ticket to Indianapolis and support herself for several months in a new city, even if she couldn't find a job as a maid. It was also the day she would have to return to James's farm if she wanted to make her train the next morning. In her haste to secure a ride to town with Jed Zwebel, she'd completely forgotten she had no way of transporting her trunk from James's farm to the Zwebels'. She'd made the mile trek with only her valise. Now she had to return to retrieve it.

She pressed her fingers to her temples. A headache was building.

Delia took a seat beside her. "If you change your mind, my brother can get your trunk by himself. You don't have to go with him."

"No," Ann answered firmly. "Frederick said James was due at the mill today, and I never said goodbye to Uncle Mac. If I don't, I know I'll always regret it."

The last thing I need is something else to add to my long list of regrets.

"You are more likely to run into him in town than you are at his own home," Delia agreed.

Ann laughed grimly. Her friend was right. The youngest Ludlows delighted in sharing their sightings of James around New Haven, though they didn't understand why their reports were of such importance. Outside the mill. Walking by the courthouse. Inside the library. The reports had died away the last few days, but she was still perpetually on edge. The Ludlow home sat a short distance from town, which meant Ann had confined her walks to their garden. Better to become a recluse than to risk seeing James, even from a distance. Her breath caught in her throat at the mere thought of catching a glimpse of his sandy head.

She might have felt differently if she'd thought there was some hope they could part as friends, but the last weeks had shown her a friendly goodbye was not to be. Everyone in town knew she was at the Ludlows, and James couldn't have missed the gossip. If he had wanted to see her, he would have arrived by now.

"What about George and Sadie? Will you visit them?" Delia asked.

Ann's middle tightened. "No, I don't think I should. Not after what they've been through. They don't need another person saying goodbye."

Ann stood and stretched her arms above her head. "I'm going to miss this sofa," she admitted. Despite the discomfort, tonight would be the last time she would lay her head down surrounded by friends. The day after next, she would awaken in a new city of strangers. Delia hadn't even met the cousin who'd agreed to take Ann into her home. Even Mr. Davis and his family, whom she barely knew, wouldn't arrive for months.

She turned to the still-seated Delia and wrapped her arms around her shoulders, finally able to give her tall friend a proper hug. "I'm going to miss you, too, Delia."

Delia squeezed her in return. "Tomorrow won't be goodbye. I can visit."

"But I can't visit you," Ann said wistfully. Delia nodded in understanding. They'd had so many conversations about her parting with James over the past two weeks, there was nothing more to say. Delia knew Ann could never return to New Haven, for the same reasons she couldn't bring herself to venture much beyond the Ludlows' front gate.

After breakfast, Delia and Ann went to Mrs. Williams's shop. A storm cloud had sprouted above, casting an ominous shadow over the town square. Cyclones of dust scuttled along the plank sidewalks as men and women ran for cover. Ann alternated between keeping her head down to protect it from the wind and glancing up to scan the streets for signs of James, but the square was almost empty. Everyone had taken refuge from the imminent downpour.

Priscilla Vollrath was waiting for them when they arrived, and she turned up her nose and huffed loudly to show them her displeasure at having to wait.

"She arrived not thirty seconds before you," Mrs. Williams whispered as they arranged a tea tray for Priscilla and her mother.

The young girl made great attempts to maintain her annoyance, but her pinched face spread into a smile when the dress appeared.

"It's breathtaking," she gasped, as her mother nodded along in approval. "Every girl at my wedding will be so envious. I can't wait to see their faces!"

"I'm sure you can't wait to see Victor's face, dear," Mrs. Vollrath added.

Priscilla waved a dismissive hand at her mother. "Of course, of course," she said as if her fiancé was a mere cog in her grand scheme to throw the most magnificent wedding imaginable.

They helped Priscilla into the dress, and the girl probed over the lace and material inch by inch. Even under her critical eye, her only demand was the satin sash around her waist be shortened by two inches. An hour later, Priscilla stepped out onto the blustery street with her cheeks aglow, and Ann stepped out shortly after with her payment for the lace.

Delia's brother, Homer, had already hitched the wagon by the time they arrived at the Ludlows', and he waited impatiently beside it. At fifteen, Homer was already several inches taller than Delia, but possessed only a fraction of her mirth.

"We best get going, Miss Cromwell," he insisted soberly as she approached. "Some storms are coming and I don't want to get caught."

Delia placed a hand on Ann's arm. "Maybe you should wait until tomorrow morning," she suggested. She pointed to the darkening skies.

Ann shook her head. "I've put this errand off long enough." Truthfully, she'd put off retrieving the trunk in the hopes James would deliver it himself. As the days dragged on, it became apparent no such thing would occur. "My train leaves at noon. If we wait and don't make it back in time, I'll have to wait a week to catch the next one." She gave her friend a quick squeeze. "We should be back by supper."

Their drive was uneventful for several miles, other than the odd gust of warm air tickling her neck. Her chest twinged as they drove past the Zwebel farm. Their home sat too far back from the road for her to see more than the wind shield of bushes stretched across their lawn but she imagined George and Sadie inside and prayed that they were well and content.

James's farm loomed in the distance, and they were still a half mile away when the wind chose to grow a temper. It blew so fiercely Ann had to hold her hat against her head with two hands to keep it from flying away. Soon she gave up and tucked it beside her on the seat. A few minutes later it began to sprinkle.

"I'm sorry to bring you out in this," she apologized to Homer.

The boy shrugged. "I guess we're going to get wet."

Within minutes the clouds crackled and poured their

contents onto the land. Ann knew the umbrella she'd brought would be ruined in the wind, and so she gritted her teeth and allowed the late-summer shower to soak her to the bone.

"This isn't really so bad," Homer mused beside her. "At least it's warm."

Ann laughed at the sullen boy's suddenly bright outlook. He was right. The day was still warm, despite the damp, and like a typical summer storm, it was over as quickly as it began. The clouds parted and the sun returned at the same moment they turned onto the lane leading to James's house.

"I was hoping to be a while," Ann called over her shoulder as she hopped down from the wagon. "Though I can manage the trunk myself."

"No problem, miss. If you don't mind, I'm going to visit my friend Abner a little ways down the road since we're so close."

"Could you meet me here in two hours?" Ann doubted her goodbyes with Uncle Mac could take more than a few minutes, given his muteness, but she had plans on how to say a proper goodbye, and those plans required time.

Homer agreed and guided the horse back to the road.

Ann stood before the door and took a deep breath. This was to be her last time in James's home. The place she'd arrived at the beginning of the summer believing it to be her new home. The place where she'd seen James for the man he truly was. The place where she'd fallen—

She didn't let herself finish the thought. Instead, she chanted the same words she'd said so many times over the past week. *He doesn't want you. He never wanted you. He deserves a wife who can give him everything.* She knocked on the door four times, waiting approximately one minute between each.

No one came.

She turned the knob and found it unlocked as always. Inside, the house smelled mustier than she remembered, and she moved from room to room calling Uncle Mac's name. The last thing she wanted was for him to mistake her for an intruder.

After several rooms and several minutes, the stairs creaked and Uncle Mac appeared in the dining room doorway, carrying a copy of *Moby-Dick*. He grinned and opened his arms wide when he saw her. Ann embraced him and drew in his scent of old books.

"Welcome…home," he grunted into her ear.

She pulled back and stood at arm's length. "Uncle Mac, you know I came to say goodbye, don't you?"

The older man dropped his head and his weathered features turned down into a frown. "Y-yes."

She squeezed his shoulders. "I'll write. I promise."

Uncle Mac whisked an invisible tear from her cheek with a weathered thumb, all the while ignoring the stream of tears coursing his own face. "Yes."

Ann took the old man by the arm and steered him down the hallway toward the kitchen. On the way, she caught a glimpse of her reflection in the polished oval mirror. Damp curls plastered her forehead, and limp strands had blown loose from her bun and straggled down her back. The crisp sleeves of her dress were now wrinkled and flattened. She plucked a stray leaf that had affixed itself to her throat like a brooch.

"Lovely," she murmured.

She directed Uncle Mac to take a seat at the table.

"Stay here," she directed. "I have something to give you before I leave, but it may take a while."

Ann snatched an empty bowl and headed outside. She returned ten minutes later with a bounty of apples. "One more Apple Brown Betty," she explained.

Uncle Mac's face creased with smile lines. "Good, good."

Ann peeled and cored and sliced the apples, and cubed the old johnnycake she knew she would find tucked under an oilcloth. She smiled to herself as the dish slid into the oven. It seemed she might learn to cook after all, even if it was only one dish at a time. She'd mastered eggs, and then this. In her time with the Ludlows, Delia had patiently walked her through enough basics to keep from starving should she have to cook for herself—and had taught her enough about following cookbook instructions that she felt moderately more comfortable with the idea of experimenting on her own. In a year she might be able to prepare an entire meal without making anyone sick.

She took a seat at the table and stared into Uncle Mac's weathered gray eyes. She wished she could have met this man a few years ago, before he'd been robbed of his voice. Now, she could only pat his hand and hope the gesture conveyed her despair at having to leave. The image of Emily, James's demanding fiancée, came into her mind. Had she really treated Uncle Mac as terribly as James described? No, she imagined Emily had been much worse. Her heart quickened in anger as she pictured the girl James had almost married.

It doesn't matter. She shook the image from her mind. She could only pray whomever James did marry was caring, and she treated both James and Uncle Mac with kindness.

Ann left the kitchen in search of her trunk. She found it exactly as she had left it, at the end of her bed. Not a thing had been touched in the room, and a fine layer of field dust had already settled over everything. Ann wiped down the furniture and swept the floor before she carried her trunk downstairs and set it on the front porch.

The humid kitchen was soon permeated with the scent of apples and cinnamon. She set the dish on the counter to cool, and gave Uncle Mac one last hug.

"Is there anything else I can get you?"

His clear gray eyes studied her, and his lips moved but no sound came out. As she waited patiently, the lines on his forehead deepened, and his mouth grew taut. Still, no words passed his lips. He stomped his foot in frustration.

"Can you show me?" Ann offered.

He took a deep breath, and the crease on his forehead eased. He pointed to the hammock hanging on the back porch.

"James's hammock? James?"

Uncle Mac grinned. He pointed to Ann.

"Me?"

The grin grew wider. He jabbed a crooked finger toward her, then toward the porch, before pressing a palm to his chest. He repeated the motions again and again as Ann puzzled over them.

You, James, chest? You, James, heart? You, James...

"Love," she blurted. Her heart skipped a beat. He asked if she loved James. Uncle Mac nodded vigorously and gestured for her to continue. What could she say? It didn't matter how she felt. There was nothing she could do to become the woman he deserved. Of course she loved him. She'd struggled against it with all her strength, but it couldn't be denied.

"I—I really need to be going." She fumbled through her pockets and pulled out a fold of bills. "Please, give this to James." It was more than half of what she'd earned from her lace. He'd never told her just how high the agency bill and her passage had been— she could only hope that this covered it. "And know I'll always write, even if you don't respond."

Uncle Mac hung his head and nodded. He walked with her to the front door where he kissed her lightly on the cheek. She glanced around one last time at the simple foyer and drew in a deep breath. Even if it brought her pain, she wanted to remember this place forever.

Outside, the storm had long since passed, and the sun shone high and bright. Her dress and hair were still damp from the rain, and she stood in a ray of sunlight on the lawn in an attempt to dry them. The clip-clop of hoofbeats grew in the distance, followed by the crunch of stone beneath wagon wheels. Homer was a little earlier than expected. Ann sighed and drank in the sight of the house in front of her. The barnyard to her right. The Schneiders' house in the distance on the left. She stared until there was no chance she could ever forget.

"Whoa," the driver of the wagon called to the horse.

Her heart stopped and she shivered despite the humid day. It was not Homer who had turned down the lane. It was James.

Chapter Twenty-One

At first, James was sure his eyes deceived him. As he drew closer he knew he wasn't mistaken, yet his mind couldn't reconcile what his eyes were seeing. His heartbeat quickened as he dismounted Old Harriet and stepped closer.

She kept her back to him until he was only a few feet away. Ann's hair and clothes were a mess. She'd clearly been caught in the recent rainstorm. When she turned and saw James she put her head down and rushed to move past him. "I only came for my trunk. I can wait by the road until my ride returns."

James caught Ann by the arm. "You don't need to leave."

Her cheeks flushed. "I'm sorry, I was certain you wouldn't be here."

"Please, at least wait on the porch." He kept his voice steady, even as his heart raced faster.

She hesitated. James saw his opportunity. "Look." He pointed to a clot of dark clouds in the distance. "It's sunny now, but another storm is headed our way. You don't want to be caught out in it."

His mentioning the storm must have reminded Ann of her appearance. Her hands flew to her hair and she opened her eyes wide. *Don't tell her how beautiful she looks right now.* He couldn't let himself be caught up in that again. He knew all too well how easily he could say the wrong thing around Ann, and he needed to make the most of this opportunity.

Ann glanced at the distant dark sky and wordlessly moved to the porch. James remained rooted to the spot.

Please, Lord. Give me the right words.

He ran his hands through his hair and prayed again— this time for courage—before joining her. She stood on the far corner of the porch, her arms crossed, and stared out over the fields.

"Why did you think I wouldn't be here?"

Ann visibly stiffened at his words. She'd likely hoped he would leave her alone. But he had to say his piece.

"I'd heard you'd taken on many weeks of work at the mill. Every day but Sunday until harvest."

"Did Frederick tell you this?"

She sniffed. "Among others."

"What else did you hear?"

She dropped her arms and faced him. "What does it matter? I'm leaving tomorrow and you'll never have to see me again."

His heart dropped. So he'd gotten the date wrong. He'd thought her last fitting with Priscilla was still two days away. James took one step toward her. "I didn't know you were leaving so soon. I was going to come see you."

"Please don't lie to spare my feelings. I know you were in town almost every day. If you'd wanted to see me, you would have."

He took another step forward. "Please, if you could give me a chance to explain."

Ann sighed. "I don't want to leave things this way. To leave angry. You were kind to let me stay here those many weeks. I've left money with Uncle Mac to repay you, as I promised."

James inched forward, his throat constricting. "You didn't have to do that."

She crossed her arms again and tilted up her chin. Were those tears in her eyes? "It's what we agreed upon, isn't it? Or rather, we agreed my true match would repay you for my fare. It doesn't matter that there is no rich banker. No oil baron. I would never have used the agency if I'd had the fare to come to America on my own. You helped bring me here. The least I can do is repay you."

Her voice rose as she spoke and her eyes flashed with anger and imminent tears. He could feel opportunity slipping through his fingers. "Can we sit?" He gestured to the porch swing, purposely ignoring the high-back rockers beside them. He breathed a sigh of relief when Ann nodded and walked solemnly to the swing. He took a seat beside her, and the swing swayed lightly beneath their weight. Ann stared straight ahead.

"It's true I was in town almost every day, working at the mill, but I was also sending telegrams to the East Coast and speaking with anyone who ever knew the Schneiders. In fact, I just got back from Pittsburgh."

"Pittsburgh?" She turned toward him in surprise, only to remember herself and glance away again.

"The day after Hal died, Jed and Frederick and I combed Hal's house looking for any clues about his relatives, and we found lots of letters from a few addresses in Pittsburgh. That's where I sent the telegrams. But there's only so much correspondence one can do through telegraph. Once I found an old neighbor, I took the train to meet him."

Ann crossed her hands on her lap. "So did you find George and Sadie's family?"

James's heart thudded in his chest. "We found someone to take them in. And I think they're going to be happy there."

"I'm relieved to hear that."

He watched her from the corner of his eye. Ann's shoulders had relaxed and a sad smile played on her lips.

They rocked in silence for several minutes, though it was anything but silent in James's head. *Tell her! Just tell her!* At any moment she could walk off the porch and out of his life forever. He drew several deep breaths, until his head was light and dizzy. He grasped for courage, but it felt very far away.

Lord, give me strength.

The same prayer he'd sent up when Ann first arrived. Only then he'd prayed for strength to keep her at arm's length. Now he only wanted to draw her up in his arms and never let her go.

"Ann?"

"Hmm?" She still gazed out at the fields, not making eye contact.

He reached for her hand and exhaled in relief when she didn't wrench it free from his grasp. If she didn't want to look at him, that was alright. But he had to feel her hand between his. Strong, brave Ann. That first day, he'd thought her the most beautiful women he'd ever seen. If he could have only known how beautiful she'd become.

"You have every right to be upset with me. If you only knew how many times I wanted to come see you these past weeks. It took everything in me not to turn down the Ludlows' street and knock on their door."

"Why didn't you?" Her voice was barely a whisper.

He plowed a hand through his hair. "I'll explain everything in a minute. But I need to tell you something first."

She looked at him for the first time. Her exquisite blue eyes opened so wide he could practically fall in them and drown. Ann's rose lips trembled, and it took everything he had to fight against their pull for a few moments longer. This was it.

"Ann, I'm in love with you."

Blood coursed through Ann's ears, deafening even the sounds of a robin chirping in a nearby tree. She couldn't have heard him correctly. She stared back into his hazel orbs.

"What did you say?"

His hands had not left hers, and now he grasped it tighter. "I said I'm in love with you. Desperately in love. I should have told you the night of the accident, but I didn't get the chance. And after I was stupid enough to let you leave, I thought you'd never believe me, even if I did tell you."

Ann's head spun. None of this made any sense. Her heart pleaded at her to fall into his arms, but she'd spent too many days replaying their last night together. The look of shock and disappointment on his face when she'd revealed the circumstances of her barrenness. The silence when she'd said goodbye and he'd said nothing in return. Her heart twisted in pain as she realized what was happening. This was not love from James. This was pity.

"You don't have to say these things, James. Your sense of duty is admirable, but you deserve much, much more. And if you're worried about me, I assure you I'll be quite fine."

Ann's heart jumped as James's face fell. His eyes misted over and he moved ever closer to her on the porch swing.

"Don't you see?" His voice was low and raspy now. "This isn't about duty at all. I want to protect and provide for you from now until eternity because I love you in a way that I could never have imagined. I thought I loved you before, when I got the letter from Mrs. Turner, but I didn't realize how deeply that love ran until you walked away. I would do anything for you. Absolutely anything."

Her entire body trembled as the sincerity in his pleas washed over her. He did love her. But with that realization came the crushing reality that she still couldn't give him the life he deserved. Ann buried her face in her hands and James pulled her close. She surrendered to his embrace and buried her face into his chest. The heat from his body pulsed through his shirt and scorched her cheek. "You say you'd do anything for me, but I can't say the same in return. And you can't make me believe you don't want children. I've seen your heart for them, and I could never deprive you of that," she explained.

His strong hands stroked featherlight touches over her hair and back so gently she shivered. He pressed his lips against the top of her head and murmured into her hair. "That's what I was trying to explain. I don't need to have children with you, Ann. I only need you.

I was certain you wouldn't believe me, so I had to find a way to prove this to you."

She lifted her head enough to look into his eyes again. "But how could you prove such a thing?"

His full lips spread in a mournful smile. "George and Sadie need a home, Ann. Judge Vollrath has the paperwork all ready. The three of you are more than I could have ever hoped for in a family. The roads that brought us all together were paved with trials, but I believe God guided all our paths."

Ann's heart thudded. "You're going to adopt them? I thought you said you found their family."

He shook his head and a lock of sandy hair fell over his brow in the way that always made her heart quicken. "Their neighbor in Pittsburgh said Hal and his wife spoke often of being only children, and how happy they were Sadie and George had each other. And though we picked through every last letter in their house, not a one referred to relatives of any kind. So the new family I referred to was me—and you if you'll only say yes."

Without warning, he leaned down and placed the softest kiss on her lips. Flames ignited on Ann's cheeks and spread down her neck. His hands slipped behind Ann's head and pulled her closer. She never wanted the kiss to end. She never wanted their faces to part.

After an eternity and an instant, he broke his lips free. "Marry me, Ann," he murmured as his mouth hovered over hers. "I don't care about your past. I only care how it's shaped you into the woman I love today. You think you can give me nothing, but your love is everything to me. Please tell me you love me, too."

Ann sprang forward and returned the kiss. Her arms wrapped around his neck and her fingers entwined with his thick hair. She never wanted to let go, but he broke his lips free and locked his eyes with hers.

"Is that a yes?" He winked.

"I still can't cook."

He kissed her again. "I've come to believe there's nothing in this world you can't do. You are an extraordinary cook in the making, but if you never want to prepare another meal, you don't have to. You can work on your needle lace, and I can teach the children how to cook. However—" he pressed his lips briefly to hers yet again "—I do hope you'll still make your coffee. I don't think I can survive much longer without it."

She playfully pushed him away, but he only drew her closer. "Please, Ann. Say you'll marry me. Tell me you'll become Ann McCann."

Only one thing about this moment kept it from being perfect. James knew very nearly all of her secrets, and yet he still loved her. She longed for him to know every part of her now. It was time for a true new start.

"James, I must tell you one more thing. My name isn't really Ann." Her heart thudded as she watched for his reaction.

He didn't relax his embrace for a moment, but he did raise a brow. "You aren't Ann Cromwell?"

"Ann Cromwell is my name, but it was not my given name at birth. Not exactly. You see, when a young girl in England enters service, sometimes the lady of the house objects to her name. So she bestows on her a new one. In some households the cook is always Mary, and all the chambermaids are Tillies."

"So your name is Tillie?"

She laughed and impulsively kissed him. His ease chased away all her doubts. She could be herself with

James. Even as she sat here still damp from the rain, she'd never felt more comfortable and content. "No, it's not. Sometimes the girl's name is deemed too fancy for a girl of her standing. Too regal. In my case, I shared a name with Mrs. Atherton, and she was not about to let a poor little maid go by the same name as she."

James laughed softly. "How very vain. So she changed your name to Ann?"

"Decent, respectable and plain. The name Ann was judged to be far more suitable for me. It's the name I've gone by ever since."

"Please tell me what I'm going to call my wife for the rest of my life."

Shiver upon shiver coursed over her spine. She felt so full of joy that she could hardly stand it. "I haven't been called by my Christian name since I was ten years old, so it may take some getting used to."

His arms tightened around her waist. "Enough stalling. What is it?" He kissed the tip of her nose.

"Elizabeth." The name tasted strange in her mouth. "My name is Elizabeth."

James's eyes crinkled at the corners and he drew her so close his face looked fuzzy. His heart beat against her and matched her own heartbeat in perfect time.

"Elizabeth Cromwell, will you marry me?"

"Nothing could make me happier than being your wife. With all my heart, yes!"

Epilogue

Mr. Davis paused in sweeping the sidewalk in front of his store and took the bundle wrapped neatly with brown paper and tied up with a string. "Six handkerchiefs this time," James told the shopkeeper. "This should be the last of them before you leave. She has your address?"

Mr. Davis nodded as he untied the string and peeked into the package. He whistled under his breath. "Beautiful as always."

Sadie's dark head bobbed up from the wagon bed. "I wanna see!"

James laughed and pushed the child gently back into the cocoon of blankets with her brother. Both Sadie and George had jumped at the chance for a trip into town, despite the biting February cold.

"You've looked at them more times than I can count," James teasingly admonished. "I've no doubt you have them memorized."

The little girl giggled as he tucked the blankets back under her chin. "When will Lizzy be back?" she asked.

Lizzy. Even after nearly half a year of marriage, the nickname they'd all come to adopt for his new wife still made his heart jump to hear it.

"I'm not entirely sure, Sadie girl." Delivering the handkerchiefs to Mr. Davis had been the last of his many errands. Lizzy said she had just one. He turned to the shopkeeper, who was about to return inside. "My wife isn't tucked inside your store, is she? She's supposed to meet us here."

"No, but you're welcome to come inside and warm up while you wait. I have some candy that's getting a little stale. Maybe someone can help me throw it out."

George and Sadie popped up like jackrabbits and George scrambled over the wagon's side. "Don't throw it out!" the boy exclaimed, his dark brows knit in concern. "We can help you eat it!"

"Is that so?" Mr. Davis stroked his mustache as if deep in thought. James stifled a chuckle as both children danced about both from cold and in anticipation. He scooped Sadie out of the wagon and into his arms.

"I think George has had a fine idea," James announced, and both children sent up a cheer as they followed Mr. Davis into the store. Once inside, he set Sadie down and she dashed with her brother to the counter where they each received a paper sack of peppermint sticks, licorice rounds, butterscotch and lemon drops, all of which he suspected were not in danger of becoming stale anytime soon.

The warmth of the store and the children's laughter settled over him like a soft blanket. The Lord had created a new family out of tragedy, and now James couldn't imagine his life any other way. The children darted to the corner where Mr. Davis stocked the wooden toys, and James drank in the sound of their laughter as they played.

The bell over the door clanged. "Good to see you, Mrs. McCann," Mr. Davis called from behind the counter.

James strode to the front of the store and wrapped an arm around his wife's waist. They'd only been apart for an hour, but he'd already begun to miss her terribly. Her face was flush from the cold and her blue eyes sparkled. It took everything he had not to pull her into a dark corner and kiss her deeply right in the middle of Davis Mercantile.

"I thought I'd find the three of you in here," she said.

"I was beginning to worry about you. I thought you might have gotten lost," he teased.

She nudged him gently with her hip but he held lightly to her. She leaned back into him and sighed. "My appointment took longer than expected."

"Were you with Mrs. Williams? I heard a woman from Philadelphia passed through last week and bought your last handkerchief."

His wife didn't react to this news, though she normally rejoiced at each and every sale. Instead, she pursed her lips and gazed deeply into his eyes. "No, I was at the Hendersons'."

"Oh, was Mrs. Henderson commissioning something?"

Instead of answering immediately, she turned and drifted toward the children playing. James followed close and gave her a discreet hug from behind.

"Not exactly," she murmured, so quietly he almost didn't hear. "I was there to see Doc Henderson."

The children both dropped their toys with a clatter as

the couple approached and wrapped their arms around Lizzy's waist before letting go to resume their playing.

"Why didn't you tell me you were seeing the doctor? Is your stomach still bothering you?" James whispered in her ear. His chest tightened. She'd been unwell the past few weeks, but had repeatedly waved off his concerns. If she felt sick enough to see the doctor, her symptoms must be getting worse.

His wife ignored his questions. Instead, she plucked a piece of doll-sized furniture from the shelf and turned it over in her hands. James mussed his hair and willed his heart to slow. Ann didn't appear sick or even concerned. If anything, her countenance was one of extreme peace. So why did he feel a strange charge in the air between them?

"Can the mill make me something like this?" she asked. Her eyes were wide and bright as they stared up into his. She looked to be the picture of health. But still his stomach knotted.

"You know we don't make doll furniture."

"Not doll-sized. I'd like one full-size." She placed the wooden toy in his hands and then stood on her tiptoes to place a kiss on his lips. George snickered in the corner.

"What on earth are you—"

His exclamation was cut off as she lifted his own hands in front of him. The toy he held was a doll's cradle.

Time slowed as his brain beat through the fog of confusion. Then realization ran through him like a shot.

"You need a full-size cradle for…"

"A baby," she whispered. She flushed crimson and

buried her face into his coat. He wrapped her in his arms, scarcely believing the news.

"How?" he finally managed to ask.

She shook her golden head and laughed. "Matthew 19:26."

He pulled her tighter into his chest and blinked back tears.

With God all things are possible.

* * * * *

If you enjoyed this mail-order romance, don't miss these other stories from Love Inspired Historical!

HIS SUBSTITUTE WIFE
by Dorothy Clark

PONY EXPRESS MAIL-ORDER BRIDE
by Rhonda Gibson

FRONTIER WANT AD BRIDE
by Lyn Cote

MAIL-ORDER MARRIAGE PROMISE
by Regina Scott

Find more great reads at www.LoveInspired.com.

Dear Reader,

The setting for this story is very close to my heart. As I write this, sunlight streams into the room through the wavy glass of the 150-year-old window in my office. When writer's block strikes, I stare out that window toward a barn raised with hand-hewn timbers or out over rows of corn or soybeans growing just beyond.

My husband's great-great-grandfather built this house, and we are raising the fifth generation to make it their home. Though James and Ann are fictional, I picture Ann scrubbing these same wooden floors as I buzz my vacuum cleaner across them and James toiling in the field as our tractor plows the same expanse with ease. Though life has changed dramatically since these walls were first erected, my one hope is for faith and family to be the focal point of our generation and each generation to come.

Whitney Bailey

Get 2 Free Books,

Love Inspired HISTORICAL

Plus 2 Free Gifts—

just for trying the *Reader Service!*

*When a child arrives with the Wells Fargo delivery
with documents listing Heather O'Connor and
Sterling Blackwell as the baby's parents, they are forced
to marry to give the baby a home—and save
their reputations.*

Read on for a sneak preview of
MAIL-ORDER CHRISTMAS BABY
by **Sherri Shackelford**, *available*
November 2017 from Love Inspired Historical!

"The only way for us to clear our names is to find the real parents. If Grace's mother made the choice out of necessity," Heather said, "then she'll be missing her child terribly. Perhaps we can help."

Grace reached for her, and Heather folded her into her arms. By the looks on the gentlemen's faces, the gesture was further proof against her. But Heather was drawn to the child. The poor thing was powerless and at the mercy of strangers. Despite everything she'd been through, the baby appeared remarkably good-natured. Whatever her origins, she was a resilient child.

The reverend focused his attention on Grace with searing intensity, as though she might reveal the secret of her origins if he just looked hard enough. "Who is going to watch her for the time being?"

Sterling coughed into his fist and stared at the tips of his boots. The reverend discovered an intense fascination with the button on his sleeve.

Heather's pulse picked up speed. Surely they wouldn't leave the baby with her? "I don't think I should be seen with her. The more people connect us, the more they'll gossip."

"It's too late already," Sterling said. "There are half a dozen curious gossips milling outside the door right now."

Heather peered out the church window and immediately jerked back. Sure enough, a half dozen people were out there.

If she didn't take responsibility for the child, who would? "I'll watch her," Heather conceded.

"Thank the Lord for your kindness." The reverend clasped his hands as though in prayer. "The poor child deserves care. I'll do my best to stem the talk," he added. "But I can't make any promises."

Sterling sidled nearer. "Don't worry. I'll find the truth."

"I know you will."

A disturbing sense of intimacy left her light-headed. In the blink of an eye her painstakingly cultivated air of practicality fled. Then he turned his smile on the baby, and the moment was broken.

Heather set her lips in a grim line. His deference was practiced and meant nothing. She must always be on guard around Sterling Blackwell. She must always remember that she was no more special to him than the woman who typed out his telegrams.

He treated everyone with the same indolent consideration, and yet she'd always been susceptible to his charm.

She smoothed her hand over Grace's wild curls. They were both alone, but now they had each other.

At least for the time being.

Don't miss
MAIL-ORDER CHRISTMAS BABY by Sherri Shackelford,
available November 2017 wherever
Love Inspired® Historical books and ebooks are sold.

www.LoveInspired.com

Love Inspired®

Inspirational Romance to Warm Your Heart and Soul

Join our social communities to connect with other readers who share your love!

Sign up for the Love Inspired newsletter at **www.LoveInspired.com** to be the first to find out about upcoming titles, special promotions and exclusive content.

CONNECT WITH US AT:

Harlequin.com/Community

 Facebook.com/LoveInspiredBooks

Twitter.com/LoveInspiredBks

LISOCIAL2017

Once both twins were bundled, snug between Papa and Erica, Jason sent the horses trotting forward. The sun was up now, making millions of diamonds on the snow that stretched across the hills far into the distance. He smelled pine, a sharp, resin-laden sweetness.

When he picked up the pace, the sleigh bells jingled.

"Real sleigh bells!" Erica said, and then, as they approached the white covered bridge decorated with a simple wreath for Christmas, she gasped. "This is the most beautiful place I've ever seen."

Jason glanced back, unable to resist watching her fall in love with his home.

Papa was smiling for the first time since he'd learned of Kimmie's death. And as they crossed the bridge and trotted toward the church, converging with other horse-drawn sleighs, Jason felt a sense of rightness.

Mikey started babbling to Teddy, accompanied by gestures and much repetition of his new word. Teddy tilted his head to one side and burst forth with his own stream of nonsense syllables, seeming to ask a question, batting Mikey on the arm. Mikey waved toward the horses and jabbered some more, as if he were explaining something important.

They were such personalities, even as little as they were. Jason couldn't help smiling as he watched them interact.

Once Papa had the reins set and the horses tied up, Jason jumped out of the sleigh, and then turned to help Erica down. She handed him a twin. "Can you hold Mikey?"

He caught a whiff of baby powder and pulled the little one tight against his shoulder. Then he reached out to help Erica, and she took his hand to climb down, Teddy on her hip.

When he held her hand, something electric seemed to travel right to his heart. Involuntarily he squeezed and held on.

She drew in a sharp breath as she looked at him, some mixture of puzzlement and awareness in her eyes.

What was Erica's secret?

And wasn't it curious that, after all these years, there were twins in the farmhouse again?

Don't miss
SECRET CHRISTMAS TWINS
by Lee Tobin McClain, available November 2017
wherever Love Inspired® books and ebooks are sold.

www.LoveInspired.com